"You should try living up to your namesake, Cleopatra—trust no one."

She considered his words, and his warning, and tried to understand why, other than her still being alive, she *did* trust him. Perhaps it was the foolishness that often comes with fear and despair—clinging to a rock protruding from the ocean though one knew it was as dangerous in its barrenness as the great wide sea.

Yet she did trust him, and it worried her. Trust meant lowering one's guard and that meant... trouble. She tried to put her thoughts into words but they scuttled away, like night crawlers before an encroaching lamp.

For a moment the darkness settled on them again as the fire dimmed. Then a spark shot upward, followed by a lick of flames as the fire found more to feed its hunger. It lit his profile against the fading light on the horizon.

"I rarely do trust anyone," she said tentatively. "I do not mean I trust you wholly, but I think, if I am right about you, you will try to fulfill your bond and that is far more than most men...most people do."

LARA
TEMPLE

—

The Return of the
Disappearing Duke

HARLEQUIN
HISTORICAL

Recycling programs
for this product may
not exist in your area.

ISBN-13: 978-1-335-50570-5

The Return of the Disappearing Duke

Copyright © 2020 by Ilana Treston

This edition published by arrangement with Harlequin Books S.A.

For questions and comments about the quality of this book,
please contact us at CustomerService@Harlequin.com.

Harlequin Enterprises ULC
22 Adelaide St. West, 40th Floor
Toronto, Ontario M5H 4E3, Canada
www.Harlequin.com

Printed in U.S.A.

Lara Temple was three years old when she begged her mother to take dictation of her first adventure story. Since then she has led a double life: by day an investment and high-tech professional who has lived and worked on three continents, but when darkness falls, she loses herself in history and romance—at least on the page. Luckily her husband and two beautiful and very energetic children help weave it all together.

Books by Lara Temple

Harlequin Historical

Lord Crayle's Secret World
The Reluctant Viscount
The Duke's Unexpected Bride
The Return of the Disappearing Duke

The Sinful Sinclairs

The Earl's Irresistible Challenge
The Rake's Enticing Proposal
The Lord's Inconvenient Vow

The Lochmore Legacy

Unlaced by the Highland Duke

Wild Lords and Innocent Ladies

Lord Hunter's Cinderella Heiress
Lord Ravenscar's Inconvenient Betrothal
Lord Stanton's Last Mistress

Visit the Author Profile page
at Harlequin.com for more titles.

This book is for all those who love life, but lie awake worrying. For those used to shouldering burdens, but wish for a shoulder to lean on, even if only for a day. I wrote Rafe and Cleo's story just for you...

Prologue

Greybourne Hall, Hertfordshire
—Christmas 1800

The day he ran away was the day the lake at Greybourne Hall froze.

It wasn't a thick cover of ice, just enough to glaze over the last dark jade glimmer of water like a dead fish's eye staring heavenwards. Snowflakes frosted the reeds and swirled up the banks in fairy-tale gusts into the open door of Greybourne Chapel. Safely inside, they hovered for a moment to glint in the pale morning sun, before falling to the unusual chequered floor in abeyance, just like all the unhappy people crowded inside.

Unlike most chapels, there were no pews or cushions and no one was allowed to sit on the carved stone benches that lined the wall. Everyone from the Duchess and her son to the grooms and scullery maids were on their knees.

Everyone but Rafe's father, the Duke of Greybourne. The Duke stood above them like a rearing bear, his fists clenched and raised, his voice spewing damnation upon them all.

Rafe had years ago ceased listening to the roaring rumble of his father's morning sermons. When he'd been younger he'd distracted himself with daydreams about great feats of bravery. Now he would soon be sixteen and had other things on his mind.

A month ago, the object of his fantasies had been Lizzy, the very pretty daughter of the postmaster in the village near his school. But that was a whole month ago and now his mind dwelt with delight on the new parlourmaid Susan who was kneeling across from him.

She had big blue eyes and freckles over every inch of her that he could see, which was not very much, but his mind imagined much more. She was some years older than he and he'd heard from the servants that she fancied Lowell, the head groom. He knew, too, that this…*tingling* had little to do with courtly love, but she was so…so everything. She was plump and had the most charming giggle that would make his insides clench and his outsides perspire.

She was also, at the moment, the only reason to be grateful for his father's daily Hell and Damnation sermon. So while his father ranted about descent into sin and something about frogs, Rafe's gaze kept slipping back to Susan's bowed head, her rounded shoulders, the generous bosom not even the unflattering apron could hide…

She peeped up suddenly and caught him. Embarrassment struck him even harder than lust. There was nothing he could do to stop the scalding blush that rushed upwards. Her mouth curved and even through the fumes of his combusting body he could see the compassion there and felt its sting.

They both looked away and, if his father had not reached the apex of his sermon, the incident might never have happened. But just then the Duke's voice boomed. 'Fornication shall bring thee down!'

And Susan giggled.

Silence.

As swiftly as the scalding heat had come it fell away, because he knew his father. They all did. Silence during a sermon was an ill omen. Rafe barely had time to gather his wits before his father lunged. He saw the Duke's hands, great twisted claws, reaching, closing around her freckled throat, raising her clean off the stone floor. Rafe had never seen such horror as in her blue eyes. She gaped up at the Duke of Greybourne, her mouth twisted, her cheeks both pale and stained with colour, the freckles like specks of blood.

No one had yet moved when Rafe launched himself at his father. He saw them all, like chess pieces rooted on their ivory and ebony seats. Then he saw nothing.

The next thing he knew, his face was half in the snow, the flakes dancing in and out of his mouth as he breathed in harsh coughing bursts. He was aflame with pain and something was burying him in the frozen ground. He could see white and dark and the length of his arm flung out to his side. The snow about it was pink.

'That's right, Master Rafe, deep breaths.'

It was Lowell, the groom.

'Susan…' Rafe croaked and there was a moment's silence which made Rafe struggle to rise once more. But Lowell held him down.

'Susan is well, Master Rafe. You stopped him afore he did harm and there's many that's grateful. You stop thrashing and I'll let 'ee be. You've nothing broken that I can see, but you took some blows before we got you away and you'll likely be sore. Best come inside now.'

'I wanted to kill him!' The words burst out, chasing away the new flakes that fell.

'Ay, well,' Lowell said as he took his substantial weight off Rafe. 'Brave words, but best learn to fight proper afore you try next. You're a right big lad and like to be bigger yet, but you'd best put some brawn on those inches.'

Rafe shoved to his shaky feet, twisting away from the groom's attempt to help him. The cold pinched at his skin and tears at his eyes and he stalked away before they came.

* * *

He was shivering by the time he reached his room, but he stopped in the doorway. His mother was on her knees again, but this time by his school trunk. A maid placed a stack of shirts into the half-full trunk and at a signal from his mother she scurried out the door.

'What are you doing?'

'That should be evident, Rafael. I have ordered the carriage to be prepared and you will depart within the hour.'

For a moment he stood in shock but then anger came once again to his rescue.

'I didn't do anything wrong! This is Edward all over again—he did nothing wrong and you sent him away. Where will you send me, Mother? To Egypt as well? Or perhaps to the Antipodes?'

'Do not be dramatic, Rafael. Until term begins you will stay at up at the Lakes. You like it there.'

'In the summer,' he exclaimed.

'Do lower your voice. Dr Parracombe is with your father and has given him something to calm his nerves, but…'

'Calm *his* nerves? He…he tried to *kill* Susan! How many more times will dear Dr Parracombe have to *calm his nerves* when he attacks one of us or the servants? He doesn't need a doctor; he needs a cell in Bedlam!'

She surged to her feet—he was already over six feet, but though he towered over her she was absolutely in control. Her face was as cold as the lake, her eyes grey and flat.

'You will never speak those words again, Rafael. Ever. Your father's religious convictions merely lead to occasional…unbefitting effusions. That is all it is. One day you will be Duke of Greybourne and you must learn that life demands sacrifices.'

Sacrifices.

'So you are sacrificing me,' he said, far more calmly than he felt.

'If that is what you choose to believe.'

'I will tell you what I choose, Mother. If you send me away instead of him, I swear to you I'll *choose* not to return to Greybourne so long as he lives.'

They stood in silence for a moment, then she inclined her head.

'Perhaps that is best. Now go wash and change. And say goodbye to your sisters.'

Rafe leaned his bruised cheekbone glumly against the cold glass of the carriage window and watched the snow-flakes melt and slither down. They'd stopped again to change the team of horses. They were probably close to Manchester because the courtyard was full of gigs and carriages and carts, with ostlers and passengers weaving between them, hunkered against the cold. Everything was in shades of brown and grey and again he felt the same rising choke of misery and fury.

Then at the edge of the courtyard he saw a flash of bright red, like fresh blood on the snow. He took his purse and stepped out on to the cobbles. A crowd had gathered to watch, some cheering, some less enthusiastic, but all curious as some two dozen red-coated soldiers marched along the muddy road.

The soldier bringing up the rear was a rather squat man, with the face of a cheeky gargoyle under his dark stovepipe shako. He stood very straight for his short stature. A little boy dashed out from the courtyard and marched alongside him for a moment and the soldier smiled down at him and patted his head without breaking step.

As the young boy ran back through the courtyard Rafe stepped forward, pulling a coin from his pocket.

'Who were those soldiers?' he asked. The boy stared at the coin, but was as quick to answer as he was on his feet.

'Thirty-Sixth Foot returned from Ireland, sir. That was Sergeant Birdie, sir. My brother served with him, sir.' All this was spoken in a hushed whisper, but with such pride

Rafe smiled for the first time since coming down from school.

'Sergeant Birdie,' he repeated, flashing another coin. 'Which way are their barracks?'

'Over Bolton way, sir.'

'Bolton...?'

'That's north, sir.'

'Excellent. I'm heading north myself.'

'Are you, sir?' the boy asked, a little dubious, but his curiosity was nipped in the bud as Rafe slid him a third coin and stepped back into the carriage.

Bolton. Birdie. Brave new beginnings.

He'd need a new name, too...

Something simple that would draw no attention. Common, unobtrusive...

Grey...

Chapter One

Syene, Upper Egypt—1822

'*Ta'al.* Come in.'

The deep voice was entirely English.

So far, so good, thought Cleo as she took a deep breath and opened the warped wooden door.

The stone floor was hard under her feet, but she knew she was standing on a paper-thin bridge over an abyss. Her next step would either move her towards safety or perdition.

She entered the room and stopped, her hand still on the door, because the man who turned to face her was not at all what she'd expected.

Certainly he was large. Very large. She was a reasonably tall woman, but he would tower easily over her brother's six feet.

More to the point, he was very bare. At least his chest was, but there was a great deal of it.

Not that bare-chested men were entirely unusual in Cleo's experience. Over the years since she and her brother had joined her father on his travels, she had been to places where bare-chested men and sometimes women were not unusual. Still, this man was not what she was accustomed to.

Then there were the scars. They mantled his shoulder and streaked along the right side of his neck. Between his size and his scars and the fear that had taken up lodging in her belly this past week, he was an intimidating sight.

Except for the shaving lather.

A lathered jaw should not make any difference to whether he was to be feared or not, but somehow it did.

'What do you want, boy?' The man wiped his razor on the towel and turned back to the gritty mirror propped on a high windowsill.

At least his words confirmed what she'd overheard in the marketplace—he was English, thank God.

'I'm afraid I'm lost, sir.'

'Lost? This is a rather unusual part of the world in which to lose yourself. How did that happen, Mr...?'

'Patrick.' Cleo offered her usual name, watching as the giant worked away at his shaving, the muscles of his back rippling like the Nile over the boulders of the cataracts. Acting the boy had once been quite easy, but she was out of practice. She cleared her throat and continued. 'I've been in Meroe looking for my father and brother, but they disappeared so I decided to return to Cairo and see if they are there.'

The giant was watching her in the mirror, the speckled glass giving his pale green-grey eyes a strange blank tint.

'Yet here you are in my humble rooms instead of on a boat down the Nile. Would you care to rephrase your predicament?'

'I don't quite understand, sir.'

'Don't you? At least half a dozen *dragomen* approached me the moment I entered town, offering various services. If you only need help reaching Cairo, any one of them would be willing to help for a reasonable price.'

The giant wiped his face with the linen towel and turned. For a moment surprise and a surge of pity chased away her fear. The scars were more evident from the front.

They climbed up the side of his throat like ivy, twisting along his jaw and ending in a whitish blade just at the base of his ear.

She should not be surprised. The merchants she'd overheard in the market had called him *nadab*, or scar. But he was otherwise so alarmingly perfect his face could have modelled for a fallen angel, with pitch-black hair and stormy eyes. Apparently, this angel had not managed to evade the fire in his fall. The whitened skin along his jaw twisted as he smiled.

'Squeamish, boy?'

'No. I can't help thinking how it must have hurt. I'm sorry I stared, sir.'

His smile softened. It felt like a door opening a little wider.

'Staring is honest,' he replied. 'It's the looking away I can't abide. So, what is it you want from me other than directions to Cairo?'

Cleo glanced over her shoulder, listening. She'd sneaked past the innkeeper, but the men would likely search all the inns in Syene. And then… She did not know what would happen then and preferred not to know.

'I'm afraid to travel on my own. I heard in the market you might be on your way north. I don't have much, but I can pay my passage.'

The giant gave one last swipe to his jaw with the towel and draped it over his shoulder as he approached. He was definitely enormous and there were more scars decorating him than she'd realised. They were dwarfed by the burns, but they danced across his bare flesh like decorations— whiteish flicks and weals, as if someone had used him for dart practice. She forced her eyes upwards from the expanse of bare skin and the dark hair that trailed down his chest towards his trousers. His eyes weren't any more comforting—they were a strange metallic greenish-grey and she could discern nothing in them but her own reflection.

He was closer than was wise given her masquerade. But she kept her feet planted. She was just a boy, just a boy…

'Does anyone believe this Patrick nonsense?' He tugged at a lock of her hair. She usually kept it short, yet unruly enough to hide her arched brows. They'd always been her undoing. She debated arguing, but there was something in the giant's face, a lack of both curiosity and censure, that stopped the lie from forming.

'It used to work well enough when I was younger.'

'Much younger, I would imagine. This local garb is doing a poor job of hiding your bosom. If you weren't so gaunt-looking, I would suggest trying for a portly look and padding out your stomach, but you'd just look ridiculous. You should put some flesh in those cheeks first.'

Gaunt-looking. It was true the past few months had been difficult, but…gaunt? Not that it mattered. She glanced down at her chest. She'd bound it, but obviously not rigorously enough. It was rather disappointing to realise it was this and not her face that gave her away.

'Thank you for the advice, sir, but since I can't do much about it at the moment, could you help me? I can pay.'

'Can you? How much?'

Hell. She'd hoped he'd take pity on a fellow Englishman and perhaps even more now he knew her to be female. But clearly this was not that kind of Englishman, despite his cultured voice.

'I have this.' She tugged at the chain around her neck, extracting a pendant from under her *gallabiyah*. The metal setting was tarnished and twisted from when a trunk fell on it; but nothing could mask the quality of the emerald.

'Good God, someone must have disliked you thoroughly to gift you that monstrosity.' The giant plucked it from her hand and the chain tugged against her nape. She resisted the urge to pull away as he inspected it, turning it to catch the afternoon light. This close his eyes were even more intimidating. The green was pale, like peridots, held in by a band of dark steel. They were shaded by long straight lashes that rose as he looked from the stone to her. She was not often intimidated by men, but the hairs on her arms rose in alarm and she kept as much distance between them as the chain allowed.

'Where did you get this?' he asked.

'My mother. It was a family heirloom.'

'That's what people call things when they feel guilty about wanting to toss them on the rubbish heap.'

'I was told it is a small but fine emerald. It is yours if you see me safely to Cairo.'

'No, I don't think that's a good idea. I'm most likely to toss it in the Nile at the first opportunity or hand it to the first blind beggar. Put that devil's eye away.' He finally let the pendant fall and she eased away, slipping it back under her *gallabiyah*. It felt strange against her skin now, as if he'd held it over a fire.

'You won't help me?'

'Help you in what way? The river is all of a hundred yards from here. If you've already made it here from Meroe, which I admit is impressive, why do you need my help on what must be the final and easiest stretch of your journey?'

'Because...'

She fell silent at the sounds outside. Horses, several of them. An unpleasantly familiar voice calling in Arabic for the owner of the guesthouse.

'Never mind.' She headed to the window, but the giant was faster than she, his arm creating a bar across the wooden shutters.

'Not a good idea. If those men are clever, they'll have a man in the back. Are they clever?'

'I don't know... Yes, I... Oof!' Her breath left her as he picked her up and deposited her behind a thick cotton curtain stretched along a corner of the room to create a makeshift cupboard. Behind was a warped wooden dresser and pegs with clothes. He squeezed her between the dresser and the corner and planted his hands on the wall on either side of her.

'You will remain absolutely silent, no matter what I say or do. Understood, Patrick the prevaricator?'

She nodded, between shock and gratitude.

She ought not to feel thankful. No doubt he would hand her over with as much emotion as he'd shown at discovering her sex, but somehow she was beginning to hope she might have made her first correct move in days.

She stared at the thick curtain as it fell back into place. She hadn't even noticed the dun-coloured fabric closing off that part of the room. Still, she felt certain anyone entering would look directly at the curtain and through it. What if she had to cough? She looked around for something to stifle herself with. A white cotton shirt hung from a peg and she took it, burying her fists in its softness and raising it like a weapon.

In a tiny corner of her mind not given over to fear and exhaustion, she thought—*expensive.*

In another corner, far less sensible, she thought—*it smells so good.* Like the woods behind her childhood home where the stream created a little brush-covered island. She'd left there half a lifetime ago, but could almost imagine it lay just beyond the flimsy curtain.

Perhaps the heat and fear were finally melting her mind.

The knock on the door was like a hammer's strike.

'Go away. I'm shaving,' the giant called out, but the knock repeated, sharper. 'Oh, for heaven's sake, what?' The door squawked as he jerked it open. 'I said I was busy. Who the devil are you?'

'We apologise most strongly, *basha,*' said the hated voice, not in Arabic this time, but in English. 'We search for a young Englishman.'

'Well, go find him, then. Simply because I'm English doesn't mean this is a congress of that feckless breed.'

'He was seen coming in this direction from the market.'

'And?'

A few breaths passed and when the man spoke he was rather less peremptory.

'We were thinking that perhaps he might seek out a fellow countryman.'

'Why? Homesick, is he?'

'No. Frightened. He has stolen something from my master.'

'Not a very clever fellow, then. How much will you give me if I find him?'

Cleo froze, pressing the shirt over her mouth even as her heart tried to leap out of it.

'How much…?' The man sounded bemused now and she heard one of the men behind him mutter a colourful curse in Arabic about greedy foreigners.

'I presume your master is paying you for your services. I'm a mercenary myself so I am perfectly willing to have a look for the felon. But if I do find him, what will you pay for him and the stolen property? What is it, by the way? Something valuable?'

'Ah…no, no, not valuable to anyone outside my master. A book. A…a family bible. It is of sentimental value.'

'A strange thing to steal.'

'Indeed. But perhaps the young fool was misled as to its worth. My master is very sad. Naturally, we will offer a reward if—'

'How much?'

'Two hundred piastres.'

The door creaked.

'Five hundred piastres!'

The creaking stopped.

'I'll think about it,' said the giant with a grunt. 'I'm just bored enough to try for the fun of it. Where do I bring this bible-filching fellow if I find him?'

'To the house of Bey al-Wassawi. Ask the servants for al-Mizan.'

'Bay Wassa We. Al Meezan. Good. Now go away. I wish to dress. And you, landlord, find my rascally valet. He went out two hours ago to have my knives sharpened. You'll probably find him at whatever brothel this city boasts.'

The door snapped shut. In the silence she heard the men descend the stairs, their argument fading. Then the scuffle and whinnying of horses as they rode away. Still nothing. Then three heavy treads and a large hand pulled aside the curtain.

'I was beginning to wonder if you'd melted through the wall, Pilfering Pat. What the devil are you doing to my shirt?'

She shook her head, the fabric brushing over her lips.

'I was afraid I might make a noise,' she whispered hoarsely.

'So was I.' He smiled. It lit his face, transformed it. The pull of his scarred skin on his jaw gave it a wry twist, but did nothing to dim its magnificence. No wonder those men had turned tail. This brusque, ill-mannered man possessed the strange magic of charisma.

She knew about charisma. It was as untrustworthy as building a fortress on sand dunes.

She shook out the shirt.

'I apologise. I hope it is not too badly wrinkled.'

He tossed it on to his shoulder to join the towel.

'I don't think the tabbies of Almack's will notice. Now, who the devil was that and why are you stealing bibles?'

'I never stole anything in my life!'

'Not a thing?'

His incredulity flicked at her nerves and absurdly a memory returned…a length of blue ribbon dangling over Annie Packham's bedpost at school.

'A ribbon. When I was at school. It was sky blue and I wanted it. My mother always bought plain ribbons because they were easy to wash.' She snapped her teeth shut. She was truly losing her mind. But at least his smile was back—with blinding effect.

'I think I believe you, Pat. Do you happen to know if there *was* a bible or was everything he said a fabrication?'

For a moment she debated sharing what little she knew. But that was weariness and hunger talking. She shook her head.

'I have no idea why he is following me.'

'No idea? None at all?'

Blast, it was hard to hold his gaze. She decided to offer something to satisfy him.

'I…perhaps it has to do with my father. He dealt in antiquities.'

'One of those fellows who dig holes wherever they go?'

'My father preferred to make copies for collectors rather than dig for originals.'

'You sound as if you prefer he remain above such practices.'

'Naturally I would. He kept claiming he would stop once he found something of true value.'

'Ah. One of those. *"Tomorrow, I promise, dear."'*

She clamped her teeth shut against the need to defend her father. This man was only reflecting her and Dash's thoughts and frustrations, but somehow they rankled coming from a stranger. He smiled at her silence.

'So, what happened to your enterprising father and why aren't you with him?'

'He is dead.'

'I see. Lucky you aren't with him, then. Is this recent?'

She blinked a few times. Dash had often told her she lacked sentimentality, but this man exceeded her by several leagues.

'I don't know. The last letter we received from him was several weeks ago.'

'We?'

'Do we have time for this family history, sir? Or are you merely drawing it out while you consider whether I am worth five hundred piastres?'

The lurking smile extinguished like a candle in a rainstorm. He stepped closer.

'You aren't worth a single piastre to me, *Patrick*. And I certainly don't need that gaudy emerald. You forced your way in here asking for help. I am considering offering it. Don't press your luck. Who is *we*?'

'My…my brother, Dash… Dashford.' Damnation, she was stuttering like a child.

'Dashford? I hope that's a title and not his given name.'

'He has no title. Most people call him Dash.'

His mouth quirked upwards again and relief flooded her. He was a volatile man, this giant, but at least he calmed as swiftly as he stormed.

'Dashford.' He drew out the first syllable. It sounded like a mincing dandy. 'Tell me you are named nothing more objectionable than Patricia?'

How she wished that were true.

'Pattie? Petra? Patience?'

She shook her head.

'*Patrice*. You're half-French. That might account for the dashing Dashford flourish.'

'Do we have time for this? Aren't you worried those men will return?'

'We will hear their horses and you will hop right back behind the curtain. Patsy?'

'Cleopatra,' she snapped and he threw back his head in a shout of laughter.

'Dashford and Cleopatra. What were your parents thinking?'

'As little as possible, I think. What does it matter what I am called? Will you help me?'

'I'll not leave you here at this al-Mizan's mercy, that is certain. But it's damned inconvenient.'

'I'm dreadfully sorry,' she said, unable to keep all traces of acid out of her voice. To her dismay, her voice cracked and she cleared her throat. He inspected her again.

'You aren't about to cry, are you?'

'Of course not. I…perhaps…perhaps if I might sit?'

He grunted and guided her to the table like an old lady. She sat, resting her elbows on it and barely resisting the urge to lean her head on it as well.

'When did you last eat?'

'Breakfast. Yesterday.'

'Idiot.'

'I am not an idiot… I was hiding. Then I went to the market to try and buy bread, but I heard al-Mizan again.'

He rubbed his jaw and her own palms tingled. She laid them flat on the table.

'My friend went to buy food, but you need something to settle your nerves.' He went to the cupboard and took out a bottle. She watched his back as his muscles bunched and relaxed. It was like the sand dunes in the Western Desert—a smooth, sculpted landscape broken occasionally by a jagged scar. His skin looked warm—pliable but firm. She leaned her chin on her hand, feeling a little warm herself.

Hunger and weariness explained a great deal.

'Are you truly a mercenary?'

He glanced over his shoulder. 'Do you even know what that is?'

'Of course I do. A soldier of fortune.'

'Well, fortune is debatable, but, yes. You're lucky I am currently not employed and can act as knight errant.'

She looked about the simple room, noting the scuffed boots and the rather ratty backpack by the cupboard. But then there was the expensive cotton shirt. She could not quite make sense of the man. Perhaps he was down on his luck?

'I can pay. The pendant may be hideous, but the emerald itself is quite valuable.'

He turned and smiled and her gaze slunk away; she felt as though she'd been caught peeking through a spy hole in a bath house. The man finally pulled the shirt over his head. Then he sat, resting his arms on the table.

Thank goodness. Trying not to stare at his chest and arms was exhausting. Clothed, he looked a little less intimidating.

'I have more than enough for my simple tastes,' he answered. 'Keep your beastly pendant for a rainy day, or an overly sunny one. I haven't seen a drop of rain since we dropped anchor in Alexandria. I am beginning to miss England, which is quite an achievement.'

'You have been away long?'

'A while. I must return though. My father died as well.'

'I'm sorry.' Her movement was instinctive, her hand settling on his forearm before she could censure herself. It was so unlike her she left it there for a moment before carefully drawing away. He didn't even seem to notice, just shrugged and uncorked the bottle, pouring two glasses.

'Don't be sorry. He was a right bastard as Birdie would say. The world heaved a sigh of relief when he finally cocked up his toes, but it means I probably must return to England and see how my family fares. Here.'

'What is this?'

'Brandy. Just a little until Birdie returns with something to eat.'

'You are being very kind, but I must pay…' She faltered as his gaze flicked back to her.

'Will you stop harking about payment? I'm not the most reliable of fellows, but I can't desert the Queen of Egypt in the middle of the desert. You asked for help, I'm offering. I'll see you to Cairo…'

The knock at the door had her back behind the curtain before she could even think. His chuckle followed her.

'It's only Birdie. Come in, Birdie. I hope you have brought enough food. We have a guest.'

Chapter Two

Rafe tried hard not to smile as the young woman's honey-hazel eyes widened at the sight of Birdie.

She had an almost unfortunately expressive face. It was like watching a battlefield, constantly changing and frequently surprising. But some reactions were thoroughly predictable—like her reaction to his scars and to Birdie's ugly mug.

To her credit, she adapted swiftly to shocks. She'd done an admirable job keeping her eyes away from his scars without appearing to do so and he'd finally taken pity on her and put on the shirt she'd crushed.

Peculiarly, it felt different against his skin and he tugged at his sleeves and rubbed his forearm where she'd touched it briefly in commiseration. Hers hadn't been the first condolence he'd received after his father's death, but it had felt surprisingly sincere.

He had probably shocked her with his unemotional response, but he refused to add sugar to vinegar. The world was well rid of the bastard and he wouldn't pretend otherwise, not even to a stranger. Certainly not to such a strange stranger.

Birdie placed the basket on the table and turned. After his first glance at the woman, he'd predictably ignored her.

'A guest, sir?'

'This is Miss Cleopatra…something. We haven't been formally introduced. She is being chased by some unsavoury individuals and we shall be escorting her to Cairo.'

'We shall, eh? What about your brother, Master Edge? He's the reason we've come to this godforsaken place and now you want to run off before we see this through?'

'We are not running off. We've done everything we can and left a trail of breadcrumbs the size of pyramids to tempt his sorry carcase through Egypt. If that doesn't knock him out of his apathy, I abandon hope for the fool. Once we reach Cairo we will know if our ruse worked. If not, I shall arrange with some friends to hit him over the head and throw him on the first boat to England.'

Birdie shrugged.

'You two were served double…no, treble measures of stubborn at birth, sir. Even if you fetch him here, there's no saying it will make a difference. You can bring a horse to water, but…'

'Yes, yes, the drinking part. All I want is to dump him in the trough for the moment. Eventually, even that idiot must drink. He's parched and won't admit it.'

Birdie grunted and began unpacking his purchases. The wide flatbread, speckled brown and black from the oven, was still warm and the scent filled the room.

The girl swallowed audibly and Rafe tore off a generous piece, handing it to her.

'Don't eat it too quickly or you'll make yourself ill, Cleo-Pat. Birdie will prepare one of his famous stews and some of the local mint tea which will help soothe your nerves and stomach. Then you sleep and tomorrow at dawn we'll find a way to sneak you past these unpleasant fellows. Right, Birdie?'

Birdie grunted again, casting her a look as he went to the door.

'I had the landlord put water on to boil. I'll be back with tea and stew.'

The woman tensed as the door closed behind Birdie and Rafe touched her arm briefly, bringing her eyes to his.

'Don't worry, Birdie is as practised at this as I am. Once you eat, you sleep. If we're to leave at dawn, I want you rested. You will need your wits about you.'

'I don't think I *can* sleep.'

'I think you'll find you can, Cleopatra. Here. Have another piece of bread.'

He had a thousand questions, but he just sat and watched as she chewed slowly, like a dutiful child, even as suspicion was practically rising off her like steam from a bath. Still, when Birdie returned with bowls of the pungent stew and sweet tea she did justice to them with the same careful but methodical approach. Her face was no longer expressive, but as sealed as one of the statues they'd passed along their route. Perhaps it was only hunger and weariness that had left her so exposed.

'More, miss?' Birdie stood with the brass teapot poised over the girl's cup. Unlike the previous three times, she shook her head, casting Birdie a fuzzy smile.

'No more, thank you, sir.' Her voice was slurring and she kept straightening her spine, only to have her shoulders sink under their own weight. Rafe would wager she was so far gone she thought no one was aware of the epic battle she was fighting against sleep.

She'd thanked him as well, but without the smile; warily, like a street dog being offered a scrap and suspecting a trap, but too hungry to keep away.

Pity—she had a smile that completely altered her face. It certainly worked on Birdie, because his usually taciturn friend was beginning to return her smiles, exposing his broken front tooth. That was an honour almost never bestowed on friends, let alone strangers. He was also digging through the stew to find the choicest pieces of lamb for her, something he'd never do for Rafe.

Rafe watched this peculiar blossoming of ease between the two even as he gauged how close Miss Queen of the Nile was to utter collapse. She'd unwrapped her dingy cloth turban from about her head, revealing short hair that fell in feathery swathes across her brow and nape. It was a burnished chestnut colour, like sunlight on wood. Her eyes were also shades of wood and light, with a ring of gold around the increasingly dilated irises.

With her cultured voice, her simple cotton *gallabiyah*, and woodland faerie hair, she was unlike anything he'd come across. Perhaps if he caught her on the cusp of sleep, with her belly full and her head heavy, she might be more liberal with her secrets.

Her lids drooped again and snapped open.

'Thank you, sir,' she recited.

'You're welcome, Miss Cleopatra. So tell me about this book they are after.'

'Book… I don't know. I *told* you.'

'Tell me again. Everything you know.'

She smothered a yawn and rubbed her forehead.

'My father disappeared. More than two months ago. He does sometimes. Disappears for long periods. Looking for objects to buy and sell. My brother went to look for him…'

'Why?'

'Why?' She dragged the word out, her eyes meeting his. He couldn't see any gold in them now, they were all brandy and darkness. The poor girl was half asleep, but he needed to learn a little more.

'Why did your brother go after him if you were accustomed to his absences?'

'Oh. Because Farouq, my father's servant, left him and returned to Cairo.'

'You were worried about your father being alone?'

'*I* wasn't. Dash was. He's nicer than I.'

Well, that was honest.

'Dash didn't return. I was worried. I thought…if something happened and I had not tried…'

'Ah. Guilt.'

'Not only guilt. Dash is too good. My father takes advantage.'

She waved a hand, narrowly missing her cup. Again she seemed to fade, leaning her arm on the table. Her other hand was absently fingering the scabbard of the knife attached to the cloth belt wrapped about her *gallabiyah*. He debated disarming her, but thought better of it. She would feel safer with that toothpick at her disposal.

'So you dressed as Patrick and headed south… Surely not alone?'

She shook her head and yawned again, covering her face with two hands.

'No. I hired a dragoman. He ran away in Meroe.'

'That is unchivalrous. Why?'

'He heard al-Mizan was looking for an Englishman. My description. Dash and I look alike.'

'I see. What did you discover of your father and brother?'

'My father fell ill and died, and I missed my brother by two days. I'm so tired. I must…'

She pushed aside her cup, laid her arms on the table, her head on her arms, and with a little sigh she was asleep.

Rafe looked over her recumbent form at Birdie who had been listening as avidly as he.

'What do you make of that, Birdie?'

'Not much, Colonel. Plenty of holes in that tale. But we can't leave her here.'

'No, unfortunately not. Well, we shall have to change our plans. This sleeping stray here has hired me to deliver her safely to Cairo.'

Birdie gave a snorting laugh.

'Hired you. With what?'

'A tale full of holes.'

'You're an easy mark, Colonel. Beware.'

'She's no threat. Look at her.'

They both looked. She snuggled deeper into her arms. Rafe sighed.

'I'd best put her to bed. Could you find another mattress for me? And not a word to the landlord about our guest.'

'Naturally not. You take my room and I'll bunk on the floor here.'

'No, Birdie. Go speak with Gamal, quietly. Tell him to meet us with the camels by the desert road well before daybreak. That al-Mizan fellow will likely still have people watching the port so we must leave town by the back door.'

'Pity. Gamal was looking forward to selling those camels at market and going home and I was looking forward to a gentle sail down the river.' Birdie sighed and gathered the cups as Rafe came round the table, inspecting his sleeping charge.

'So was I, old man. You are a right nuisance, Miss Patrick Cleopatra. Come along now, into bed with you.'

He was prepared for panic or resistance, but there was none. He held her with one arm around her waist and she went as boneless as a rag doll, her head falling against his chest and her legs buckling. With a grunt he tucked another arm under her legs and swung her up.

She was a tall woman and he'd been right that there were some very pleasant curves under her *gallabiyah* and robe. Her hair was silky under his chin, and beneath the smell of dust and hay was an elusive scent, something cool and green, like a field of wildflowers caught in a late frost. It was totally out of place in a land of browns and ochres.

He smiled at his unusual flight of fancy, but as he laid her down carefully on the narrow bed he allowed himself to breathe it in, her hair just tickling the tip of his nose as she turned to the wall and curled into a ball.

'You are a very peculiar beast, Miss Whoever-You-Are,' he murmured above her and went to fetch a blanket for his new employer.

Rafe stood by the bed. It was still dark and only the occasional sound of an animal—the faint bray of a donkey or yowl of a cat—broke the silence. The girl was still curled up against the wall, taking up a fraction of the long bed. She slept like a hedgehog being sniffed at by a dog.

He rolled his shoulders.

It was time to wake her.

He'd been right to assume the men chasing her would have people at the docks. He'd gone there himself after she'd fallen asleep and seen a couple of the men who'd stood behind that al-Mizan fellow delivering orders to the boatmen. There would be no leaving by that route without having to contend with their knives and the might of the local Bey. It was possible, but risky, and he always preferred the path of least resistance.

Which meant another ride through the desert.

Not his favourite.

He'd told Edge years ago he had no interest whatsoever in visiting his beloved Egypt, being burnt to a crisp by the brutal sun and having what was left flayed by sandstorms. His experiences of the land thus far had only partially changed his mind. He wasn't averse to a nice trip downriver on one of those dahabiya boats, but camels...

Damn, he was getting old.

She sighed, shifting, and the dim light of the oil lamp on the table glinted on her short hair. Even in the pallid light, it was obvious that colour would look magnificent if left to grow long. She'd done a poor job in the back, leaving a tangle of warm waves that gave him a rather clear idea of the magnitude of the offense. Pity. He'd have liked to see that warm chestnut silk in its full glory. Since he'd have her back in Cairo within a week, that was unlikely, but a man could dream.

He leaned over the bed and touched her shoulder and almost fell backwards as she catapulted on to her feet, skidding along the wall.

'Shh…' he cautioned, praying she wouldn't scream. 'It's only the scarred mercenary. It's time to leave.'

She was breathing as if she'd run up four flights of stairs, her hands pressed to the wall. Her eyes were just pale slashes and then they closed as she breathed in very slowly.

'I was dreaming of al-Mizan.'

'I'm sure he'd be flattered.'

'That is *not* what I meant.'

'I'm relieved. I don't see much of a future for you two. Unions should be based on more than a shared appreciation of criminality.'

Her gasp was followed by a little snort of laughter.

'I am not a criminal. I told you, I did not steal anything.'

'I don't particularly care if you did. Mercenaries aren't choosy about their employers, Pat. Now dress so we can slink off into the dark while it is still dark.' He held out his hand and she carefully detached herself from the wall. Her hand was warm in his as he helped her down and, despite her violent awakening, it had the softness of sleep in it. It felt…comforting—a peculiar feeling and not an unpleasant one. He wanted to slip her fingers between his so he could capture that softness, but he let go and turned to take the folded cotton scarf she'd used to cover her head from where Birdie had folded it over a chair.

'You are looking a little better for your rest and food. How are you feeling?'

'I feel…' She paused, her eyes widening in surprise, 'I feel better. That stew was life-giving. But I cannot remember anything after that.'

'I'm not surprised. You were exhausted. Fell face forward into your stew.'

'I did not!'

Her hands, pale smudges, rose to touch her face and he couldn't help smiling at her embarrassment. It was so out of place in this strange situation.

She was out of place.

Hell, *he* was out of place.

Even in the dim light he could see her face turning bright red and he took pity on her.

'I caught you before you landed. It would have been a waste of a decent stew.'

'I don't believe you.'

'Well, I am exaggerating a little. You were coherent enough to put the plate aside before you folded your arms on the table and fell asleep. Don't look so pained, Pat. Amazingly you did not make a fool of yourself, though I would be sure to tell you if you did.'

She glared at him.

'That's right,' he approved. 'Annoyance is healthier than embarrassment. Have at me.'

She surprised him again, her hands dropping, her brows drawing together almost in sorrow.

'You must think me so selfish.'

'I must? Why must I?'

'I did not even thank you or your valet.'

He moved towards the table, tucking his favourite knife into its scabbard and strapping it on before pulling on his coat. He had no problem with people showing their gratitude, preferably in monetary terms, but her remorse made him uncomfortable, as if he'd cheated it out of her, which made no sense.

'You thanked me twice last night, Pat. And Birdie three times. Every time he brought you tea. You drank like a camel.'

'Did I? I…it is all a little murky…but that is not the point. I am truly grateful. And I am sorry you must leave here because of me.'

'Yes, well, we were leaving anyway. You have ten minutes to get yourself in order, Cleo-Pat. I'll wait for you by the stairs.'

He picked up his pack from the table and left the room before she said anything else. Her mercurial transformations were unsettling and he didn't like being unsettled. It was bad for longevity.

Chapter Three

Cleo had lived through many strange days. Certainly stranger than skulking through the narrow roads and the palm groves out of Syene in the pre-dawn hours with two silent men.

Her father's activities had sometimes required hasty scuttlings off in the dark, but the emotions that accompanied those exoduses—a gut-tightening amalgam of fear, anger, frustration, exasperation and weariness—weren't present that dawn. Other than her fear for Dash, she felt surprisingly calm.

Still, she kept glancing over her shoulder, expecting to see al-Mizan and his men materialise out of the dark alleys, but no one followed and only a few stray chickens and a couple of somnolent dogs watched their departure, not even bothering to bark.

Once clear of the town they followed a rough pebbled path towards the low hills. She had little to watch now but the broad back of the mercenary ahead of her. He wore a pale coat that blended well with the desert and he walked with long but light strides.

She was following him without knowing a thing about him other than that he was English and a mercenary. Surely that was a flimsy base upon which to place her trust?

He had a nice smile, her mind offered.

Plenty of scoundrels had nice smiles. '*A man could smile, and smile, and be a villain,*' as Hamlet had said. In fact, it was often their stock in trade. Her father, when it suited him, could smile and beguile with the best of them.

And a marvellous physique, the same treacherous voice chimed in, and she gave it a firm shove back where it belonged. She'd fallen once into that trap and had sworn never to do so again. William had looked like one of the Greek statues he so admired and he'd been a thorough scoundrel in the end.

As always, thoughts of William made her hackles and suspicions rise. She should at least demand to know their destination. It was clear they were heading into the desert, but surely these two men did not think they could get far in this brutal land on foot and with nothing but what they were carrying in their backs.

The mercenary raised his head, scanning the low cliffs, the dawn light turning his scars milky grey.

Was he looking for someone? Perhaps he had struck a deal with al-Mizan while she slept and was delivering her to him in the privacy of the desert...

She slowed, reaching under her robe to grasp the knife attached to the cloth belt wound about her *gallabiyah*.

The giant turned and stopped, his eyes catching the first light of the sun rising sluggishly behind her. Her instincts, usually so reliable, were still as groggy as she'd felt yesterday. Perhaps she *was* still light-headed despite the tea and stew.

She didn't even know his name. That was wrong, wasn't it? To trust one's life to a man when you didn't even know his name?

'What now, Pat?' He sounded impatient.

'I don't know your name.'

'For the love of Zeus... You want society introductions? Here?'

He swept an arm to take in the ragged hills around them and she backed away another step.

'Why won't you tell me your name? Two words. Even one will do.'

'I could just as easily lie to you about it, you know.'

'Yes, but then I'll know you're lying. About everything.'

He sighed. 'And you were so sensible yesterday. My name is Rafe. Now get moving before our guide Gamal decides to continue without us and trades our camels for a bride.'

Rafe. It wasn't much, but it wasn't a lie. Strange name for a strange man. And apparently there were camels and a guide awaiting them.

She took a deep breath and moved forward. He nodded.

'Good. Now stop acting like a skittish foal and keep quiet. I don't want anyone passing through these hills to hear a female speaking in English. So assume you've taken a vow of silence until we're safely in the middle of nowhere, understood?'

She opened her mouth and closed it as he raised a brow.

She nodded, annoyance doing a fair job of chasing away her fear. There was no need for him to snap at her like that. Any sane person would hesitate under these circumstances. Skittish, indeed!

She continued this bracing inner dialogue until they passed through the ravine on to a broad plain. Several camels were tethered together by a copse of palm trees, one camel hobbled, his front leg bent upwards and tied to prevent him from running off. A young Bedawi was seated on the rim of a square well and he jumped down and flashed them a grin, sweeping the scene with his arm as if he'd produced the whole oasis from thin air.

Still wary, she approached the closest camel, a cow with a swan-like neck and eyelashes as thick and curling as their guide's.

'She likes you,' the Bedawi said in French as he adjusted

the cow's bridle, smiling at Cleo. Cleo returned his smile and was just reaching out to pat the cow's neck when a large camel to her right gave a resentful grunt and stretched out his neck to nip at her robe with large yellow teeth. She leapt back and the young man shoved the hairy face away, but gave it a quick rub on the chin and the grunts subsided.

Cleo rubbed at her shoulder though the camel had done no damage.

'I don't think he likes you flirting with Gamal, Pat,' Rafe said beside her. 'Pity you two got off to a bad start, especially since you'll be riding him.'

'I… *Him?* You must be jesting!'

'Best way to make sure you don't turn your back on the brute is to be on *his* back, right? Pat here will be riding Kabir, Gamal.'

She was quite certain the giant was making game of her, but the Bedawi took him seriously, raising his hands in horror.

'No, *nadab*. Kabir no like women. He al-Shroud. Only men ride him. Boy will ride Gamila.' He patted the cow.

Well, Gamila wasn't as pretty as her name proclaimed, but her soft muzzle brushed Cleo's shoulder, as if to compensate for Kabir's bad manners. Cleo smiled into her doe-like eyes and stroked her wiry neck.

'You're nothing like that great brute, are you, darling?' she cooed. 'You're a beautiful little sweetheart, aren't you? Yes, you…*ack!*'

She gave a whoop of surprise as Rafe raised her by the waist and deposited her on the blanketed saddle.

'Do try to remember you've taken a vow of silence until I say otherwise, Pat. And if you must talk, try not to sound as though you're making love to the blasted animal— anyone hearing you will see through that disguise faster than I did.'

He strode off and Cleo glared after him. It hadn't hurt,

but her skin tingled where he'd touched her none the less, as if she'd left it exposed to the desert sun.

They rode in silence, Gamila falling into an easy rolling gait, her long neck swinging a little from side to side as if to some unheard tune. Occasionally Rafe glanced back at her with a half-amused smile, as if remembering a good joke, or as if convinced his demand she remain silent was proving a true penance.

Which it was, blast him.

Silence was usually no hardship for her. She'd long ago developed the skill of daydreaming her way through interminable and uncomfortable hours of travel. But now the temptation to demand he tell her his plans was churning inside her like the cataracts of the Nile.

After what seemed like hours he checked Kabir's pace and came alongside her.

'You may speak now, Pat. All those thoughts bouncing about inside of you can't be good for your health. Or my longevity. I should have remembered to take away that little toothpick tied to your belt while you slept before you're tempted to wield it against me.'

She pressed her hand to the 'toothpick' and narrowed her eyes against the glare of the sun as she looked at Rafe. He and Birdie had wrapped linen cloths into turbans to protect their heads like the local *fellahin* and he had tucked the cotton end of it so that it covered the scarred side of his face.

'Where are we heading?'

'To a port further north.'

'Is that wise? Once al-Mizan realises I am no longer in Syene, he will likely search the neighbouring port towns.'

'Not when he hears your brother hired two men to take him to the Red Sea port of Berenice yesterday evening.'

'What? Why did you not tell me? I must return…'

She tugged on the reins and at Gamila's protesting grunt Kabir's long neck snaked out, his teeth bared and heading for Cleo's knee. Fortunately, they closed with a snap just short of her as Rafe angled the animal's head away.

'What the devil is wrong with you, you hairy tortoise? He really doesn't like you, does he? And there is no call to hare off in pursuit, Miss Osbourne. Your brother is not on his way to Berenice. That is what is termed a *diversion*.'

Her excitement fizzled.

'Al-Mizan is too intelligent to fall prey to a trick.'

'Which is why I paid two men to leave town in a highly secretive manner after spreading rumours of taking a furtive, honey-eyed *hawagi* to Berenice.'

'What will happen to them if al-Mizan catches them?'

His gaze moved over her face.

'What a sensitive conscience you have, Pat. Once they provide your admirer with the information they were well paid to deliver, he will let them go.'

'You cannot be certain of that.'

'I am certain of nothing, but I choose my pawns well. They are cousins of Bey al-Wassawi and were in pressing need of some funds. It would not serve al-Mizan's purpose to harm the relations of the local Bey with no cause.'

'And what information were they to pass along?'

'That Birdie and I are on the run from Mehmet Ali after I tried to…ah, elope with his niece and that we presumed al-Mizan came to my rooms using the tale of an English thief as a cover to gauge my defences.'

She tried not to smile. 'That is…elaborate.'

'I thought so, too, but Birdie concocted it and he has an affection for tall tales. To give him his due it did possess the right elements—honour and revenge and cowardly foreigners and all that.'

'No element of truth?'

'Did I elope with the Khedive's niece?' His brows rose in mockery.

'No, I meant…are you on the run?'

'Only from myself. But this wasn't what you were anguishing over just now, though, was it?'

'I wasn't anguishing.'

'If you'd squeezed your lips together any tighter, you'd have lost them. Now that we are a safe distance and can talk I think it is best you tell me more about your predicament so we can be prepared for the worst.'

Suspicion came back with a roar, chasing away her amusement—what if all this openness and charm was aimed at coaxing the information out of her without risking violence? What if he and al-Mizan—?

'There. You're anguishing again,' the mercenary interrupted her thoughts. He looked cross and impatient now, not the kind of expression one expected of a crafty killer. Still, she looked around—they were truly in the middle of nowhere. If he chose to kill her, the only beings to witness her demise would be jackals and vultures and the creepy crawly things that feasted on carrion and…

'Where are we heading?' She forced the question out, her voice as rough as the ground under Gamila's sure hooves.

'I told you, Gamal is taking us further up the river.'

'Which port?'

'You needn't concern yourself with that. Gamal knows what he's doing. I hope. Now, why don't you tell me—?'

She spurred Gamila forward until she came up beside Gamal. Rafe sighed and clicked his tongue, spurring Kabir after her.

'May I ask you a question, Gamal?' she asked in Arabic.

'You speak Arabic!' The young man's eyes widened, accentuating the lines of kohl under his eyes that protected them from sun and disease.

'I learned in Acre.'

'Ah! Far away.' He glanced past her and switched to his lilting mix of French and English. 'She speaks good

Arabic, *nadab*. Now someone understand Gamal and I not speak as to little children.'

'Just remember this little child here is the one paying you,' Rafe replied, tapping his chest. Gamal's smile widened.

'I shall keep your secrets, *nadab*.'

'You don't know my secrets, Gamal.'

'Then it will be easy, yes?' He winked at Cleo and she smiled and answered him in Arabic.

'I don't want to cause you trouble, but could you tell me where you are taking us?'

'*Biltakid!* Of course! To Daraw. We shall reach it by nightfall. There is a small port there where a fishing boat could take you to Luxor and from there you could find a proper *dahabiya*. That would be fastest.'

She thanked him and allowed her mount to fall back again. Unfortunately, Rafe did the same.

'Why didn't you tell me you spoke Arabic?' he demanded.

'You didn't ask.'

'True. Would you have told me had I asked?'

She considered that.

'Probably. I don't enjoy lying unless I must.'

'Good. So now tell me what you spoke of and why it worried you.'

'How do you know it worried me?' she temporised.

'Because when you aren't impersonating a sphinx, your face is as expressive as a toddler's.'

'Ah, I see you are still smarting from Gamal's child comment.'

'No, I merely don't like people talking behind my back.'

'We were right beside you.'

'Don't quibble, Pat. Tell me.' He paused, his gaze holding hers. 'I see. You don't trust me…'

She waited for another flash of panic, but it refused to

come. Somehow facing his scarred and frowning visage made him less fearsome.

'All he said was that we are heading for Daraw, a small port not far to the north. There are only fishing boats there, not the larger *feluccas* or *dahabiyas* that could transport us to Cairo.'

Rafe tapped his hand on his thigh and scanned the horizon.

'I wish we had a decent map of this place. Mine shows nothing between Syene and the temples. I'll have a word with Gamal and Birdie and decide what is best.'

'I'm dreadfully sorry to be such a bother, Mr... Rafe.'

'How very English of you, Miss Pat. And it is either Rafe or, if you are clinging to the codes of civilisation, Mr Grey.'

'Mr Grey.' She smiled at the wholly inappropriate name. Mr Grey had to be one of the least grey men of her acquaintance. 'I am pleased to make your acquaintance, Mr Grey.'

He smiled back and gave a little bow.

'The pleasure is all mine, Miss Cleopatra... What *is* your full name?'

'Osbourne. Cleopatra Osbourne.'

'*Osbourne?* Well, well. The pleasure is all mine, Miss Cleopatra Osbourne.'

Chapter Four

'Tired?'

Cleopatra-Patrick Osbourne glanced up from staring at her saddle and shook her head without a word.

She was proving to be one of those rare people who only spoke when they had something to say. There was even something a little intimidating about the way she made no requests for either sustenance or rest as the hours melted away in the blazing heat. She'd eaten when Birdie brought her dried dates and bread, bestowing that same surprisingly warm smile upon his friend, but otherwise she seemed miles away, as unapproachable as the desert.

The broad, padded saddles were far more comfortable than he'd expected and the camels moved with impressive balance and occasionally speed over uneven ground, but the desert was just as uncomfortable as anticipated. It was mostly rock-strewn plains between stark hills, tufted with thorny trees and bushes. It was nothing like the illustrations of rolling sand dunes he'd seen in his brother's books. He'd have to have a word with Edge about authorial integrity.

It was also empty. He'd seen not one living soul the entire day other than a few lizards poking their snouts at the sun. It was daunting as hell and hot as Hades. The only positive was that it would be impossible for anyone to approach them without being seen. He untucked the cloth that covered his face and breathed deeply.

'Gamal said we are stopping for the night at the end of this plain,' he said to the girl and she glanced up from her contemplation of her saddle.

'So soon? We could cover quite a few more miles before dark, surely.'

'*You* could, perhaps, but there is a well there and I think the camels might prefer to stop and drink. They've been doing the hard work all day, after all. You've only been sitting there scowling and stewing.'

Even under the film of dust that covered her face he could see her colour rise, but then the lines at the corners of her eyes crinkled in laughter.

'You are a strange man, Mr Grey. I cannot tell if you are trying to annoy me or make me laugh.'

'I haven't yet decided. Either will serve the purpose better than you sinking into a brown study. Though to be fair, brown is pretty much all there *is* to study out here.'

She laughed and unhooked the cloth covering her mouth, shaking off a small cloud of dust.

'I love it.'

'You and my brother.' He sighed. 'I wish you would explain what it is about the desert that appeals to you, for I am yet to understand this passion for sand.'

'Now you are being facetious. There is so much more than sand here.'

'Rocks. Thorny bushes and stunted trees.'

'Have you seen none of the antiquities?'

'A little. Birdie and I have been on a forced march, or rather forced sail up the Nile.'

'You said as much before. Why *are* you here if you are not interested in these lands? Has it to do with this brother of yours?'

He found himself on the verge of telling her about Edge

when he realised she had done it again—very neatly deflected attention from herself.

'Miss Osbourne—'

'Look!' she interrupted with a little sigh of pleasure. 'An oasis.'

They'd just come around an outcropping and a burst of blessed green met their eyes—palm trees waving above a clump of bushes and a streak of low green grass marking the run off from a well.

'Thank the lord,' he said with equal pleasure. 'Miss Osbourne, would you care for a cup of tea?'

Rafe held the two chipped cups as Birdie poured from the kettle.

'Campfire tea again, Colonel,' Birdie said with satisfaction. 'It has been a while, no?'

'You have a peculiar sense of nostalgia, Birdie. We had perfectly respectable tea only yesterday. Without the mud. I hope the boiling killed whatever that is that's floating in it.'

Birdie poked at it with the tip of the stick he'd used to stir the fire, adding flecks of charred wood to the brew.

'Looks dead to me. You drink that and give her the other.'

'*Thank* you, Birdie.'

'You're welcome, Colonel.' Birdie grinned unrepentantly and Rafe sighed and walked across to where the young woman was seated on a wide boulder. She was staring hard at the ground, oblivious to the spectacle of the setting sun turning the hills around them into a dance of red-orange fire. She might be dressed like a man, but she looked the image of a desert princess being conveyed to some unwanted fate—resolute but inwardly resisting.

'May I join you, Pat?'

She cast him a guilty look, as if she'd been caught thinking very uncharitable thoughts of him and their little camp.

Well, he'd been thinking the same.

She met his gaze but he felt her thoughts were several leagues away. She did not even appear to notice he was holding out a steaming cup of tea so he raised it, making the steam weave tipsily between them.

'Here. For you.'

She blinked and took the steaming tin cup warily. 'What is it?'

'Tea. Sugar. And something murky at the bottom, so drink carefully.'

Her sudden laugh was even more a surprise than her smile—it was rolling, joyous…irresistible. It took years off her face and he found himself smiling as he sat down on the boulder beside her.

For a few moments, they sipped their tea and watched the sun melt into the hills. The wind was rising, sweeping away the baking heat of the day, and the scent of earth and tea soothed the edges of this stark world.

He knew it was time to discover more about his charge, but the moment was so…peaceful, he didn't want to let it go just yet.

In the end she spoke first.

'The last time I had tea in the desert was with my brother.'

'Tell me about him.'

'He is two years younger than I. Very clever. We write articles together for the *Illustrated Gazette* about our travels under the name D.C. Osbourne. Do you know the *Gazette*?'

'I don't, I'm afraid. A local newspaper?'

'Oh, no. They are London-based and very selective.'

'Impressive.'

She glanced at him as if gauging whether he was being serious. Birdie had given her soap and she'd washed her face and hands and her lashes were still spiked together. With her short hair uncovered and the wind teasing it against her cheeks and brow she could easily have been a model for Leila, the heroine of the *Desert Boy* novels his brother penned. He smiled at the silly notion and she frowned.

'It *is* impressive,' she insisted, mistaking his smile. 'We have had almost a dozen articles appear in the *Gazette*. Do you know how many journalists would give their eye-teeth to achieve that?'

'Many, I presume. I have no idea what eye-teeth are, but they sound valuable.'

Her frown gave way to laughter again.

'They are the pointy teeth, like a dog's, though I am quite certain you know that. You are a strange man, Mr Grey.'

'That has been pointed out to me before, for various reasons. What is yours?'

'I cannot make out what you are thinking.'

'That is a good sign. I've spent many years working to achieve that effect and it is comforting to know I've succeeded. Do you always expect to know what people are thinking, Miss Osbourne?'

'No, that would be presumptuous of me, but few people make the effort to truly hide their thoughts and even fewer do so while appearing so amicable and reasonable on the surface.'

He pressed a hand to his chest.

'Are you implying that I am duplicitous, Miss Cleopatra-Patrick-on-the-run-dressed-as-a-boy?'

'No, I am saying you possess a singular talent, Mr Grey. It was a compliment.'

'I shall return the compliment by telling you precisely what I am thinking, which is that though I find your singular talent for not chattering very impressive, at the moment I need you to tell me as much as you can about your situation so I know what lies ahead of us.'

She sighed and touched the tip of her tongue to the dry

skin of her lower lip. His tongue tingled and he pressed his teeth into it. Down, boy. Wholly inopportune.

'I don't particularly enjoy talking about my family's affairs, Mr Grey.'

'Perfectly understandable. I myself would prefer to share my bed with a dozen warthogs rather than do that, but, given the circumstances, you will have to overcome your distaste.'

'I know that. I am not certain where to begin. With my father, I suppose. He is rather hard to explain. He was a…a collector.'

'Of?'

'Curios. He travelled the world collecting whatever he thought people might have an interest in buying. Masks, statues, anything really. Since we came to Egypt he concentrated on statues and ancient jewellery. And mummies.'

'Mummies? As in…mummies? *Dead people* mummies? Your father was a grave robber?'

'Of course not, mummies aren't…they…he…well, I dare say you are right. Amongst other things. For the most part he worked for a French antiquities trader in Cairo named Boucheron, but he recently tried to find independent sources of income.'

'Such as selling decomposing corpses.'

'They are remarkably well preserved; that is the whole point. He recently sold a shipment of some three dozen mummies to a man named Pettifer in London who also has an interest in Egyptian curiosities.'

'He shipped three dozen dead people to London.'

'They weren't all people. There were also some baboons and cats and even a crocodile…' She must have seen something of his thoughts on his face for her honey-brown eyes filled with laughter. 'Never mind. I know it is ghoulish, but there is a market for them thanks to the likes of Belzoni and Drovetti. People pay to watch them unwrapped.'

'Good God.'

'You are very squeamish for a mercenary, Mr Grey.'

'Having my life almost forcibly removed from me on too many occasions, I have a healthy respect for it. I don't like the thought of my body being…tampered with.'

'Well, I don't think you need worry about that as you are unlikely to be mummified.'

'I prefer not to think about it at all, Miss Morbid. Shall we return to your father?'

'I dare say we must. The point is that my father was a scavenger. Rather like the ibises by the Nile—he collected what he could and hurried away when bigger prey arrived. That is why we moved so often.'

'And this is how you were raised?' That explained quite a bit.

'Not wholly. Until I was fourteen I lived with my mother in a small town near Dover. After she died…eventually we went to live with my father. He was in Acre at the time, searching for Templar treasure.'

Eventually. There was a wealth of possibilities tucked into that word. Curiosity plucked at him again, but he concentrated on his objective.

'I presume he found none?'

Her dimples appeared though her mouth merely gave a small quirk, as if struggling against invisible constraints.

'Naturally not. We were quite hopeful for a while, though.'

'So was I at fourteen. What happened next?'

'He ran afoul of Suleiman, the local Mameluke ruler.'

'What did he do? Try to steal his mummy?'

'I see you find this amusing, Mr Grey.'

'No, merely trying to raise a smile out of you. I'm improving, aren't I?'

Her smile won out over the dimples and he found himself smiling back.

'So you left Acre for Egypt?'

'No, first we went to Greece where Father found someone who made wonderful statuettes which he then made to look ancient by staining them with tea and cracking them. Dash and I enjoyed that part of it. Then they shipped them to accomplices of theirs in England until he was requested to leave after…after his partner returned to England and my father could not pay his debts. From there we went to Zanzibar because he had heard from Mr Pettifer that there was demand for more exotic findings. We lived there until—'

'Let me guess. Until he fell afoul of the local ruler and was forced to leave. Again.'

'No, his searches meant we sailed a great deal along the coast and at one point the ship we were on was captured by pirates.'

'Good God! How old were you? Were you…hurt?'

She tipped her head on one side, considering the undercurrent he could not hide from his question.

'Ever since I came to live with my father I have often been Patrick. He said he could hardly take in a girl and was planning to send me to some horrid convent school in the desert. I refused to go and leave Dash alone with him. Patrick was a compromise.'

He digested this piece of information, adjusting his thoughts and curbing his temper, but it wasn't easy. Fathers were a sore point with him, but hers was shaping up to be someone he most definitely would not have gone out of his way to help.

'Do you mean to say you have been masquerading as Patrick Osbourne from the age of fourteen?'

'Well, only part of the time. It was far simpler than it sounds. We were children and there were very few Europeans where we were and many tended to be associated with the various churches and therefore naturally my father avoided them. The most creditable Englishwoman I met during this period was Lady Hester Stanhope and she was dressed far more outrageously than I.'

'You met her?'

'I did, though not in the best of circumstances. My father tried to insinuate himself into her expedition to Ascalon, but once he realised she planned to surrender whatever she found to the authorities he left. She was very kind to Dash and me and thoroughly approved of my man's garb, having adopted it herself long before. She even gave me a pair of her embroidered trousers.'

'So she, at least, knew you were a girl.'

'Oh, yes. It is usually the women who see through my disguise, but they rarely tell the men.'

'The world in a nutshell.' He grinned and she finally turned to him fully.

'*You* saw through it, Mr Grey. What does that make you?' Her smile, complicit and full of mischievous light, felt like an invitation to step over an unseen barrier... Into what, he had no idea, except that it was probably not a line he ought to cross. He pulled back on the reins he hadn't realised were slipping.

'Observant by necessity. My livelihood depends on it, Miss Osbourne. Now that we have established your father's dubious activities, tell me what happened here in Egypt.'

She shrugged and swirled her tea.

'The French led by Drovetti protect the antiquities trade jealously, sometimes violently. That is why Father decided it was safer to work with them. Boucheron hired him to help set up workshops to produce what they term *souvenirs* for sale in Paris and London and Vienna.'

'Sounds sensible. What went wrong?'

'My father never abandoned his dream of making a great discovery and he felt Boucheron's activities demeaned him. He wanted to be a Belzoni.'

'What on earth is a Belzoni?'

'Not what, who. Belzoni made his name transporting the statue of young Memnon to England and explored as far south as Ybsambul. He is all the rage in England now. My father abhorred him.'

'I thought he wanted to be him.'

'Precisely. Envy is a strange beast, isn't it?'

'I wouldn't know,' he said primly and won another smile.

'In any case, my father decided he would go even further south, to the pyramids of Nubia. There are dozens of them there, more even than in Egypt.'

'There is also an ongoing war, as best I can gather. Hardly the best place to take one's family.'

'That was why I…why Dash and I decided not to go with him.'

'I see. And how did he react to that?'

'He was…upset. He is accustomed to us tending to the practicalities of his life. But he had his servant with him. At least he did until Farouq also decided he had had enough and returned to Cairo where he went to work for Boucheron, my father's employer. By this time Dash and I had already decided it was time to leave Egypt. We'd been talking for a long while that we no longer wished to live like… fugitives. We planned to return to England and set up house and write articles and perhaps Dash could find employment at a university or a newspaper. We began making arrangements and sent a letter to our father to inform him.'

'Let me guess, he wrote back denouncing his ungrateful offspring.'

'No. He never wrote back at all. I told Dash that was an answer in itself as we should leave, but Dash is far nicer that I. He decided he could not leave without speaking with my father directly.'

'Leaving you alone in Cairo?'

She scuffed her boot on the pebble-strewn ground. The sun had sunk lower still and the hills and scrubby trees were casting long shadows, like fingers straining to envelop them. He could feel the struggle inside her.

'Tell me, Cleo-Pat.'

'It's all so complicated. I don't know if there is anything to tell. Dash tells me I am absurdly suspicious by nature.'

'I am glad to hear that. Here is your chance to unburden those suspicions to someone who has plenty of experience in that field.'

'Very well. A couple days before Dash left for Nubia, Boucheron came to our lodgings and told us our father stole something from him before his departure. He demanded we find my father and force him to return.'

'I thought you said your father spent several months in Nubia? If he stole something before he left, why didn't this Boucheron demand it's return earlier?'

'Precisely. I presumed Boucheron only realised my father's transgression because Farouq revealed something when he went to work for him.'

'Strange. Did he not tell you what it was?'

'No. When he realised we had no idea what he was speaking of, he merely said our father would know and that when we found him we should tell him that, unless he complied, Boucheron's Janissaries would resolve the issue. I knew what that meant. He'd once sent one of his servants to "resolve an issue" with a Maltese merchant. We never saw the merchant again.'

It wasn't calm, but iron control that held her voice flat. Probably years and years of expecting the worst. Rafe's hands tightened on his thighs but he didn't speak, just waited, and after a moment she continued.

'I decided right then that enough was enough. Boucheron might just as easily decide to kill one of us to make his point and I wanted Dash out of there.'

'Why didn't you offer him the emerald?'

'I did. He tossed it back at me. It seems no one wants it.'

'Interesting.'

'I thought so, too. I told Dash we needed to leave immediately and at first I thought he would agree—we even made travel arrangements—but then he disappeared to Nubia and left me a letter telling me he'd arranged for me to travel with a family returning to London on the same ship who were willing to provide me with lodging until he arrived.'

'Since you're here I presume that plan fell through.'

'I could not leave Egypt not knowing what had happened to Dash. Besides, the Mitchums were extremely proper and quite shocked with me. I think they were pleased I reneged on my brother's plan.'

'I can imagine. So, tell me what you discovered in Nubia and how those fellows, whom I assume are Boucheron's men, came to be chasing you?'

'It is complicated…'

'I have gathered that. Since we have nothing better to do at the moment you have plenty of time. Tell me.'

She sighed. 'Very well. When I reached Meroe I discovered my father had died and that Dash had been and already left to return to Cairo. But when I reached Wadi Halfa an innkeeper warned me a man called al-Mizan was looking for a young foreigner matching my description. Clearly he was searching for Dash. We are very alike.'

'I'm impressed the innkeeper didn't hand you over. You must have some hitherto undiscovered ability to charm.'

The dimples punctuated her cheeks, but her voice remained dispassionate.

'That was when my dragoman left me, so apparently my charm has its limits. I managed to remain hidden until Syene but when I tried to hire a felucca the owner ran off to find al-Mizan so I went back into hiding. I thought the longer I led them astray, the more time Dash would have to reach Cairo and then leave for London.'

'Wait. Why would he leave for London if you hadn't?'

Her shoulders rose and fell on a long sigh.

'Because I left a letter saying I had left for London as

agreed. If something happened to me on the way to Nubia, I did not want Dash searching for me.'

Rafe shook his head, but he understood sibling loyalty. The only reason he was presently sitting on a boulder in the middle of the desert, with aches in places he hadn't even known existed, was because of his brother.

But what the devil was he going to do with her? Simply conveying her to Cairo was no longer a viable solution.

They sat in silence for a while, watching the last glimmerings of the sun as it melted behind the hills. A pleasant breeze began to stir the dusty green bushes and cooled his face.

'So what shall we do next?' she asked, interrupting his musings.

'Go to sleep.'

'You know perfectly well what I meant, Mr Grey. Should we not go and try to slip into Daraw under cover of darkness?'

'No. Arriving in a new city in the dark draws attention.'

'I would have thought the opposite.'

'Foreigners entering a new town will always be remarked and Birdie and I doubly so. We are safest hiding in plain sight. A foreigner and his Bedawi guide will draw attention, but hopefully not suspicion. Tomorrow you and Birdie will remain here while Gamal and I have a look about Daraw and if it is safe we will hire a boat and then sneak you on board. So there. What say you to that brilliant reasoning, Master Pat?'

'I say your superior reasoning is not matched by superior mathematical skills. There will be a foreigner and two local guides. Birdie can remain to watch the camp.'

'I didn't miscount. Two guides would be suspicious. You will remain here with Birdie.'

'Two is no more suspicious than one.'

'You will remain here with Birdie. If anyone is watching the port, they might see through your disguise as easily as I did.'

'So you *do* think there might be trouble.'

'I always think there will be trouble. It protects me from being either surprised or disappointed.'

'True, but it is an awfully wearying way to live.'

She sounded like someone who spoke from long experience.

'Your father has a great deal to answer for,' he said in a burst of annoyance and she smiled with surprising lightness.

'He was not all bad. People rarely are. Surely there is something you remember fondly about your own father?'

'Not a thing. He wasn't a sweet old thing like yours.'

'Well, at least my father had some sense of duty; he could have abandoned us when we were dropped on his doorstep, but he didn't.'

'Good God, Pat, that's no measure of a father's worth.'

'True. Perhaps I feel guilty I never truly liked him. Is that terrible of me?'

'Terribly honest. I never met the fellow and I'm not very fond of him myself.'

She laughed.

'You are very flippant for a mercenary.'

'We are a surprisingly flippant breed.'

'That is not what one would expect.'

'Have you ever met any?'

'Only some of Boucheron's Janissaries. I think their senses of humour were beaten out of them at birth, poor souls. Are there others like you?'

'I'm afraid to ask what "like you" entails to your mind, other than flippancy.'

She considered him, brushing aside a tangle of hair the wind had blown over her brow. Despite her masculine attire and haircut, he was finding it very hard to believe anyone could possibly be fooled by her masquerade.

'I don't know,' she said at last. 'You are not at all what I would have expected.'

'Another ambiguous statement. You are very skilled at those, Cleo-Pat.'

'I shall be even more ambiguous, then. I am glad you are not what I would have expected. Thank you for coming to my aid.'

With the sun hidden it was already pleasantly cool, but he flushed as swiftly and as absurdly as a boy. For a moment his mind went peculiarly bright and blank, like stepping from darkness into a well-lit room. He searched for something to say. Something flippant and safe.

The breeze was rising and it flicked the edge of her cloth scarf against her cheek and she brushed it away, unwinding it from her neck.

She had taken off her robe and her *gallabiyah* hung loosely about her, but now he could see her throat and collarbone, paler than her hands, just the hint of a silver chain disappearing beneath the fabric. The image of it lying against her skin, with that tangle of metal and vivid green stone nestling between her generous breasts… He tried to stop the downward spiral of his thoughts and blood, but with a sense of fatality he felt his body clench with anticipation of following those thoughts with touch…with taste…

He gathered himself, pushing away his libido's wholly inappropriate response. It was not as if she was making any effort at all to be seductive. In fact, she was one of the least artful women he had ever met. For all he knew, all those years playacting a boy meant she was unaware of her attractions and, as far as he was concerned, it was best to keep it that way.

She laid her folded scarf on the boulder and took another sip of her tea, closing her eyes, her tongue brushing across her lower lip as if to gather every drop of the beverage. Again there was absolutely no reason for his body to lurch like a poleaxed camel, but it did.

'Don't do that.' The words were out of him before he could think them into silence and she straightened in surprise.

'Don't do what?'

'W-wet your lips.' Hell—was he stammering? He hurried on. 'It will only dry your lips further. I will fetch more tea. And food. I'm starving.'

He strode off, relieved to put some distance between them. Perhaps the desert thirst had caught him and this strange, sensitised heat was the outcome. Or perhaps this land of ancient gods and strange tales was affecting him more than he wished to admit.

Another complaint to set at his brother's door.

Chapter Five

Birdie and Gamal were preparing flat loaves of charred bread on stones set on the fire and the earthy scent mingled with the smoke. Rafe's stomach growled in anticipation even as his mind moaned.

'I need a decent meal soon, Birdie. I'll waste away on this regime of bread and cheese.'

'You've gone soft these years, Colonel. A little hardship won't hurt you.'

'Devil take you, Birdie. I don't need any *"It will be good for you"* advice. I shall turn thirty-seven soon.'

'Huh. I was forty-six last month, young 'un.'

Rafe tried to school his smile.

'Forty-eight. And we celebrated in full style on board Chris's pleasure ship.'

Birdie's crooked teeth reflected the flickering firelight.

'Did we? I don't recollect much. The mead that rascally Catalan of his brewed would have been useful against the French. Hopefully we can celebrate yours on board there as well after we bring the young miss back home. She'll be safe there?'

Rafe brushed the sand from his hands.

'I don't know. I don't think so. We may have to improvise something.'

'Hmmm…'

'What does that mean?'

'It means, my fine buck, that you have found another way to avoid coming to terms with your future.'

Rafe stilled.

'Birdie, we do not discuss this.'

'*You* don't. Nothing stopping me from doing so. Only a few months ago you said now the old Duke is dead you had no choice but to return. Then you concoct this plan to bring Edge back from Brazil by counterfeiting your death…'

'You know why I did that. The stubborn idiot wouldn't have moved otherwise.'

'Aye, but don't tell me you weren't considering turning that fiction into something permanent and having your brother assume the title.'

'I considered it for all of two minutes. I wouldn't do anything which meant I could no longer see Edge.'

Birdie's face softened.

'I know. Those two years you spent with him and his son were your best. All the more reason why you should have your own children. And that means going back to England, putting your hand on what's rightfully yours and settling down. I'm not saying you shouldn't help Miss Cleopatra reach Cairo, but after that it's time to go home. No more lost souls.'

Rafe shifted uneasily.

'I don't want the damn Duchy; all I have of Greybourne are bad memories. That place will sap my soul. I enjoy what we do, Birdie.'

'You enjoy solving other people's problems and you were a fine officer. I dare say having a few hundred people under you as the Duke of Greybourne won't be much different. You'll make your own memories to chase away the old. I've never seen you dragged down by fate, Rafe. Not when you stomped into barracks twenty-odd years ago and demanded I take you on and not when you near lost your life when you pulled McAllister and Cates from the fire at Los Piños.'

Rafe instinctively rubbed at the marbled skin of his neck. He might have saved two of his men from the fire at the gunpowder depot, but it had been Birdie who'd saved his life and nursed him back to health. Another on a long, long list of debts he owed him.

'Don't talk rot, Birdie. Fate not only dragged me down, but stomped me into a pulp when Jacob died.'

'I know you loved your nephew like your own, Rafe. I was there with you at Chesham those two years, remember?' Birdie answered softly. 'Fate dealt you and Edge a vicious blow, but it didn't fell you. You saved your brother from drowning in grief and you're still trying to save him, but at some point you will have to stop trying to save others and do something about yourself.'

'What the devil is wrong with me? I like my life, Birdie.'

Birdie shrugged, which only made Rafe angrier.

'You're a fine one to talk. You've no more roots than I do.'

'That's true, but I'm coming to regret it, Colonel, and it may be well too late for me. You've made me a rich man, but I told you when we began this voyage it would likely be my last.'

'You've said that a dozen times before.'

'Aye, well, that's my problem. I'm as scared as you.'

'Scared.'

'Shaking in my dusty boots. Elmira told me so and she is right.'

Rafe fell silent. He knew Birdie and the rather taciturn widowed housekeeper they employed at Tarn Cottage had an arrangement, and he was glad for Birdie, but he hadn't realised it went beyond mutual convenience.

'I didn't know it was that serious, Birdie,' he said a little weakly.

'Well, neither did I for as long as I could ignore it. I

never expected a woman to want to look at my ugly mug day in day out, but the truth is I've come to admit I want that. When we return... I think I will stay. I'll be there if you need me, that will always be the case, but...'

Rafe touched Birdie's shoulder briefly.

'I'm happy for you.'

'Well, don't say that yet. She might have come to her senses and changed her mind by the time we return. But if she hasn't... I would rather see your children born before Elmira kills me with her cooking.'

Rafe smiled, but he didn't feel it. The sick feeling was only growing. He'd known this moment was coming since the day he'd received news of his father's death.

Birdie had known him longer and better than anyone and yet he still could not explain to him the deep, sick sensation that rose up in him every time he thought of returning to Greybourne. He'd built a whole new life, a good life, well away from that dank pit. His brief return to it when Edge's son was born had only provided more proof of precisely how dank it was.

He'd returned, expecting to find Edge and his wife Lady Edward happily celebrating the birth of their son. Instead, he'd found Edge alone with Jacob, a happy but sickly babe, while Lady Edward had been whisked away to Bath by her mother to recover her strength. As the doctors shook their heads in despair over Jacob's health and Lady Edward kept extending her stay in Bath, Rafe had abandoned all thought of leaving Edge and Jacob.

His resolve to remain had received an extra boost when a month after his arrival his father descended on Chesham unannounced, spewing his usual vitriolic concoction of doom and damnation. The Duke proclaimed the infant an abomination to God and demanded he be sent away so Edge could beget a healthy heir for Greybourne since Rafe's seed was clearly not going to bear fruit.

That had been a day Rafe would prefer to forget. If it

had not been for Birdie and the swift arrival of his mother, accompanied by the ever-ready Dr Parracombe and his sedatives, he and Edge might well have committed patricide. If ever he'd needed a reminder of the poison that was Greybourne, he'd seen it that day. He wanted nothing to do with it. He would do his duty by the estate and the welfare of his tenants and not a hair's breadth more.

'I think you'd best look elsewhere for someone to dandle on your knee, Birdie. But you are right that I must at least make provisions for the management of the estate. It will be damned strange going back there. It feels as though I'm willingly stepping into a pit full of vipers.'

'There'll be naught but old snake skins by now.'

Rafe wasn't at all certain of that, but he shoved that thought aside.

'That is just as unappetising an image. Speaking of which, isn't that ready? I am so hungry I could eat your cooking.'

Birdie tipped the plate he was in the process of extending and Rafe rescued it before its contents slid into the fire.

'Now, now, Birdie. I thought you had a tougher hide than that.'

'I need one with you about. Go feed the young lady before she blows away. And watch yourself over there.'

Rafe took the plate and shot a look at his friend.

'What is that supposed to mean?'

'She might come to like you all too well if you go on as you are and then you'll be sorry.'

'What the devil do you think I was doing?'

'Making her smile. And laugh. And liking it.'

'I was making her tell me the truth, which is rather necessary under the circumstances. That is all.'

'If you say so. Now go feed her. *That* is necessary.'

Cleo watched the two men talking by the fire. The contrast between them could not have been more marked.

Even with his scars, Mr Grey was a splendid specimen of a man. His size and patrician features only served to accentuate Birdie's squat ugliness. But as she watched the easy, smiling communication between the two it was evident that contrast was lost on them.

'Love looks not with the eyes but with the mind...'

She shoved the foolish quote away and shifted her gaze to the hills once more.

Perhaps she had been too honest with Mr Grey. In his rough and sardonic way, he'd charmed the truth out of her. He'd cleverly made her relax her caution, lean into his warmth that made the world sag a little in his direction. She hadn't even noticed it until he'd moved away. For those brief moments she'd felt utterly natural sitting here with him. Unthinking, un-calculating, just…herself. It was so rare a feeling she only recognised it when it was withdrawn.

She shook her head. The events of the past weeks must be addling her brain.

It was a little mad to allow someone else to assume custody over her fate. She'd never done it before, but in truth it was a wondrous sensation.

A dangerous one, too. All she knew with certainty was that this handsome, scarred giant was a walking deception. He instilled confidence, made her lower her guard, yet she knew he could be ruthless. It was obvious in the way he watched the world, the ease with which he'd faced al-Mizan and dismissed him and then orchestrated their departure with a minimum of fuss. The way he accepted the change in their plans and the annoyances it must bring without any sign of discomfiture. It was as if he expected life to be full of rocky shoals and murky pits. It was unfair that he should convey such an air of calm and humour when he was no doubt eternally alert beneath. His was the behaviour of a man who did not rest, who did not trust.

And if a man did not trust, he could not be trusted.

'*"There's no trust, no faith, no honesty in men; all perjured, all forsworn, all naught, all dissemblers,"*' she muttered at the desert floor.

'Well, that's a miserable philosophy. Here. You'll feel better once your belly is full.'

She looked up, startled. She hadn't even heard him return. She would make a horrid mercenary.

He waved the plate at her and the flat bread slid tipsily across. She caught the plate, the warm, doughy aroma overlaid by the tangy smell of goat's cheese. Her mouth watered and her stomach rumbled like approaching thunder. She leaned forward, embarrassment flooding her once more.

'Who was the dismal fellow or lady who had such a poor opinion of men?' he asked as he sat down, placing his own plate on the boulder and tearing a strip of bread.

'Shakespeare. Juliet's nurse speaks those words to Juliet after Romeo kills her cousin. I didn't mean to...' She foundered, worried he would think she had been referring to him. Which she had.

'Shakespeare. Of course. It's always Shakespeare that's trotted out to bolster one's beliefs. Still, it's always good advice to keep your expectations low. Like expecting this bread to be inedible and then discovering it is delectable. I must be growing desperate indeed to think that.'

She relaxed once more. Flippant had its advantages.

'*"Nothing is good or bad but thinking makes it so,"*' she offered and took a bite of the hot, pungent combination of bread and cheese.

'Shakespeare again? I don't think I agree with him here. There is plenty that is categorically bad and no thinking otherwise could make it good.'

'I believe he meant we can shape our perception of the world. If we always expect evil, then we will perhaps miss the good.'

'A fair point,' he conceded with clear reluctance.

'Dash tells me I have a sad habit of quoting Shakespeare,

but one of the few possessions we managed to always take with us were his plays and I have reread them dozens of times. I shall try to restrain myself.'

'No, don't. It appears you've had to restrain yourself far too much in your short life, Cleo-Pat. Enjoy your unfettered freedom while you can, because once you're safely in London, you will face restraints aplenty. Now eat up. You'll need your strength for what's ahead.'

Unfettered freedom.

Cleo turned over on the thin pallet Gamal had placed for her by the fire and pulled her robe more tightly around her, tucking her fist under her chin. A few feet away the dying fire glittered at her. A short distance behind her was the substantial bulk of Mr Rafe Grey stretched out on another pallet.

She knew she must sleep, but she'd never felt so wide awake in her life. As if she'd swallowed a sackful of shooting stars and they were slamming about inside her like fireworks.

It made no sense. She was exhausted, weary to the marrow of her bones, her legs and back aching from the interminable ride.

And afraid she might never sleep again.

This is absurd, she told herself. Last night she had fallen asleep with her head on a table. The previous night she'd curled behind a stack of reed baskets in an empty market stall, convinced she'd wake up to the tip of a knife. Tonight she was blessed with a mattress of sorts, a blanket and a mercenary who was literally watching her back.

And she couldn't sleep.

She *needed* to sleep, but his words kept bouncing about in her head, butting against her worries like a goat at a gate.

Unfettered freedom...

If all went well she would be returning to England after more than a decade away.

To what?

To a great gaping blackness, greater than the enormous night sky above them.

She breathed in and out slowly, trying to focus on the world around her and not the panic inside her. Over by the well a camel groaned and then came the faraway ululation of a jackal. The mercenary behind her stirred and settled. She could not tell if he was awake and was struck by an urge to turn over and check. She shifted on to her other side as quietly as she could.

Oh. *Not* sleeping.

His eyes looked black, the last flickers of the fire sparking them with stars. He lay on his side facing her, his head resting on his bent arm and folded coat. The moonlight stripped half his face of colour and cast the rest in shadow.

'It's only a jackal,' he whispered.

'I know,' she whispered back. 'They won't come near. It isn't that. I can't seem to sleep.'

'That's not good. Surely your beloved bard had something to say about the importance of sleep. He seems to have something to say about everything short of how best to boil an egg.'

She smiled, absurdly relieved by his nonsense.

'He says sleep is the *"balm of hurt minds"* and something about stealing us away from ourselves, and knitting unravelled sleeves of care, and then of course there is Hamlet's famous—'

'I regret asking,' he interrupted. 'In any case, take his advice, close your eyes and begin knitting.'

'I am trying. I cannot stop my thoughts.'

That was more honest than she wished, but he merely raised himself on his elbow.

'Annoying little bastards, aren't they? Send them over here and I'll give them a talking to.'

A laugh huffed out of her and she untucked her hand and cast an imaginary object at him.

'Put them in a sack and drown them, please.'

'You're a merciless little thing. No need for such measures, I'll just dust their jackets for you and send them back on their best behaviour.'

'That sounds more nursemaid than mercenary.'

He did not answer immediately and she worried she'd offended him. Then a different smile tugged at his mouth. Not jesting. Warm and intimate and yet distant.

'I will have you know I am a fine nursemaid, Cleo-Pat.'

'You have children?' Her thoughts leapt to children far away, wondering where their father was…

'I had a nephew, but he died. Jacob. He was all of two years old.'

'Oh, no. Oh, *no*! I am so, so sorry.'

'So am I. He charmed everyone who knew him. Well, almost everyone.'

'Your brother's son?' she asked. 'The brother you came to Egypt for?'

'The same.'

'What happened to him?'

'My brother or Jacob?'

'Jacob.'

He sighed.

'He was ill for a long time and then he died. I didn't mean to add my ghosts to yours. There is something about sleeping under the heavens that loosens the tongue. Go to sleep, Queenie.'

He turned on to his back, his profile etched against the darkness behind him. She felt he was tempted to turn his back to her completely, but was resisting the urge. For a mercenary he was very considerate of other people's feelings.

Fair play would be to turn over herself and give him the privacy of his thoughts, but there was something comforting about the sharp-cut lines of his profile. She could feel the strange sink and jerk of sleep and in that floating moment before her eyes sealed themselves against her will she wished one could embrace someone in pain without a thought to propriety or consequences.

It might have been the jackals that woke her, or the grunt of the camels. Whatever it was, sleep dropped her from its embrace and she landed flat on her back, her eyes wide and staring at the moon. She turned immediately, half expecting to see a wild beast crouched, ready to leap, but instead there was nothing.

Not even a sleeping giant.

Mr Grey's pallet was empty, the blanket neatly folded, and at the edge of her vision, between the boulders, a dark shape was moving. Away.

No…two dark shapes. She rose to her knees, squinting into the ink of night. They moved lightly and quickly eastwards. She could still hear the faint rumble of snoring near the trees—probably Birdie asleep by the camels.

She knew she had not been asleep for long—the stars and moon had barely moved. She rose, pulling her robe about her and attaching her dagger. Her mind tumbled through possibilities but one held firm above all—the path between the boulders led down towards Daraw.

Rafe watched the band of stars shimmer above him, cold and bright like shards of crushed ice scattered on the darkness. Without even looking he could feel sleep weigh Cleopatra Osbourne down, long lashes lowering over her intense golden-brown eyes.

He closed his eyes as well, willing everything away, willing himself not to turn and look at her. Then he turned on his side and watched her after all, wondering what on earth he was going to do with her. Eventually she gave a little puff of a sigh and her body relaxed as she sank into a deeper sleep.

He rose carefully and went towards where Birdie was leaning against a boulder.

'She's asleep,' Rafe whispered, motioning to Gamal to join him. 'We'll back as soon as we take a look at this port and the lay of the town. I don't want any surprises tomorrow.'

Birdie yawned widely and nodded.

'She won't like you doing this behind her back.'

'I can handle her dislike. It's her mistrust I have a problem with. If I tell her, she'll insist on coming and that might prove dangerous. I want her here where it's safe.'

'What do I tell her if she wakes?'

'Hopefully she won't, but if she does, tell her the truth.'

Birdie cast a glance towards the fire.

'Just come back quick like, will you?'

'As quick as we can.'

On this side of the Nile the village was a small one. He and Gamal made their way to the north of the village to where they could see the feluccas and fishing boats tied to the two simple wooden wharves that spanned the reedy shallows. The small open space by the wharves was surprisingly full for such an hour and small port.

'Is the port always so crowded at this hour, Gamal?'

'No, *nadab*. This is the hour for home and *shisha* and *kahwa*, the coffee place. I do not like this.'

'Neither do I. Blast…' Rafe shifted further back into the shadow. 'See that man, the tall one just at the edge of the port talking to the fat one?'

Gamal leaned a little past him.

'You are right, *nadab*. It is al-Mizan speaking with the Sheikh.'

'Devil take him.'

'Al-Shaitan is more likely to take us, *nadab*.'

'Good point. Come. There's nothing for us here. We

shall have to keep to the desert until the next—' He stopped
as Gamal's hand clamped on his arm.

'Anzur!'

Rafe had no idea what that meant, but he followed Gamal's gaze towards the other end of the wharf where the
reeds took over. Beyond, the half-moon was a shattered
reflection on the inky water and the pale blur between the
reeds might have been a large bird looking for frogs, but
somehow he knew it was not. He motioned Gamal back
the way they came.

Coming round the north of the village, they found her
easily enough. She'd chosen a good vantage point to watch
the port, but was so intent on the figure of al-Mizan as he
stood talking to the rotund Sheikh she did not even notice
Rafe approach until he was three feet from her.

He found himself praying she would not cry out. He
never liked to employ force, but in this case… Just as he
was wondering if indeed he could do it, she turned on her
haunches, her hand dropping to the ground as if ready to
propel herself forward. He touched his finger to his lips,
his eyes locking with hers in the darkness.

They remained like that for a moment and for a second
her gaze flickered over to where al-Mizan was standing.
There were two other men with him now and they were
conferring and looking about them. When her eyes returned to Rafe's he shook his head and pointed into the
darkness behind them. Finally, she moved to follow him.

They were halfway back to the camp before he felt capable of speaking calmly.

'What did you think you were doing?'

'I woke and you were gone,' she replied. 'I thought—'

'You thought we'd gone to sell you out.'

He'd been betrayed often enough through the years and
he rarely took it personally. He *shouldn't* take it seriously,

but somehow this show of mistrust after everything she'd told him…everything he'd told her…

He tried to tell himself it was understandable—she was frightened, worried, and all too used to thinking the worst of people. He should not be angry with her.

Well, he wasn't angry with her, he was *furious*. He'd forgotten what that felt like—like molten steel filling him. He felt as though he had to do something or explode, but there was nothing he *could* do. He did not understand this volcanic pressure inside him, but he knew it would, it *must* pass.

'I had to be certain,' she whispered as they entered the encampment. Her voice was low but insistent, on the verge of a plea. Gamal cast them a worried look and slipped off towards his pallet by the camels where Birdie's snores still rumbled gently. Rafe drew a deep breath, but the expected calm didn't follow.

'Go to sleep, Miss Osbourne.'

'You are being unreasonable…'

'*I* am being unreasonable?' He dragged his voice down and she sighed.

'Yes, you are. You are in a temper because I disobeyed you, but you should have told me of your plans.'

'I would have you know I am a model of good temper when dealing with *reasonable* people, Miss Osbourne,' he snapped.

'I think it very reasonable to insist on taking part in deciding my fate.'

'That is not what happened and you know it! You knew full well you were meant to stay at the encampment!'

'And I decided not to. That is my prerogative. I am after all paying for your services, Mr Grey. I am not obligated to follow your advice.'

'You aren't paying me a scuffed piastre, Queenie, and if you don't want to find yourself alone in the middle of the desert, you *are* obligated to follow my advice.'

* * *

Cleo rarely felt truly angry. Long ago she'd often felt this kind of impotent fury at her father as he'd dragged them from one disastrous venture to the next. But her anger had faded into frustration and finally sloughed off her altogether. She'd forgotten how hot and cold and confusing it felt.

It also felt alive. Vivid. Bubbling inside her more powerfully than fear.

Amazingly, it felt *good*.

'Do you often issue threats you won't act upon, Mr Grey?'

'How do you know I won't act upon them, Queenie? You don't know the first thing about what I am capable of.'

She snorted.

'I know you are capable of dismissing perfectly good advice. I told you Daraw was too close to Syene to be safe, but you had to go sneaking about at night just to prove me right. What if al-Mizan's men or someone in the village had seen you?' She was well aware she was fanning the fire and perversely she was enjoying it.

'The only person they almost saw was you, Queenie, and the only time I and Gamal were at risk was trying to stop you from putting your neck into al-Mizan's noose!'

Her anger faded a little at the thought that she had endangered them as well. She tried for dignity instead of righteousness.

'If you had discussed your plan with me, I would have happily complied—'

'Ha!' he interrupted. 'You wouldn't recognise compliance if it kicked you in the backside. You may be used to ruling the roost, but if you plan on spending the next few days haranguing me and ignoring my directives, I'll happily leave you here.' He snatched his pallet from the ground and stalked off towards the camels.

Cleo lay awake for a long while, her cheeks stinging

with a swirling contradiction of heat and anger and hurt. She watched the last glimmer of embers die, very aware of the emptiness behind her.

Chapter Six

'Tired?' Birdie asked as helped her dismount at the end of the following day's ride. It was the first word any of them had spoken to her since they'd set out that morning. Concern was writ large on his puckish face so she managed an almost-smile and shook her head.

She wanted to tell Birdie the truth—she wasn't tired, she was exhausted. With the look on Rafe's face haunting her, it had taken hours to fall asleep. Even admitting his anger was justified, she didn't know why it affected her so. He wasn't her friend, so she could hardly lose his friendship. Yet it felt precisely as if she had.

The closest thing she'd felt to this was when they'd been forced to leave Acre after living with the Tawil family in their sprawling house just north of the port. But that had been a real loss—a loss of love and friendship built over years. Her father had hardly given them a chance to say goodbye to the people who'd become their family. It was absurd to feel the same deep wrenching sensation merely because a man she hardly knew was angry with her.

She glanced at Rafe's broad back as he helped Gamal remove the saddles while Birdie set out his pots by the fire. It was the same scene as the previous night and yet she felt they were already excluding her.

If he hadn't been a mercenary, and a flippant one at that, she might almost believe he'd been hurt by her mistrust.

'Here, miss.' Birdie approached her and held out a steaming cup. She took it and bent her head over the steam to hide the pricking of grateful tears.

'Thank you, Mr Birdie.'

'Just Birdie, miss. That's not good for the heart, you know.'

She started and some of the tea splattered over her hand. He handed her a surprisingly clean handkerchief and she dabbed at the stinging liquid.

'What's not good for the heart?'

'Worrying when you can't do a thing about it. It was my fault for falling asleep, but next time just give me a good kick and wake me before you go off on your own so I can calm your worries.' He hesitated. 'We've been in far worse situations than these, believe me. And if something happens to him I'll see you through.'

She breathed through the burn of tears. These men hardly knew her and yet somehow they were more committed to her safety than her own father ever had been.

'Thank you, Birdie.'

He flushed and frowned. 'No need. Best thing to do is keep yourself busy. Finish your tea and go draw more water for those thirsty beasts while Gamal and I prepare supper.'

The brusque order calmed her far more effectively than empty reassurances. She finished her tea and went to unhook the water gourd by the well. She'd watched men and women work the wells, but doing it herself was harder than she anticipated, the rope burning her palms as she dragged up the heavy leather buckets.

How the women who filled large clay jugs with water carried this weight on their heads over miles back to their villages or tents, she had no idea. She tried not to spill the precious water as she poured it into the trough and was concentrating so hard on her task that the blow caught her completely by surprise. She landed neatly on her behind in the mud and found herself staring up into the bulbous eyes of Kabir as he ambled past her to the trough. Her nemesis looked well pleased with his victory as he slurped noisily at the water.

'I'm doing this for you, you ungrateful wretch. You might at least show some respect,' Cleo muttered as she struggled to her feet. The other camels approached, Gamila huffing gently and batting her long, curled eyelashes at Cleo as if in apology for Kabir's behaviour. Cleo stroked Gamila's neck as they both stood and watched the slobbering Kabir with what Cleo was certain was shared disgust.

'Typical male. No consideration or manners,' said Rafe behind her and Cleo turned in surprise, her hands covering the muddy patch on her behind.

His comment sounded like an olive branch, but his expression was as blank as it had been all day. They stood for a moment in silence before he jerked his head towards the campfire.

'Supper is ready.'

Unlike the previous evening, supper was a subdued affair. The tension between her and Rafe was palpable and both Gamal and Birdie exchanged glances and ate in silence. When Birdie poured out the last of the tea, she gathered her courage and turned to Rafe.

'May I know where we are heading next, Mr Grey?'

Rafe put down his cup.

'I was wondering how long before you started making demands.'

'It is not a demand, merely a question.'

Birdie directed a frown at Rafe. 'We've decided the ports are too risky, miss. Gamal suggested we go by way of the camel route and take a boat from Asyut, which is too large for them to control.'

'Asyut! That means several more days in the desert.'

'That's right, miss. So we'd all best catch some rest now.'

She took her pallet and followed Rafe to arrange it by the fire, searching for some way to ease the tension that strummed between them.

'I am sorry you have had to extend your journey because of me.'

He shrugged. 'Never mind. Hopefully we have confused them sufficiently to give your brother time to reach Cairo and leave Egypt. That is your object, no?'

'Yes. Yes, of course. I only hope Dash acts immediately once he sees my letter.'

'So do I. Was he named for his speed or for his dashing manners?'

There was a hint of lightness in his voice and her relief bloomed.

'Neither. An ancestor of ours from Ashford in Kent went to France and took to calling himself d'Ashford. My mother decided to perpetuate that foolish vanity in Dash's name. She was very...poetically minded.'

'So she's to blame for you quoting Shakespeare?'

'She'd be proud to accept that blame.' She smiled and turned away to unfold her blanket, surprised by the burning in her throat. It seemed so long, long ago—those evenings reading with her mother in their small back parlour where it was warmest because it shared a wall with the kitchen. She'd thought that was her life—simple and safe and happy, just the three of them with occasional visits from her father. Now it felt far less real than sitting in the desert with a mercenary.

But it was still there, that memory—of warmth, her mother's deep voice as she read, holding the book a little away from her because she always misplaced her spectacles...

'You miss her.'

His voice was brusque but not unkind and she both shrugged and nodded, waiting for him to move away. To her surprise, he spread his pallet between hers and the desert once more and came to sit on a boulder by the fire. He picked up a twig and traced neat little rows on the ground. The sand rushed into them like raindrops into a crack in the pavement.

'I'm sorry, Cleo-Pat.'

'It hardly matters. It was so long ago.'

'Some things never stop mattering. Was she responsible for you name as well?'

'Of course. She said it was part tribute to Shakespeare's play and part tribute to my father. In Greek it means "glory of the father". All the Ptolemaic queens were named Cleopatra and all the kings Ptolemy, which means "warlike".'

'Well, that says it all. Name the kings after violence and the queens after kings.'

She laughed. She'd always hated that aspect of her name, but somehow his words blew away that slight with a puff of laughter. He smiled and the knot of tension in her stomach unravelled further.

'I'll call you Cleo, then. Or Glory.'

'Not Glory, please. Besides, you already appear to have far too many names for me.'

'Cleo, then. Or I rather like Cleo-Pat. Osbourne doesn't suit you, though. Do you know what it means?'

'I…no, I never thought it meant anything at all.'

'It's old Norse. It means the bear god…*os bjorn*.'

'Does it? I rather like that. Do you actually speak Norse?' She couldn't keep the scepticism from her voice and he gave that grunt she was coming to recognise was a mix between amusement and annoyance.

'I know some odd bits. I lived with my brother for a couple of years, after his son Jacob was born, while I recovered from my burns. The boy never fully escaped the rheumatic fever and needed to be watched closely. He loved being read to and I soon made my way through most of

Edge's mythology collection, including a tome on the significance of names in old Norse. Jacob was particularly fond of that. Perhaps it was my ludicrous accent.'

Strange how well she could imagine Rafe holding a somnolent babe in his arms, reading aloud in his deep purr of a voice. She didn't want that image in her mind; she had enough to unsettle her at the moment.

'Does Rafe also mean something in old Norse?'

'Yes. Wise wolf.'

'How apt. So I am a bear god, you a wise wolf, Birdie can be a kind, resourceful bird and Gamal the handsome camel named Camel.'

His smile flashed in the dark.

'We sound like one of Aesop's fables. Except in my case, Rafe is nothing more impressive than Rafael shortened.'

'Rafael,' she repeated, and the sound rolled outwards, warm and liquid in the darkness. 'God heals. An archangel's name.'

'I know. I was definitely misnamed.'

'I don't think so. Raphael saved people.'

'Even less appropriate. I'm a mercenary, remember?'

'Of course I do. You saved me.'

He snorted.

'You hired me to do just that. I might as easily have handed you over to that al-Mizan fellow if he'd been more generous. I don't think Raphael haggled with God over his fee.'

'You didn't haggle over the fee either.'

'I don't think he could have matched your offer. That grotesque green gewgaw is worth a couple of months' lodgings at least.'

Her hand groped for the chain that held her little treasure and closed on it.

'You could take it now and still hand me over to al-Mizan.'

'Even mercenaries have their principles, Queenie.'

'I think you make a better bear than I do, Mr Rafael Grey. You are long on brawn and bluster. I know you weren't even considering handing me over to that man.'

'You know nothing of the sort, as you proved by following us into Daraw. You should try living up to your namesake, Cleopatra—trust no one.'

She considered his words, and his warning, and tried to understand why, other than her still being alive, she *did* trust him now. Perhaps it was the foolishness that often comes with fear and despair—clinging to a rock protruding from the ocean though one knew it was as dangerous in its barrenness as the great wide sea.

Yet she did trust him and it worried her. Trust meant lowering one's guard and that meant…trouble.

For a moment the darkness settled on them again as the fire dimmed. Then a spark shot upwards, followed by a lick of flames as the fire found more to feed its hunger. It lit his profile against the fading light on the horizon. He had a profile worthy of a coin—strong and sharp, as if the winds of life had hewn him down to his elements. The only imperfections were his scars. She wondered what had happened to him.

Trust no one. It was excellent advice, but…

'I rarely do trust anyone,' she said tentatively. 'I do not mean I trust you wholly, but I think, if I am right about you, you will try to fulfil your bond and that is far more than most men…most people do.'

He actually squirmed, raising his eyes skywards as if beseeching the heavens for deliverance. She smiled and continued. 'Also I don't know that Cleopatra didn't trust anyone. She appeared to trust both Julius Caesar and Marc Anthony enough to have children with them.'

'That was good political sense, not trust. Or trust in her ability to direct her fate by whatever means at her disposal. A very sensible woman, that illustrious lady.'

'I agree. But being sensible doesn't preclude trust. You

strike me as a sensible man, but you trust Birdie. And your brother.'

'What do you know of my brother?'

'Nothing but what you said yourself. But I know love when I hear it. Your brother is a lucky man to have you.'

'You are damned annoying, Pat.'

'That is the second time you have damned me, Mr Grey.'

'I have a suspicion it won't be the last, Miss Osbourne.'

Chapter Seven

Desert travel was strange.

Almost a week had passed since they'd left Syene and, though they were always in motion, it seemed to Rafe as if they never truly made any headway. The pinkish cliffs gave way to dunes and plains and then again to cliffs. The shadows of the camels marked the passing of the day—long and fuzzy into the west, shrinking and darkening as the day passed, scrunched beneath them, like an oily puddle, and then stretching out into the east once more until everything began to glow orange and dim to purple as the sun expired.

Gamal set a brisk pace and it was too hot and dusty to talk during the day, but at night by the campfire, the four of them settled into the easy camaraderie of soldiers on the march. Ever since he'd enlisted in the army at sixteen he'd come to love these times—sitting around a fire, talking and listening.

It had been a way of life for him and Birdie and it was also in Gamal's blood, but Rafe was surprised how naturally Cleo fitted into their little troupe. Perhaps this was what came of a life adapting to circumstance. She rarely complained and whatever snaps of temper and impatience she allowed herself were directed solely at him. Strangely, he welcomed these chinks in her defences.

He watched her helping Birdie. The two of them were talking and laughing, the evening breeze sifting through her short hair and every so often she shoved it away from her eyes with the back of her hand.

His mind was still struggling to resolve her contrasts. Her clothes and some of her gestures were boyish, yet she looked as feminine as Venus rising from the sea. Her voice, too, was all woman—deep and warm and with a dash of spice, like winter cider. Especially when she laughed. Her laugh was as generous as her curves and he really had to stop trying to coax it out of her.

He sighed again at the pity of it all. His body had crossed the Rubicon with her and was having a grand time thumbing its nose at him from the other side. He knew he would do nothing about this attraction, but it was a damnable nuisance.

She came and sat cross-legged on the pallet beside him without a word and they both watched the sky succumb to the night.

He'd heard the desert was a strange and deceptive place, but he'd assumed that referred to its physical nature, not a spiritual effect. And yet it didn't feel at all logical that anything bad could happen to them in this elemental place. He felt…peaceful.

He should and would do well to keep in mind that the desert…in particular this desert and in this strange woman's company…was not at all peaceful.

It was a jackal who broke the silence. The howl went on so long he felt it begin to reverberate inside him. Finally, it broke into a series of sharp yaps and stopped.

'It sounds lonely,' she said.

'I know, but it likely isn't. Gamal said they almost always live and hunt in packs.'

She nodded. 'I saw a mother jackal playing with her

pups once. They were the sweetest things—with enormous ears that looked as though they would tip them over. It was beautiful—I know some people believe animals do not possess emotions, but you could see how much pleasure they took in one another.'

Her voice was deeper than usual and its rawness plucked at him.

'Is that what you want? A pack of your own?'

'Is that so wrong?'

'Not wrong… It depends.'

'On what?'

'Whether you know its limits. Families aren't a magic antidote to loneliness. We of all people should know that.'

'I do know that. I'm not…' She gave a little laugh. 'I am an awful liar. I cannot even lie to myself. I envy *jackals*, for heaven's sake.'

He could feel it. Of course she was lonely. So was any reasonably sensible human being. Sometimes every cell in his body ached with bone-deep loneliness. It was part of being alive. Belonging to a pack could temper, but not eliminate, it.

'I hope Dash is safe. I hope…' Her voice quavered and she stopped, her hands fisted on her thighs. Without thought he put his arm around her, cursing himself.

Her breathing was still shallow, stuttering. He wished she would cry. It was better than this…drowning. She was drowning in the desert and it was his fault.

'Cleo… Please…don't listen to me. I'm no authority on anything. You'll have your family.'

She shivered, pressing her forehead against his neck. He could feel the contours of his scars against her skin and started pulling away, but her hand curled into his shirt, her fingertips dragging the fabric against his ribs.

'We come from a long line of soothsayers,' he whispered against her hair. 'I can see you'll have a dozen children—six girls, six boys… No, better have more girls, they are less trouble.'

She gave a little huff of a laugh, her breath cooling the perspiration on his throat, and he stopped himself from tightening his arms.

'*I* am trouble…' she whispered hoarsely, but he could hear the glimmer of a smile there and a wave of gratitude rushed through him.

'That's true. Serious trouble. Perhaps we'll change that to more boys than girls since you are likely to have a bevy of little warrior queens. You'll never have a moment's rest.'

Her hair was soft and he rubbed his cheek against it, just turning his head a little so that it skimmed the corner of his mouth. He breathed her in again, trying to reach that enticing core. It was unfair that she smelled so good despite everything and he probably smelt like one of the camels by now.

'I don't want a dozen children,' she murmured. 'I want two or three. The more you have, the more you worry.' Her voice was creaky, but he could tell she was back. Which meant he should let her go.

He didn't want to. She was warm and soft against him and it took every ounce of his will to sit still. To remind himself he was comforting her. That he had nothing to offer and no right to take. They sat in silence until the words were dragged out of him.

'I'll find your brother for you.'

She sighed and pulled away a little.

'It isn't your place to find him, Rafe. You are doing more than enough helping me. I'm sorry I…fell to pieces. Thank you for being so patient.'

She took his hand and rubbed it gently between hers. He'd been simmering already and her touch was fire set to dry hay. It spread so fast and so hot he couldn't do anything but sit there as the heat flayed layers off him.

He must have made some sound because she untangled

herself, murmuring a stifled apology and went towards the well. He walked in the other direction, chased by images that had nothing to do with reality—of spreading her out in the middle of the desert, discovering every curve and line and taste of her. Of pulling her on top him so he could watch her body against the starred sky as they moved.

It would pass. These little fevers always did—they dragged him back to his youth, twisting his view of the world and convincing him he wanted something he didn't really. But they never lasted. Eventually they ran out of tinder and went ashen and dull. It was only that her foolish, pointless yearning had infected him for a moment. Like jabbing an old wound.

It would pass, all he had to do was wait it out and one day he would wonder why on earth it had caught him so hard.

'We are almost at the end of Darb al-Arba'in. Asyut is past those hills,' said Gamal, pointing eastwards over his camel's neck. He'd kept them at a fast pace that day to reach the oasis and though Cleo was grateful to see the shadowed grove of palms that promised rest, his words caused a sharp twinge in her chest. Beyond those hills was the Nile and the end of their journey.

Gamal had told her he would be leaving them in Asyut. He would sell all of the camels but Kabir and Gamila and then return to his family, wealthy enough to marry.

Rafe and Birdie would likely proceed to Cairo in search of traces of his brother, and she... Once she reached Cairo she would know more. There was no point in worrying unnecessarily. Worrying had made her blabber about jackals and loneliness last night and forced Mr Grey to comfort her like a child.

She'd held on to that sensation last night as she tried to sleep. The warmth of his body around hers, his scent—earthy and cool. His hand between hers, large and rough

with a warmth that sparked fires through her like a field
of thorns in summer. It was foolish to indulge these sensations, but she did anyway. All too soon she would be on
her own again and life would snatch her back in its talons.

'What is Darb al-Arba'in?' Birdie asked and she welcomed the distraction.

'It is the forty-day camel caravan road from Nubia to
Asyut. Asyut is quite large so we can probably find a boat
there without drawing too much attention. I doubt al-Mizan
will be there. If he persisted in looking for Dash at all, he
would most likely have gone to Luxor.'

She glanced at Rafe, but if he was relieved they were
near their journey's end, she could see no sign of it. Or of
anything, for that matter. When he wished, he could keep
his face as blank as a rock.

'Look at that, Colonel!' Birdie exclaimed as they passed
through the last line of palm trees. Out of the ochre plain
before them rose the palmiform pillars of an ancient temple. Either design or time had left only several separate
structures standing and a row of half-buried sphinxes. She
loved these small temples in Egypt—they were as delicate
and sturdy as life, with their exuberance carved and painted
on their walls and pillars.

She wished Dash were there with them. He would have
loved to see this.

As they watched, a goat and kid ambled up the alley
of sphinxes, the kid skipping and bucking over the sand
as they headed into the shade of the palms. Kabir huffed
in disgust at such frivolity and Gamila nudged him in the
neck.

'I think that is a hint, Kabir.' Cleo laughed.

Gamal smiled. 'Kabir is stubborn.'

'I place my faith in Gamila,' Cleo replied, patting the
cow. 'Please tell me we may set camp near here and explore the temple a little?'

'You'd think we were on a Grand Tour,' Rafe said drily,

but then added, 'Setting camp here sounds like a good idea. We could even sleep inside. What do you say, Gamal?'

'Very good. But I will sleep with the camels and keep them safe from thieves, *nadab*.'

'So will I,' Birdie said. 'You won't find me stepping inside a tomb until it's my turn to fill it. But you enjoy yourself, miss. No telling what tomorrow brings.'

'I know precisely what tomorrow brings, Birdie,' Rafe said as they moved towards the temple. 'More dust and wind, more dry cheese and burnt bread and dates, and more aching muscles and sulky camels. I'd trade my kingdom for a bath, a feather bed, and a slab of sirloin.'

'I thought I already won your kingdom for a glass of whisky several times over, Colonel.'

'Well, I wish you would do a better job hanging on to it, old friend. I don't want it.'

'So you say, but duty has a way of sinking its teeth into our tail, Colonel. Now you and Miss Cleo go have a look at your new lodgings. And try not to fall into a pit or come across a snake in there and make this all a wasted trip.'

'You two sound like a married couple,' Cleo said as she slipped off Gamila.

'Birdie sounds more like a mother hen. He's picked up some bad habits since I met him twenty-odd years ago,' Rafe said as he followed her past the staring sphinxes and between the pillars that rose like stone flowers out of the sand.

'You've known him twenty years?'

'Since I enlisted in the army.' He must have seen the surprise on her face for he gave a wry smile. 'I'm thirty-seven. Almost.'

'Your parents did not mind you enlisting so young?'

'I ran away.'

'Why?'

He shrugged, waving her inside, and after a moment's hesitation she entered the temple. Inside, the heat dropped sharply and the rising afternoon breeze made the dust dance and flicker like gold flecks in the shafts of sunlight poking through the cracked roof.

Rafe followed her over the sand drifts into the depth of the temple, pausing beneath the carving of a pharaoh with one hand upheld and the other outstretched and balancing a bowl. They went deeper, past carvings of humans with animal heads, birds with long curved beaks, a large baboon seated on a pedestal, and endless rows of hieroglyphs.

'Think,' she whispered as she unwound her turban, her voice shivering the still air. 'This has been here for thousands of years. Created at a time when Egypt was as great as any empire. I wish I had my notebook and a pencil here. This would make a wondrous tale for the *Gazette*. If only I knew who they were…'

'They are ashes and dust just like everyone else.' His voice was so flat she knew he was still elsewhere. She turned to watch him as he stared blankly at the wall.

'Why did you run away, Rafe?'

His eyes flickered to her and away.

'I had a fight with my father.'

'What did you argue about?'

'I said fight. Not argument. No one argued with the… with my father.'

'Well, then, what did you fight about?'

'Him trying to kill a maid because she giggled.'

The air squeaked out of her lungs. He turned at her silence, his smile wry.

'I come from bad stock. Are you certain you want to be alone in here with me?'

'Don't be foolish. Whatever your father was, you are as sane as I.'

He walked along the wall, his gaze moving over the carvings, but she could feel things shifting about inside him. She wanted to stop him, turn him to her and have him tell her…everything. He seemed so open sometimes but with every snippet he revealed she felt the mystery grow. And her curiosity. He must have come from a well-to-do family—it was in the way he spoke and a certain ease, that expectation that people would follow. But there was much more and that was mostly hidden in darkness. Now she felt he was finally twitching back a corner of the curtain and it shocked her how much she wanted to pull it away completely. He remained silent so long she was certain he had no intention of continuing his revelations, but he surprised her again.

'I used to have dreams that they would come and switch me, as well.'

'Switch you? Who?'

'Whoever kept switching him into a violent fanatic. It almost made me believe in demons and possession, which would have made my father very happy. He was a fire and brimstone zealot.'

'Perhaps…perhaps it was an illness?'

'Perhaps. Since we never spoke of it, I never asked. Whatever it was, that was why I ran away.'

'But…your mother? She must have been frantic.'

'Frantic is not a word one would associate with my mother. Her object was always to keep the surface of her world calm. She was a master…sorry, mistress of control. If it calms your conscience, I did write to her after I enlisted.'

'And she didn't object?'

'She objected to my choosing to enlist rather than purchasing a commission. She told me she preferred I join the Dragoon Guards so I didn't have to mix in low company.' His voice rose in a mincing falsetto and she smiled.

'I have a notion your mother does not sound like that.'

His mouth relaxed into a smile. 'No. She's a true martinet.'

'So? Did you join the Dragoons?'

'Hardly. I joined the Rifle Corps when it was formed

and that summer I was already losing my first battle in
Spain. The next year I won my first battle in Copenhagen.'

'What did your mother say about that?'

'I have no idea. I did not speak to her until Edge's son
was born. I was thirty by then and since I was already several years into this mercenary business, the issue didn't
arise.'

Each of these lightly delivered revelations were blows
that made her heart give a heavy, painful thump before
hurrying along again. He didn't sound angry, but she was;
she was furious for him. It was burning and crackling inside her. She wanted to reach through time and space and
shake sense and love into his parents. How could they not
have cared?

'Well, I am very happy Birdie found you. He strikes me
as a far better person than your parents.'

'Undoubtedly. Though to be fair, I found him. One of
my many talents—I know a good egg from a bad one.'
He grinned at her over his shoulder and she felt a flush of
pure pleasure.

'I've never been called a good egg before. As far as
compliments go… I like it.'

His smile softened and for a moment they stood there
in silence. She'd never felt so cut adrift from life and yet
so very right where she should be. Home. The thought
shook her but before she could even pull away from it,
Rafe turned back to carving of a woman standing beside
a crowned man holding a staff.

'Could this be your namesake?' he asked, his voice curious, calm and distant. She recognised the question for
what it was. The end of his revelations.

'No. From what I understand this style is much earlier
than Greek times. By that disc I think this is Amun, god
of the sun. You said your brother is a scholar, he would no
doubt enjoy this.'

'No doubt.'

'When I was a child I always wanted to see the places my father mentioned when he came to visit us in England,' she said. 'But I never imagined I would. When we were at the orphanage…'

He turned abruptly.

'You were in an orphanage?'

'After my mother died; but only for a year. Then a ship's captain arrived with a letter from my father saying he would take Dash.'

'Only Dash?'

She shrugged.

'Well, to be fair, I can understand his dilemma. Being saddled with a girl, especially in this part of the world, is not easy. But I couldn't allow them to take Dash without me so I cut my hair and took his second-best set of clothes and we both presented ourselves at the ship and said the message must have meant sons, plural, not son, singular. I am quite convinced the Captain saw through our ruse, but he was a kind man and probably took pity on me. The orphanage was not very salubrious.'

In the gloom of the temple she found it hard to read his expression but her pulse picked up, like a camel sensing predators beyond the cliffs.

'I did not tell you about my childhood to make you pity me, Mr Grey.'

'I don't pity you. Between an orphanage and your current life, I think you chose well. But forgive me if I think your father was a complete louse.' He spoke with barely suppressed violence. 'I cannot understand people who abandon their children. If you don't want them, don't have them.'

'Perhaps that is something one does not know until one has them?'

'That is no excuse.'

'I don't understand why you seem angrier with my father than with yours.'

'I used to be viciously angry with him,' he said finally, to the pharaoh.

'Not any more?'

He shrugged.

'When I heard he had died, I thought it would come back, but I can't find it. I think…if he *was* mad it is unfair to be angry with something beyond his control. Don't ask me about my mother, though. And I mean that seriously, Prying Pat.'

His smile was back so she didn't mind the rebuke. They stood for a moment in the darkening silence. It occurred to her she'd never felt more comfortable with anyone. She didn't want to return to Cairo, or England. She wanted to stay right here, with Rafe. She saw her hand rise just as he turned towards the entrance.

'I'll fetch our belongings and we'd best eat and have an early night. We should reach the river tomorrow.'

Chapter Eight

An hour later Cleo was heading back towards the temple through the palms, her arms full of brush for the fire, when she saw Rafe by the well.

He stood with his back to her, his shirt off, his back glistening with water as he shaved. The lowering sun was adding red and gold to everything and it transformed his back into a landscape far more arresting than any she'd seen on their trip. Like the desert, its power was rough and raw. Beautiful.

She stood rooted, like Lot's salt pillar of a wife. She couldn't look away. Her heart began thumping viciously, her skin burning, and a moan bubbled up inside her. It had been building this whole week, images and thoughts and sensations knitting together into one stifling fabric of need.

She would never have imagined a week ago that one of her chief worries was an increasing tendency to daydream about a brusque and flippant mercenary. She couldn't even blame him. All he was doing was shaving peacefully. She, in turn, was on fire. She wanted to skim her tingling palms down that sculpted expanse, feel every curve and contour, slip them round to his flat abdomen until her fingertips brushed the dark hair arrowing down...

She knew she should move on, but she remained where

she was, wishing he would turn to her, not with his teasing laughter or compassion, but mirroring the heat she felt flooding her, making it hard to breathe.

He poured water from the gourd over his head and face, rivulets forming shiny stripes down his back. She swallowed as he dried his face with a strip of linen, his touch slowing and softening as it moved over his scarred shoulder.

Her heart squished itself into a little ball, shoving back the lascivious storm. What she wanted more than anything was to wrap her arms around him and touch her lips to that shattered, tortured skin. Soothe it…him…

Oh, this is not smart at all, Cleopatra. Lust is one thing, caring is another matter altogether.

Their journey was about to come to an end. In a couple of days she would never see him again.

Repeat after me: you will never see him again.

He turned, his hand still on his scars, his eyes locking with hers. She didn't know what she looked like, but she was afraid he could see *everything*. His hand descended slowly from his scars and she watched it with something like horror, as if waiting for him to extend an accusing finger. She'd been hot before, but her face blazed like the noonday sun. She swallowed and stepped back, stumbling a little.

'If my scars bother you so, you must stop sneaking up on me when I am shaving, Cleopatra.'

His voice was utterly flat and her mind utterly aghast, so it took a moment for her to register his words. She dragged her gaze up from his chest to his eyes.

'That's not… I wasn't… They *don't*…'

He walked towards her, still with that same flat look. She tried to gather her thoughts, explain…

Explain what? That's she'd stood lusting after him behind his back? That even now she wanted to reach out and take…

Perhaps if he had stood still she might have been able to think of something sensible and mature to say, but he kept coming towards her and her mind joined her body in the wishful clamour—perhaps he would not stop...he would put those big hands on her, touch her, bend down to press his half parted lips on hers...

He was within an arm's reach from her, he extended his arms... God, she would combust faster than dry papyrus if only...

With a faint, unamused twist of his mouth he took the bundle of twigs from her arms and walked past her.

She stood for a moment, heat and horror warring inside her for dominion.

It was only a few short moments but it felt as though she'd been down to the rings of purgatory and back.

Nothing like that had ever happened to her. Not even with William when she'd been young and foolish and— despite her father—still believed in love and dreams come true. She'd thoroughly enjoyed their embraces, even if they'd led to humiliation and disillusionment. But she'd never felt...fire.

She'd never felt afraid.

Already the flood waters were lowering, leaving behind the usual debris—a wincing embarrassment and frustration. It took another moment for the real sting to wake her as his words finally sank in—he hadn't thought she had stood there like a lust-struck ninny, but stricken by disgust and dismay because of his scars.

Shock held her silent for a moment. He treated his scars lightly, but there had been disappointment in his voice, his eyes. No—not disappointment, *hurt*. She'd hurt him.

She turned and hurried towards the temple, her mind tumbling over itself.

Rafe was kneeling in the central chamber of the temple, his head bent as he worked to kindle the fire. He'd put a shirt on and it clung damply to his back. He must have heard her enter, but did not look up.

'I'll be out of your way once the fire is ready.'

She hurried into speech.

'Rafe. You were wrong. Your scars don't bother me in the least. I've seen them before, remember?'

He pressed some dry weeds gently on to the flicking flames, careful not to smother them.

'You were half-dead that day and you had a hard enough time looking at me even then. You don't have to hide it, Queenie. I'm used to it.'

'But...'

'You looked as though you'd seen a ghost. So unless one of your mummy friends was making faces behind me...'

'Just *listen*.'

He stilled, but didn't turn. With his shoulders bowed over the fire, the rising flames casting gold lights on his dark hair and making the wall carvings shiver and dance, he looked like a supplicant come to beg mercy of the gods.

'That's is not why I looked...however I looked. I wasn't even thinking of your scars...no, that is not quite true. I *was* thinking of them, but they don't frighten me. The truth is...' She came forward and took a deep breath before resting her palm lightly on his scarred neck. His skin was both cool and hot, or perhaps that was her. 'I don't know you very well, but I hate the thought of you being hurt.'

Rafe froze.

I hate the thought of you being hurt...

It meant nothing, nothing at all. He'd seen people react a thousand and one ways to fear and loneliness. It took everyone differently. It clearly took Cleo into unnecessary realms of compassion.

So said his mind. His body, however, already on its knees, dropped at her feet like a panting puppy. There was nothing he could do to stop it marshalling the troops against him. It gathered the feel of her hand on his skin, the warmth of her legs close behind his back. It added images from the long, hot, dusty days—the way she wiped the perspiration from her cheeks or tilted her head back to catch the first breeze of the afternoon, exposing that little dip at the base of her throat where her scent would rise with each beat of her pulse.

He kept still, waiting for his mind to reassert dominion over his body. It was usually faster in coming to his defence, but the heat kept rising like the Egyptian sun—becoming incomprehensibly hotter, spreading from her hand like a curse, seeping through his skin into his veins and skidding along merrily to attack him from within. It bothered him far more than the erection that pulsed into life within seconds of her touching him. This heat felt far more dangerous than a lustful surge—it felt as though it was plotting against him.

What the devil was wrong with her to touch him like that? It would serve her right if he'd do what every base cell in his body ached to do.

He drew away, very carefully, as one might from a poisonous snake.

'I don't need pity, Miss Osbourne.'

'That is good. I haven't any for you.'

He uncoiled himself and stood. She stepped back and again he saw that same widening of her eyes and pupils. Damn it, he knew fear when he saw it.

'You tell a fine story, Cleo-Pat, but you have to work on not flinching or blushing with embarrassment.'

She gave a small, strangled laugh, surprising him.

'I wasn't flinching and it's not embarrassment. I'm beginning to think Birdie has grossly exaggerated your knowledge of women, Mr Grey.'

He clasped her arm before his mind even fully registered her meaning. She didn't pull away, just stood there. He had been right—she looked flushed and flustered. But he had been absolutely, peculiarly wrong—it wasn't fear, or disgust, or even compassion. The latter had been in her touch and voice, but not in her eyes, at least not now.

She could as easily have looked away, lowered her lashes, anything, but she let him take it in—the almost sleepy look in her eyes, the sultry heat colouring her cheeks, the tension in her parted lips. It wasn't an invitation; it was an admission. She wanted him to see the truth because she would not allow him to believe the alternative—that his damage either frightened or repelled her.

He had no idea what to do with this gift.

Oh, hell.

He laid his palm gently against her cheek. It shook slightly, reverberating against her skin, his index finger resting on the impossibly soft lobe of her ear.

'I apologise, Cleo.'

'Don't. There is no need, Rafe.' Her fingers rose to brush across his jaw, her gesture mirroring his. 'How did it happen?'

It sucked him in, that gentle question. It rang with concern and an echo of pain, as if she'd been there with him those long, agonising months when he'd been tempted to take whatever path available to relieve the pain.

'Stupidity. Mine. I walked into a burning building and would have stayed there if not for Birdie.'

She shook her head, her fingers feathering over his damaged skin, her mouth a sad, tense bow as her eyes followed her fingers, making his skin burn all over again.

'There is more to it than that. Don't make light of it.'

'I'm not… I must. I don't like remembering it.'

'Yes, I can see. I'm sorry.'

'It was a gunpowder depot. We were sent to salvage what we could when their cannon fire hit the building. I was already outside, but five of my men were still inside.' The words were dragging themselves out of him, just as he'd tried to drag out McAllister and the others. 'Birdie and I went in to find them. We pulled two out and I went back...'

He could remember the smell—acrid, evil—and the sound—snapping and sizzling. He'd just anchored his hand in McAllister's coat when the explosion hit him. He had no other memory until days later. And then the first memory was pain. For a long time.

He breathed in and out.

'It was a long time ago.'

'Some memories defy time. They're carved on our minds like those walls. If we lived a thousand years, they would still be there.'

He nodded slowly. Right now it felt as if this moment was being carved in stone, too. He didn't want it there any more than those long painful weeks in Los Piños, but it was unstoppable.

'I didn't mean to pry, Mr Grey,' she said as the silence stretched and he shook his head. He didn't want her to call him Mr Grey right now. Not that he wanted her, or anyone, to call him Greybourne, but for the first time the lie felt wrong. What would happen if he just...told her? If he laid it all bare. He'd already revealed so much more than he'd ever intended. What would happen if he added his true name? Not Mr Grey... Rafael Edgerton, Duke of Greybourne...

The image reared up again—that dark-eyed, twisted beast of a man with fingers tighter than steel bands and a mouth spewing hate. His heart stuttered. That wasn't him any more than he was Mr Grey.

'Rafe,' he said, brushing his thumb across her lips as if to imprint it on her. His voice was raw. He knew touching her was wrong, dangerous. Birdie had warned him precisely of this. He could not take advantage of the situation. Not with her. Even more so now she'd given him this strange gift.

His heart, already booming like that infernal cannon, quickened its barrage. She was important. Somehow in this short, intense week, she'd become important enough to demand another level of care, from himself as well. Whatever lay in her future, it wasn't him. He figured in no one's future, hardly even his own.

But his thumb was still gently brushing her lips, gathering her breath, his fingers resting on the soft sweep of her cheek, on the pulse at her neck. Sharp, urgent…

'Rafe…' It was a slow exhalation that made his body tighten, his mind fizzle and fade as her lips seemed to continue moving against his thumb, murmuring something. Very gently she laid her hand on the centre of his chest. The impact wasn't gentle at all. A swirling miasma of heat and iciness swept outwards from his centre, lighting his body from within.

There was a snap as a twig cracked in the fire and a surge of flame lit the walls around them with sunset colours. She smiled, a slow smile that rumbled through him like a herd of wild beasts on the hunt.

'You look like a pharaoh with the carvings behind you,' she mused, her gaze moving over his face and making his skin tingle as if her fingers were doing the exploring. 'Beautiful.'

He half laughed at the absurdity of that word, but it was another layer stripped away from him. He shook his head, trying to gather his strength against the assault of his own senses, but she merely brushed her palm up his chest, his shirt no protection at all. 'Don't laugh. You *are*,' she insisted. 'You have eyes that take in the whole world and I like the way those lines near your eyes always deepen when you try not to laugh at me.'

She touched his jaw, her fingers trailing again over his scars. 'You think these disgust me, but they don't. I wanted to touch you. I wanted to do this…'

She rose against him, her breath caressing his jaw, her hair tickling his cheek and temple as she brushed the lightest of kisses over his damaged skin.

'God. Cleo…' His throat moved with her name, his hands closed on her waist. He needed to put her away from him, but she was so warm, she smelled so…*so* good… He breathed her in, that faraway coolness of the fields after the first winter rain that brings life to everything. It was doing the same to him.

He must be going a little mad.

A lot mad.

She sighed deeply against him, her lips parting to allow her tongue to taste the tense sinew of his throat. Painful pleasure unfurled inside him like smoke from the camp-fire, flickering embers into firestorms.

He couldn't stop himself from arching his neck to give her better access. She moaned encouragingly, her hands skimming up his back and he realised she'd slipped them under his shirt. They felt so damn good against his skin. So damned right.

So absolutely wrong.

Her nails trailed down his back and with a shattered groan he caught her arms and drew her away before she utterly destroyed him.

'Cleo, *please*. This is a mistake.'

A mistake.

There was such anguished insistence in his voice it muted the drums of warmth beating inside her. Cleo leaned back to inspect his face. He *was* beautiful. But he was look-ing worried and angry again. She desperately wanted him to feel what she did—as warm and doughy as fresh bread and as light as sunbeams. She knew this was not proper, but it felt *right*. How could he not feel that, too?

'It doesn't feel like a mistake,' she murmured, resting her palms against his chest. His muscles shivered beneath them and it spread to her. She *liked* that sensation. It filled the great big echoing cavern inside her with incandescent light.

She had no idea what the morrow would bring but for the first time in…she did not know how long…she felt truly herself. Cleo.

'But it is, Cleo. I can't take advantage of you.'

'May I take advantage of *you*, then, Mr Rafe Grey?'

'No!'

'In two months I shall be twenty-seven years of age. Twenty-seven!'

'What on earth has that to say to anything?'

'Twenty-seven and I have never felt this before…this fire. That *cannot* be right. Even when William and I—' She squeaked as his hands tightened briefly on her arms.

'*Who* is William?'

Clearly mentioning another man while propositioning one was not a good idea. She had a lot to learn about seduction.

'It doesn't matter. He was an antiquarian friend of my father's and just as dishonourable. But that was a long time ago and I never felt like this when he touched me. I *like* feeling like this. It feels as though you are lighting fires inside me, as though—'

'Cleo, please, *please* stop.'

'I don't want to stop. Tell me why it is so wrong to wish to kiss you? I am not asking for anything else…'

'Cleo…'

There was such an entreaty in that one word her fires doused a little further. He looked tense and miserable and with a shaft of pain she realised he really did not wish to do this.

'Is the idea so distasteful?'

'No, Cleo—'

'You think me mannish in these clothes…and ugly.'

'Are you mad? I think… I *know* you are torturing me. Believe me, I would like nothing better than to do precisely what you are asking. And more. But you placed yourself in my care. Try to understand what that would make me if I gave in to base instincts. It would be a betrayal.'

'I wouldn't hold you responsible.'

'But *I* would.'

For a moment they both remained there, facing each other in the firelit temple.

She should not argue with him. Lust had not completely killed her common sense, yet she couldn't stop herself.

'And if I weren't in your care?'

'I don't...dally with innocents.' He would have sounded priggish if his voice hadn't all but cracked midway through the sentence.

'What a silly word. What if I weren't *innocent*?'

'You're impossible.'

'Oh, just tell me the truth.'

'If you were experienced and not in my care, I would fall over myself to coax you into the nearest bed, Cleopatra. But you aren't and you are. And that is that.'

'No, I'm not and it isn't. I'm not an *innocent*. William saw to that.' Again, possibly not the best thing to reveal to a man one is trying to seduce. 'So you see, you would not be doing anything wrong.'

'What did the bastard do to you?'

She shrugged, the memories dousing her passion. Ten years later, it still stung. She'd been almost eighteen and he close to forty, her father's age. But to her he'd been... freedom. He'd listened to her and made her laugh and made her feel...beautiful. Day by day, he'd peeled away her embarrassment and prudish concerns with teasing and little fleeting touches that seduced her. Little gifts and complicit smiles and then...promises. Of a shared life, a house and a family in England. A home, children. Security.

Except he already had a home and children. And a wife.

At least he'd had the decency to tell her the truth before he'd scuttled off. There'd been some mercy in that. Amputation was healthier in the end than the slow gangrenous rot of wondering what she had done wrong. She'd told her father, still naive and hopeful enough to think he'd take her side, maybe even comfort her. Well, another lesson learned. He'd been more furious at her having chased off his partner and ruining their trade in faux Greek statuettes than at William's betrayal.

That was the last time she turned to her father for comfort or aid. From that moment on it had been her and Dash and she'd been better for it.

'Cleo. Answer me. Did he hurt you?' Rafe said insistently, dragging her out of the past.

'You needn't sound as though you want to hunt him down and shoot him. It happened ten years ago and he did nothing worse than take what I offered willingly and then tell me he could not marry me because he already had a wife in England.'

'Nothing worse? Where the devil was your father in all this?'

She gave a little laugh. 'He was blaming me for chasing away his business associate. But it was *my* mistake for trusting either of them and it has nothing to do with now.'

He drew a deep breath, as if pulling back on invisible reins.

'Cleo, these feelings are natural. Especially when you are in danger and afraid. But they wear off and when they do they leave a bitter taste because you think you are choosing, but it is not a true choice. You deserve someone who can promise you happiness.'

Somehow this hurt more than everything he'd said before.

'I don't want anyone to promise me anything and certainly not something as ephemeral as happiness. My whole life has been built around a string of empty promises, being shunted about from one dream to another, none of which were mine, and watching all of them turn to cinders.'

He did not answer and they stood in silence for a long

while. He still held her lightly, his fingers gentle against the sensitive inside of her arm. She could hear his breathing—slow and deep and forceful, like the surf beating on the stone walls of Acre. She'd always felt those waves were the sound of the whole world breathing.

'Right now the sum of my dreams is to find my brother, reach England safely, and make a life there. All I want from you is…this.' She rested her hand once again, very gently on his chest. 'Rafe…'

He let go her arms abruptly and stepped back.

'I'm going for a walk. I'll sleep at the entrance tonight.'

Rafe spread his bedding outside the entrance to the chamber and pulled his blanket over him. He settled heavily on his aching shoulder and lay still for a long while, watching the moon blur as a ragged cloud crept up on it in the dark. He heard nothing from inside the temple but the snap and crackle of the small fire. The temptation to go inside was excruciating, but he remained where he was, a solid, aching barrier between her and the world.

He waited, as tense as a drawn bow, for her to come to confront him. Even for her to wish him goodnight. But no sound came. It was hellishly unfair that she could fall asleep so easily after kicking him off a cliff into purgatory.

It didn't help that a pack of jackals was carousing somewhere in the darkness. The jackals' long yowls reminded him of drunken soldiers after a battle—caught between the relief and sadness of surviving, and the need for human touch.

He wished the pack would find some other corner of the desert to annoy.

He turned on his back, staring at the immensity of the sky, and drew his leg up to ease the thudding pressure in his groin. A whole year without a woman was bound to wreak havoc, but that was no reason to indulge his body's juvenile fascination with Cleopatra. Or her fascination with him.

I like feeling like this.
So do I, damn it.

He turned on to his side again and opened his eyes, trying to chase away the ruinous images playing across his closed lids. But his mind was busy stacking the cards against him, pulling them out one by one like a vindictive Tarot card reader—what if she was no longer under his care? After all, she said she was not a virgin...

His mind stumbled over that for a moment. William. Of course she would fall in love with someone named after her precious bard.

You're an idiot, Rafe. Lust is bad enough right now. Don't add jealousy and anger to the mix.

But he couldn't help it. Every time he thought he'd plumbed the depth of her father's callousness, she let drop another pearl. What kind of bastard blamed his daughter for being seduced and lied to by his own friend? Osbourne was very lucky he was dead because if he'd been alive...

Except he wasn't; he was dead and Cleo was alone and for the moment she was his responsibility. Which meant there could be no *'all I want from you is this'.*

He groaned and rubbed his face, blocking out the filigree of stars. He could have come just listening to her. That voice and her big gold-brown eyes all sleepy and warm and... He was so tempted to go back into that temple and curl himself around her and feel her mouth on him again, that soft sweep against his neck...

There was something wrong with this world that women had to deny animal desire unless sanctioned by ceremony. He'd turned his back on that nonsense; why should he impose it on someone as unconventional as Cleo? She wanted it honestly and that was all she wanted from him...

The pin finally fell into the groove and with it the snap of affront.

Of course, that is all anyone wanted from him—some

service to be performed: save me, solve this problem, scratch this itch...

God knew he wanted to scratch this particular itch, just not at any cost.

She was no different in the end. She'd dragged admissions out of him he'd only ever told a handful of people, charmed them out of him with the lightest of touches and that aphrodisiac tincture of compassion. Then she'd come in for the kill with those impossibly sensual eyes pouring honeyed heat over him.

'May I take advantage of you, then, Mr Rafe Grey?'

He should have said yes and the hell with worrying about being manipulated and used. He didn't care. He just wanted...

He half rose, only to lie back down.

In the end, the only thing that should matter was that she was in his care until she was safe. He had so few codes left in his life, so few truths. If he took advantage of her... and it would be taking advantage of her as much as she wanted to take advantage of him...

A shiver of heat raced through him, like a rat roused from its hiding place.

Blast and double blast the woman.

He kept his eyes resolutely closed. A stone-hard cock had yet kept him from sleep when he knew he had to be rested and he was damned if he was going to let it do so now. He had trained for years to deal with situations where he needed sleep and his body rebelled.

He began counting backward from one hundred, each number taking him down a step towards a blank door. At fifty he vaguely noticed he wasn't holding his pistol as he always did during the count. Strangely it was suspended beside him without any contact. A railing had appeared there instead, smooth under his hand. He kept counting even as he wondered where it had come from.

He started floating at thirty, much later than usual, and

even then almost lost his count when a dark-eyed little boy sitting on the steps holding a toy horse smiled up at him.

He felt his hand settle on the familiarly warm downy hair and then the numbers finally fell away.

Chapter Nine

Cairo—three days later

'Home sweet home.'

Rafe dropped his pack on to a scuffed wooden table at the centre of the room and rolled his shoulders. Cleo laid hers down more gently and looked around.

The house was well situated, close to the wharves of Boulaq, but within easy distance of the centre of Cairo. It probably belonged to a well-to-do merchant for it was large and clean and the wooden latticed shutters were in good repair. She peeked through the shutters—the sun was low and beyond the rooftops the Nile was a swathe of silver and copper scarred by the white sails of feluccas and the flat ferries cutting towards Giza. Below she could hear the shopkeepers and the distinctive gaggle of men from the coffee house, and above the scent of the river and the spice store below she caught the warm scent of coffee and the muskier tang of the *shisha* pipes.

She closed her eyes and let the sounds and smells waft around her.

Home sweet home.

For a little longer only.

She had not thought she would miss this city, but now

she knew her days here were numbered she felt the squeeze of sorrow that this, too, must be left behind. She was becoming truly maudlin. She hadn't cried when William abandoned her, yet she'd cried on Gamila's hairy neck, saying goodbye to her and to Gamal.

Gamal, wealthier by five camels and several gold coins, had reassured her it was in the stars that she would return one day to the desert with her man and children and then they would ride Gamila's calf. It was a lovely image, however unlikely, and she'd accepted it for the gift it was.

'Hungry?'

She nodded at Rafe's question. He was still by the table and was watching her. The back of her nape tingled with awareness and the resurgence of embarrassment. Neither of them had referred to the events in the temple at Kharga and Rafe had made every effort to behave as if the interlude had never happened.

Perhaps to someone like Rafe, who'd seen so much in the world, her behaviour was easy to dismiss. Still, he'd been uncomfortable with her ever since. When they'd reached Asyut and she'd curled up to sleep at the bow of the felucca they'd hired, he'd gone to sit at the stern.

'Tired?'

She nodded again.

'You look like you're propped up with scaffolding, Cleo-Pat. Take off that turban and sit down.'

'I should go to Ezbekiya and see…'

He came towards her and she tensed as she had every time they'd come within touching distance since her failed seduction. He looked even more like a corsair in this civilised setting. Nothing had outwardly changed—his plain cotton shirt was open at the neck, his dark hair disordered and his jaw covered with stubble except where the scars left it pale and bare. In the desert his raffish air looked far more natural than the rigid dress code of many visiting Englishmen. But here in the small room with its prosaic table and chairs and a faded painting of some Mameluke patron, he looked like what he was—a mercenary. Capable, dangerous, calculating.

He untucked the edge of her scarf from under her ear and unwound it, his dark brows drawn together with concentration. When he brushed his knuckles from her temple to her cheek that side of her face lit like an oil lamp and she held herself stone still, hope springing to life. But he merely moved away, tossing her scarf on to the pile on the table.

'You've brought half the desert in here with you, Queenie. You aren't going anywhere but into a bath. Everything else will wait until the morrow.'

'I must see if Dash is there—'

'Do you know what they call animals that rush into traps?' he interrupted and she frowned, well aware this was a trap in itself.

'No…'

'Supper.'

'Oh, *very* amusing.'

'Sarcasm doesn't work if you're laughing, Cleo-Pat.'

She didn't bother to deny the accusation. It was very hard to remain serious when he was in this mood. No doubt this lightness was relief at finally reaching the safety and relative comfort of Cairo and knowing he would soon be shot of her and her problems. Tomorrow he would be on his way to find his brother and she—

All her amusement and the glimmerings of pleasure were doused as swiftly as if she'd been tossed headfirst into the Nile.

He frowned. 'I don't care what mouldering mummy of a thought your tortuous mind has conjured, Queenie; you aren't going anywhere today. Come, I'll show you to your room.'

He went towards the door, but she wavered and he glanced back.

'It's not a trap, Cleo.'

'I know that. It's only… I've forgotten what it is like to be indoors.'

'After a week, miss?' Birdie asked as he entered the room with a wooden tray bearing a steaming long-spouted teapot and plate of honeyed cakes. She smiled at him with relief.

'It feels much, much longer than a week, Birdie.'

'Is that a jibe about how heavily our company weighed on you, Queenie?' Rafe asked.

'Stop that bickering, you two, and come drink.' Birdie filled the *finjans* and the scent of coffee and cardamom filled the room. 'Naguib brought this fresh from the coffee house. His son's heating water for Miss to wash and I've sent him to fetch us a good piece of lamb for supper. You'll go to the baths by the square, sir?'

Rafe drained the small cup and rubbed his hand over his jaw, but his gaze was on Cleo. 'You go, Birdie. I'll make do here with hot water and a blade.'

'No, you won't, sir. I'll keep a weather eye here, never fear.'

Cleo saw the yearning mix with hesitation in Rafe's eyes and sighed.

'I am not foolhardy, Mr Grey. I won't disappear while you are at the *hammam.*'

'Your word.'

'My word.'

He nodded but there was still a peculiar hesitancy about him. Finally, Birdie gave him an unceremonious shove towards the door.

'Off with you. Faster you go, faster you're back and it's my turn.'

When the door closed behind him Birdie smiled at her.

'Come along, miss. I'll show you to your room.'

'That sounds very grand, Birdie.'

'Well, it's not that, but right now I'd venture we'd be happy in a hayloft, miss.'

* * *

It wasn't the laughter or the scraping of some string instrument from the coffee house down the street that was keeping Rafe awake. It was a blank wall.

Behind the straw-coloured wall was Cleo's room and her equally narrow wooden bed. In essence, he lay closer to her now than he had in the desert where nothing but a couple of yards of cooling air separated them.

Except now he couldn't see her and it was wreaking havoc on his ability to surrender to sleep. She'd become a talisman, like those prayer beads the men in the coffee house clicked between their fingers. He'd grown accustomed to seeing her just before he fell asleep—marking it in his mind: One Cleopatra Osbourne, present and asleep.

Other than that hellish night in Kharga, for a week now this had been his nightly rote. He hadn't noticed it had become a habit. He certainly hadn't realised it had become a necessity.

Strange to think he'd watched her sleep more than he'd watched any other woman. He'd spent a fair share of time in bed with women over the years, but he could not for the life of him remember ever watching them sleep. If he'd thought about it at all, he would have considered it an imposition—he didn't like the thought of anyone watching him while he was unconscious, so he had done unto others as he wished to be done unto him.

He had no idea why she was different. Perhaps it was the desert—that thick but crystalline darkness, or the absence of walls to protect them from whatever dangers lurked in the darkness so he had to check she was safe.

There was also that niggling confusion—he could not quite get to the bottom of the puzzle that was Cleopatra Osbourne. She was at once so direct and so very convoluted. He found himself searching her face for some clue that would settle the question one way or another. Perhaps in sleep she would reveal that essence. But her face, free of wariness and tension, her lashes twitching like feathers as she dreamt, only confused him further.

Not that it should matter. He'd never before thought it necessary to understand his charges in order to protect them. Why he should feel that impulse now, he didn't know. It was there, though. A discomfort, like sitting on a poorly stitched saddle.

The confusion was rubbing him raw.

Having a real bed, a room and a solid wall between them should have been a relief. The last thing he would have expected was to be lying awake staring at that wall, as alert as if a pack of rabid jackals was scratching at the door.

He'd felt the same at Chesham when Jacob was ill. He and Edge had taken turns keeping vigil and he'd been terrified he'd fall asleep on his watch and wake to find his nephew dead. In the end Jacob had died snug in Edge's arms in the middle of a sunny day. It made no odds if they were awake or not, but something deep and atavistic told him it mattered. The same overpowering urge to assure himself she was well was pressing on his chest like an incubus. He needed to *see* that she was sleeping.

Absurd. Besides being improper and unnecessary and offensive.

He groaned and rubbed his stiff shoulder.

He would compromise by ensuring all the doors and windows were secured. In a few days she would be on her way to England on his friend Chris's ship and there would be no checking on her, sleeping or waking.

His stomach clenched and he stood. A thousand things could happen to a woman travelling to England. Cleopatra might be more resourceful than most people of his acquaintance, but he knew the world—it stacked the deck against women and even the most agile fox could find itself cornered if the hounds were set upon it.

Even if the *Hesperus* was still docked in Alexandria... Even if he trusted Chris with his life... Even then the thought of watching her set sail to an unknown future felt like a betrayal. Worse, it felt…frightening. Wrong.

He felt a little ill with it. Like the days before one fully succumbed to an ague. His insides felt rough, raw, miserable.

It was damn lucky he no longer depended on his skill as a mercenary to pay the bills because he'd clearly gone soft.

He padded into the corridor and his stomach clenched again.

The door to her room was ajar and the narrow bed empty. Fear was chased by anger—she could not possibly have been so foolish to have gone off alone? He strode into the room and the anger dimmed at the sight of her boots, now clean and shiny, set by the small table-cum-dresser. But that merely made way for fear to return. He did not believe they had been followed, yet…

He hurried down the corridor to the salon and stopped in the doorway.

She half turned, her eyes dark and gleaming like an animal's. She was wrapped in a cotton blanket and it trailed on the ground like a cape. She looked more than ever like a faerie being with her short hair and large eyes. A breeze was slipping through the shutters, but his body was heating up far too fast for the cool air to soothe him.

With a mixture of anger and resignation he felt it take hold. He might as well have been that blasted princess chained to the rock in the sea—there was no escaping this wave. It swept out from his centre like kindling tossed into a keg of gunpowder.

He'd wanted to feel young again, but not like this. Not overwhelmed by a need he didn't even understand. He *liked* lust—liked it fierce and hot and immediate. But not when it was laced with fear and this strange loss of balance.

It had happened before, in moments of weakness. This welling of need for some place to set down roots and grow. Someone…

But it dragged up every doubt and demon inside him, his mind mapping the future down a hundred paths to perdition. It ended in his father's madness, his nephew's death, with the murky image of the woman who might marry him realising her mistake. It ended with pain and emptiness and a loneliness worse for being shared.

He *liked* his life. There was no reason to change it only to make it worse. He had no faith in his ability to be anything but a temporary haven. That was the essence of his being. Temporary.

Cleo deserved everything her father and that bastard of a lover had denied her. She deserved her pack of jackals, a safe, good man who would help her set down the roots she'd been denied by the men who should have stood by her.

He knew as much about roots as he did about camels. Less.

He should stay away.

However much his body was waxing lyrical about her at the moment, she was only a page in a very brief chapter of his life. She had no place in his tale any more than he had in hers.

'Why aren't you in your room?' He tried to keep his voice low and authoritative.

'I can't sleep,' she whispered. 'The room feels…stifling after the desert. It's foolish, but I needed to breathe. Did I wake you?

'I wasn't asleep.'

'Oh.' She turned and touched the shutters briefly. Through the perforations of the *mashrabiya* he could see the inky shimmer of the Nile. 'I came to look at the river. It always calms me.'

'You sound as if you will miss it.'

'I think I will. Or perhaps that is only because my future is so uncertain. Better the devil one knows…'

'What will you do when you reach England?' He hadn't meant to make it sound like a demand, but she reacted as to the flick of a whip, her back straightening and her lips flattening.

'First I must be certain Dash has left Egypt. I am very grateful for your help, Mr Grey, and I will find a way to repay you, but you are under no further obligation to me.'

'If I were your friend al-Mizan, do you know what I would do once I realised you'd slipped through my net?' he said, ignoring her stilted formality. 'I would wait for you to do precisely what you appear determined to do—return to your home ground. You might as well declare your arrival in Cairo from the nearest minaret.'

'I'm not quite the fool you think me, Mr Grey. I do not plan to parade around Cairo for all to see. Besides, I doubt my father took anything so valuable from Bey al-Wassawi he'd send al-Mizan all the way to Cairo.'

'You know as well as I al-Mizan is not in the employ of Bey al-Wassawi. He came from Cairo and carried a letter of recommendation from the French consul general.'

'Why are you only telling me this now?' Her voice rose in anger.

'I might just as easily ask why you didn't tell me you knew al-Mizan was in Boucheron's employ?'

She turned her head back towards the shutters.

'I've never met any of Boucheron's mercenaries.'

'Yet you knew he employed a man by the name of al-Mizan.'

'It might have been a common name for all I knew.'

'Not at all, according to Gamal. You didn't mention it for a reason.'

Her chin lowered like a bull considering whether or not to charge.

'Oh? And what reason do you ascribe to me?'

'Two reasons. At first you didn't trust me. It was one thing for a foreign mercenary to shield you from a local bruiser, quite another to expect him to take your side against another foreigner and a wealthy and influential one at that. A sensible mercenary might have decided you and your beastly bauble were not worth the risk.'

'And the other reason?'

'The opposite consideration. You were worried you might not be so easily rid of us if we thought the source of your threat was here in Cairo.'

'You appear to think you know the workings of my mind, Mr Grey.'

'Some of them, certainly. You are too honest a person to lie convincingly, Cleo-Pat.'

'I did not lie.'

'Omitting to tell the truth is still being dishonest.'

'The same applies to you. You don't appear to be at all bothered by the fact you lied by omission.'

'Not terribly. You did not need to know it. Now you do.'

'Magnanimous of you.'

'Merely practical. It makes it clear why I cannot allow you to charge into town tomorrow.'

'He will be on the lookout for Dash, not for Miss Osbourne. Miss Osbourne left for London with the Mitchums weeks ago.'

'Yet what happens if you are recognised? Boucheron will surely be interested why Miss Osbourne, who as you say left for London, has returned to Cairo in record time. No reason for him to consider that at all suspicious.'

She crossed her arms. With her short hair and the plain cotton nightshirt Birdie had procured her she did not look like any young woman of his acquaintance. Her hair feathered over her dark brows and his hand twitched with the need to sift through it, brush it back, shape his hands over her head, her nape... He wanted so very badly to walk over and...

And nothing. It was not going to happen.

'I shall naturally not advertise my return, Mr Grey,' she replied. 'All I wish to do is go to our rooms and see if Dash is there. Perhaps I shall discover this is all a foolish misunderstanding and that all is well…' She wavered, but clung doggedly to her shrinking island. 'There is no reason to always suspect the worst.'

'There is one reason to always suspect the worse and that is one's wish to survive.'

'*"A coward dies a thousand times before his death, but the valiant taste of death but once."* That is from *Julius Caesar* in case you were interested, Mr Grey.'

'Not Old Willie again. And if you must quote him, try not to choose a quote where the character is dead by the next act.'

Her reluctant laughter rippled out.

'I concede, but my point is still valid as well. Living in fear is a dreadful way to pass through this world.'

'I disagree; it is far preferable to be a coward than valiant. As a coward I've died many times and will likely do so again before I do so irretrievably. But, unlike Caesar, for now I'm still here to argue with you.'

'Don't be coy, Mr Grey. You are certainly no coward.'

'You think not? By your definition I most certainly am. My cowardly little mind maps the world with a hundred ways my candle can be snuffed. It could be anything— from having my throat slit by one of your enemies to being poisoned by Birdie's culinary efforts. Every night I go to sleep is another temporary victory over that catalogue. I am only alive today because I am a coward.'

His anger grew with his words. She wasn't attacking him, but it felt like an accusing finger. Rafe Grey's life was based on the actions of a coward, or running away from burdens—his father's anger, his mother's indifference, even his true name. He'd escaped them all, tail between his legs. He didn't need some misguided miss spouting romantic nonsense about being valiant to him. It was a little late for that.

'Then I'm very glad you're a coward.' She spoke softly and there was still a remnant of a smile curving her lips.

It was either the smile or something in her words, but he felt a little stunned, as if he'd walked into a tree he'd not realised stood right in front of him. Of all the risks he prepared for daily, he was not prepared for her shifting moods.

'If being brave is forcing your way again and again through your fears, and I agree it is, then you are a very brave man, Rafe.'

Damnation.

'Are you buttering me up for a purpose, Cleo-Pat? I still have no intention of allowing you to run about Cairo unchecked.'

'I am not buttering you up, but cannot in good conscience continue to impose upon you. You have your own matters to see to.'

'Do you wish me to help you or not?'

'Of course I do, but…'

'Good. Then stop arguing about everything. Tomorrow we will decide how to proceed. Right now, take advantage of having a decent bed.'

He sounded sensible and authoritative. But inside a voice was pleading—*Please go to sleep before I do something my conscience will hit me over the head with.*

'Very well. Thank you, Rafe,' Cleo murmured and he shrugged, clearly uncomfortable with gratitude or praise. He looked like an overgrown, embarrassed schoolboy. She almost enjoyed saying nice things about him just to watch the confident man turn into a squirming mass of discomfort.

She enjoyed far too much about him.

What would he say if she told him it wasn't only her worries about tomorrow that had kept her awake, but the realisation that it was over? This brief, frightening, and yet beautiful adventure.

She smiled at him. She would miss him awfully when they parted ways, but she wouldn't allow that to take away from the gift he'd unknowingly helped her uncover. Somehow during their passage through the desert she'd come to feel she belonged. She'd been right there at the centre of her own world, instead of alone or an observer. It wasn't that Rafe Grey had moved into the centre of her world. *She* had. Whatever happened from that moment onwards, she would hold on to that.

Still, she wished so much she could take something more before they parted ways tomorrow... The thought was suddenly so unbearable she reached out and took his hand. Strange how well she knew it already—its size, the roughness of his callouses and the softness of the heart of his palm. She'd held it sitting by the fire in the middle of the universe and nothingness.

In the dark, with the city hushed around them, his hand was like that campfire—it became the centre of a vast universe, the point from which everything was mapped. She wanted to feel it against her cheek and neck with a need stronger than a desert thirst. Her own skin was half on fire, half icy.

'Cleo...' His voice scraped at her nerves, his hand tightening on hers for a moment, but then he stepped back and turned resolutely towards the door.

'Goodnight.'

Chapter Ten

Rafe was at the table when she entered the sitting room the next morning, the remains of breakfast to one side and a cup of coffee at his elbow as he scribbled on a sheet of paper. He glanced up as she entered, but then returned his frown to his letter.

'I need the direction of your house,' he said to his letter. 'I will go there this morning.'

Cleo took a piece of bread and poured cardamom-scented coffee into a small cup.

'I'm coming with you.'

'No, you are not.'

'I most certainly am. Aside from everything else, you will never find it without me.'

There was a distinct sound of grinding teeth, but he remained bent over his writing. She watched his hand moving in a steady dance over the paper, dipping into the inkwell, flexing. Her own hands were tingling.

He laid down the pen, but did not look at her.

'I concede you know a great deal more about Egypt than I do or will ever wish to know, Pat, but I know more about thieves and murderers than I hope you ever will.'

'Excellent. Then between the two of us we should be prepared for everything.'

'You have hired me…'

'To bring me to Cairo. Which you have. You are no longer in my employ and I am no longer your charge.'

'You are merely strengthening my case that you are not in command. I work alone.'

'That is not very kind to Birdie.'

'Birdie and I are considered a unit for the purposes of my occupation. You, however…'

'Know my way around this city and my own home, which is more than you do. Even if I were to give you the direction, several other families have rooms in that building. You will likely become lost and go into the wrong rooms if you go alone.'

'Must you always insist on having your way?'

'Only when I know I am right.'

He sighed.

'I don't know why I even bother arguing with you.'

'We are not arguing. We are conferring on how best to proceed.'

'No. I was telling you… Damnation, never mind. You may come. But otherwise you will do precisely as you are told. If I tell you to run, you pick up your skirts and run. Understood?'

Cleo paused at the corner of the road, between an open-fronted shop stacked high with rugs and another glittering with pots and pans.

The street looked the same and utterly different.

It was not as busy as Boulaq, but this part of Ezbekiya was still crowded with shops and narrow streets populated by foreign merchants and mid-level officials of the Khedive's court. Her father had always hoped their fortunes might so improve as to allow him to move to the more prosperous parts of Cairo, but Cleo had enjoyed the anonymity of this crowded corner of the city. No one appeared to know or care whether she appeared in her boy's garb or in one of her few dresses.

Now the noise and the crowds felt as oppressive and foreign as the first time they'd come here four years ago.

'Is one of those buildings where you live?' Rafe put a hand on her arm, not to guide her across the road, but to restrain her. He needn't have. She'd become as wary as he these past weeks.

'Yes, we have rooms in the building just by that little passage halfway down.'

'You have that look on your face again. What is amiss?'

'I don't know. Perhaps I am being over-cautious, but something feels…wrong,' she murmured.

'Cautious is good. Especially when a group of unpleasant men are on your tail. You should trust those sensations—your mind sees more than you do. Is there something out of place on the street?'

'No, it is merely…yes, yes, you are right—something *is* out of place. I left the *mashrabiya* shutters closed and Dash would never leave them open in the middle of the day. See upstairs?'

He raised his eyes to scan the house, his hand moving a little on her arm. It was a reassuring rub. For such a big man he had a gentle touch.

'Perhaps your landlord came to look around?'

'He has never done so before and would have no reason to. Our rent is paid through to the end of the quarter.'

'I see. Is there somewhere you can wait for me? Or perhaps I'd better take you back to Boulaq now I know my way here.'

'We agreed I was to come with you!'

'And you have. There is no need for you to go any further, Queenie. We passed a spice shop just around the corner. Wait for me there.'

'No!' It was her turn to grab his arm. It was a substantially thicker and more solid affair than hers and she added her other hand to secure her grip. He looked down at her hands, his brows rising. Embarrassment hit her like the blast of an open oven and she dropped his arm, tucking her hands into her *gallabiyah*.

'Listen to me. The buildings along the north side of the street were once part of a Mameluke palace and they've been separated into lodgings in the least sensible manner. Corridors and doors head in every direction so you might never find the right door and even then you won't know if anything has changed since my departure. Besides, I am far safer with you than on my own out here and—'

He sighed. 'Very well, you will probably only follow me anyway and make matters worse.'

'There is no need to be insulting.'

'And there is no need to take offence when you've already won the draw. Now, lead on, MacDuff.'

'It is *"Lay on"*. Why must everyone misquote that?'

'Because it is an improvement on the original.'

'An improvement on *Shakespeare*!'

'You look ready to run me through. You shouldn't idolise anyone, Pat. Not even a man who's safe by dint of being dead. He can still disappoint, you know.'

'I don't idolise him. There isn't even a *him* to idolise—it's his writing that means something to me; not the man himself. He could be a three-legged, one-horned goat for all I care.'

'Yet you still allow him to sway your judgement.'

'I do not.'

'You are standing here on a street corner, arguing with me while al-Mizan's minions might be roaming your house. I'd call that being swayed.'

'It's not… I'm merely…not ready.'

'I know, but it's always better to know the truth.'

'No, it isn't. Oh, devil take it. Let us go see.'

* * *

'Your housekeeping skills leave a lot to be desired, Queenie.'

Rafe watched her as she scooped up a pile of clothes and a bonnet from the floor. 'What are you doing?' he asked as she began laying out the clothes on the narrow bed.

'Checking.'

'What?'

'Clothes.'

'And why are you checking clothes?' he asked carefully.

She placed her hands on her hips and looked around the room.

'Dash has been here.'

'I don't know much about your brother, Cleo, but I don't think he made this mess.'

'Of course he didn't, but someone has taken at least one set of clothes—warm clothes—as well as his best shaving kit and his old writing case. The note I left him is missing as well. I doubt the thieves would have been interested in that.'

'I see. But we don't know if he came before or after the people who decided to redistribute all your possessions on the floor.'

'After. This picture frame is broken, but the likeness it held of my mother is gone. It was hanging on that wall and had it been intact when he came he would have taken it with him, frame and all.'

'Good point.' He rubbed his chest as realisation set in that had Cleo not gone in search of her brother, she would have been here when they came to search the rooms. If he'd had any lingering doubts about the need to remove her from Egypt without delay, the casual violence inherent in the ransacked room removed it utterly. By hook or by crook he would see her safe to England and be done with this.

He watched her as she continued inspecting the room. Her face was imperturbable again, except for that stubborn jutting of her lower lip. He could see no fear there, but she was no fool. She *must* realise the danger to herself. He followed her into the next room.

'This means that your brother has likely been through here in the last few days, seen this chaos and realised it was time to leave Egypt in your wake post haste. That is good news.'

'Yes.'

'You don't look relieved.'

'I should be, I know. But I don't understand what they are looking for. My father may have been many dubious things, but I've never known him to steal something outright. I cannot make sense of any of this.'

She was gathering and stacking the discarded slips of paper, the same ferocious frown cutting lines in her brow. He wanted to tell her to forget about making sense of her sire's leavings and concentrate on the future. Except that he was as aware as she must be that her future was even cloudier than her present.

She placed the stack of papers on the desk and straightened a small framed print of a very English landscape on the wall. He could see where she had done her best to give this depressing set of rooms some character—there were colourful cushions and carpets and a few framed drawings of temples and landscapes.

He followed her into the next room and stopped in the doorway, absurdly embarrassed as he realised it was her bedroom. It, too, was a jumble of discarded clothes, cushions and books and she bent and untangled a simple muslin dress from the pile in the middle of the floor. There was hardly anything untoward about the sight of a plain cotton frock, but he took a step backwards and went back to the main salon.

It was only a dress. He'd seen hundreds of them—on and off women. He wasn't merely getting old; he was becoming addled. Next he'd be blushing at the sight of a bonnet and getting hard at the mention of a reticule.

Pathetic.

After all, the simple Egyptian belted robe she wore showed as much of her anatomy as a gown. Well, not as much of her magnificent bosom. He wouldn't mind at all seeing that on display in one of the low-cut London fashions. With her height and physique and those elfin features she would probably attract a great deal of attention. She would look best in vivid colours, desert colours, that reflected the honey of her eyes and skin and the chestnut warmth of her hair. Earth and fire.

Ah, *hell.*

'We should be going.' His voice was more growl than suggestion and he cleared his throat, calling himself to order.

'In a moment...' Her reply was muffled and her shadow moved about the room, the dark length of an arm slipping across the floor and touching the bed as if beckoning him.

Seeking a distraction, he picked up a book from the desk and flicked open the cover. With a jolt of annoyance, he realised that the fates were having a grand time toying with him—it was a well-worn copy of Edge's first *Desert Boy* book, the one he himself had all but forced his brother to write. He flicked the page, his heart contracting at the familiar drawing of a cat riding a camel and the printed dedication.

To J.- My heart, my home, for ever.
And to R.- My brother and my rock.

Combating lust with sentiment was not a tactic he had tried in the past. He couldn't even vouch for its effectiveness because at that second a far more immediate peril intervened.

He could never later make sense of this lapse in his caution.

A bout of juvenile lusting, even combined with surprise at seeing Edge's book, was no excuse for becoming so pre-occupied he completely missed the man's approach. He couldn't even console himself that his near-murderer had been unusually stealthy because Cleo did hear him. One minute he'd been glaring at the book and the next there'd been a cry and a blur of movement as Cleo barrelled past him and into the man rushing towards him with a dagger, her hands fastening about the attacker's wrist, driving it upwards.

The man cursed, swinging his arm back at her and there was a dull thud as his elbow struck her head and she hit the wall, sliding to the floor. The assailant hardly changed his trajectory as he continued towards Rafe, his whole body behind the thrust of the knife. But the momentary check Cleo had provided was more than enough.

Rafe raised the book he held and gave a brutal whack to the man's knife hand and then swung the volume back to connect again with the side of his attacker's all too fa-miliar face. The knife flew in one direction and the man in the other, his head hitting the doorjamb behind him with a thud. Rafe advanced immediately, but before he could even grab him al-Mizan's eyes rolled backwards and he slipped to the ground.

'You killed him,' Cleo whispered, rubbing her shoulder as she struggled to her feet. She did not appear to be very shocked by the prospect.

Rafe's blood was still boiling, but too many thoughts were going through his mind so he focused on what mat-tered right there and then.

'He's not dead and he'll probably come out of this faint any moment, so help me. Bring me a cravat or scarf to tie his hands and then go into the hallway and I don't want to hear a peep from you. Not one word.'

She hurried out and returned with a stack of linen strips and he hauled al-Mizan on to a wooden chair and set about tying his hands and legs to it. The man was already beginning to stir and Rafe shooed her towards the hallway.

'Stay out of his sight and for God's sake don't say a word. Promise me!'

She bunched her fists, but nodded, and he picked up the man's knife and waited.

It did not take long. Al-Mizan groaned, cursed and looked as though he was well on his way to casting up his accounts, but he controlled himself, finally focusing on Rafe.

'Hello, al-Mizan.' Rafe smiled. There was a livid bruise along his cheekbone where he'd knocked against the door-jamb and another along his jaw where the book had caught him. Rafe tapped the tip of the dagger to the already swelling flesh and al-Mizan winced, shying away.

'Looks as though you are going to have quite a black eye. I suggest applying wet compresses and avoid trying to skewer people for a few days.'

'You lied to me in Syene,' al-Mizan snarled.

'Did I? I only remember turning down your less than generous offer.'

'You knew of this Osbourne. You are in league with him.'

'Not at all. It is simply that his offer was better than yours. I am merely trying to help return him to England in one piece. I assure you he neither has nor wishes to have whatever it is you are looking for.'

'I saw you this moment holding a book!'

Rafe picked up the discarded *Desert Boy* book and opened it.

'This? I applaud your master's taste in reading, but he could have saved himself great expense and trouble and bought a copy at a bookshop.'

Al-Mizan glared at him, but there was a growing puzzlement in his eyes.

'Perhaps I was mistaken about this instance, but the son of Osbourne took his father's possessions from the lodgings in Meroe. The book as well. My master did not think the boy was in his father's confidence, but then why take the book and why disappear?'

'Perhaps because a murderous fellow was on his trail?'

'He was not to know I meant to harm him.'

'You're not that stupid, al-Mizan. What else was he to think when mercenaries begin to make enquiries about him in the middle of Nubia? Of course he ran. He told me the day he came to find me he did not know why you were chasing him.'

'If he does not have the book, then who does?'

'I neither know nor care. My role is to ensure Mr Osbourne is put safely on a ship to England. I am happy to enquire if he took any books from his father's possessions and, if he has, I will ensure we deliver them all to your master, Monsieur Boucheron.'

It was a gamble. Rafe saw Cleo's shadow shifting in the hallway as she listened and he hoped she kept quiet.

Al-Mizan's eyes narrowed and he gave a tug at his bonds.

'I never spoke my master's name. You reveal yourself, *basha nadab.*'

'Not at all. It does not take a great mind to realise Osbourne's father took something from his employer. Neither I nor Osbourne the Younger have any interest in entering that feud.'

'I see no reason why I should trust you. When last I did my men wasted a day chasing two of Bey al-Wassawi's cousins.'

'Only a day? They were even more ineffective than I thought. As for trusting me, you should because you strike me as a sensible man and, more to the point, because at the moment you are tied to a chair and I could easily make away with you right now.'

'It would be foolishness to harm me, *nadab*. If you know aught of my master, you should know he possesses a great deal of influence here. He could have you thrown into one of our prisons. You would not like it, I assure you.'

'Don't waste your time threatening me, al-Mizan. You would have an easier time of it if you killed me outright rather than trying to put me in a local gaol. But having failed in that endeavour I suggest you pass along a message to your master. My only interest is in returning Mr Osbourne to England. I have no interest in stolen goods and neither does he. All I want is the man, on a ship.'

'Why? Of what value is he to you?'

'I could ask the same of you.'

'I told you…'

'You told me a tall tale about some family bible. Now we have each other's measure, al-Mizan, you know I don't believe that. Tell me what it is you are really after and I might be able to help you. I don't believe you have gone to all this trouble for a mere book. As best I understand antiquities in this country, there are no valuable books. All writing was on papyrus scrolls. Therefore, I presume it is the contents, not the book itself, that is of value. I also find it curious that your master apparently didn't send you in pursuit until Mr Osbourne's servant defected to his service. Therefore, either he didn't notice this extremely valuable book's disappearance, or, more likely, he did not know of its existence until told of it by the servant.'

Al-Mizan's mouth pressed down hard. Rafe pressed forward his advantage.

'A more romantic fellow than I might have begun to dream of a book filled with clues to a treasure Mr Osbourne was pursuing in Nubia, but since your master did not give you any instructions to make enquiries regarding

Mr Osbourne's activities there, I can discard that fantasy. He wants this book and only that.'

'How do you know he gave me no such instructions?'

'I can count, Mr al-Mizan. I enquired when you passed through Syene on your way south and by my calculation you must have turned around the moment you discovered Osbourne the Younger had been and gone and ridden hard to close the gap. Answer me one question, Mr al-Mizan. Do you know why your master wants this book? Just yes or no will do. No details necessary.'

Al Mizan sighed, his shoulders lowering a little.

'In my position, it is best not to know all the details. It is enough that he wants it and that he pays me well for my services. But I tell you, for him it is of the highest importance.'

Rafe nodded. He knew truth when he heard it. It was a sensible man who did not seek knowledge that could redound against him.

'Then perhaps I should have a word with him myself.'

'I would usually counsel wise men against foolishness, *nadab*, but in this case I need not bother. Monsieur Boucheron is not in Cairo.'

'Where has he gone?'

'He does not inform me. He ordered me to remain alert for Osbourne's son's possible return and then he left.'

'I see. In any case, if we should discover aught of it before we depart Egypt, I will see it is delivered to him. We want nothing of it, merely to return to England now that Old Osbourne is dead. Understood?'

Al-Mizan nodded. It didn't count for much, but it was the best Rafe could secure at this juncture.

'Good. Now I think it is best we part ways.'

'You will not leave me tied to this chair!' al-Mizan protested and Rafe picked up a discarded cravat and twisted it into a gag, tying it around al-Mizan's mouth.

'A few knots won't hold back someone of your skills,

I'm sure,' he murmured reassuringly as he went towards the door. 'Clearly you have paid someone in this building to send word to you if anyone enters these rooms. Make enough of a racket and I feel certain they will come running.'

Cleo was waiting in the narrow hallway, her honey eyes wide, her mouth a thin, determined line, and a broom held firmly in her hands. He waved her towards the door just as a loud crash sounded. Clearly al-Mizan meant to dismantle the chair himself. Good fellow.

Chapter Eleven

Within moments they were wending through the narrow alleyways, skirting stalls and laden donkeys, water boys and women balancing baskets and jugs on their heads. Eventually, Cleo stopped looking over her shoulder every few yards, but she did not speak until they were within sight of the river.

'Why did you tell him I was Dash?'

'Because while they think you are your brother they will be looking for him in the wrong place, giving him more time to leave Egypt unobstructed.'

'Of course. I see. Thank you.'

Her voice was brisk and Rafe realised again how grateful he was for her calm, though she had looked anything but calm as she had launched herself at his would-be killer.

The memory still formed icicles in his chest. The blur of movement, the realisation of danger, the shock. He'd made mistakes in the past and they'd cost him and others, but this…

He didn't want to think about it.

'Don't ever do that again, Cleopatra.'

The words were out of him before he could stop them.

'Do what? Ask questions?'

'Throw yourself at someone wielding a knife.'

They'd reached the house in Boulaq and with a last glance down the street he ushered her inside. She went, but her frown showed precisely what she thought of his comment. He couldn't blame her—he wasn't happy with himself either at the moment, but he couldn't help it.

'I would think you would be grateful, Mr Grey. You might now be sporting another impressive scar in your collection if not for me.'

'I *am* grateful, but I am also serious. Never do that again.'

'You prefer I leave you to be skewered?'

'I prefer you not try to skewer yourself on a trained killer's knife.'

'So do I. Very well, if you prefer to play the hero, next time I shall leave you to it.'

He stomped up the steps beside her, not sure he was pleased with her compliance.

'Do you think he believed you?' she asked.

He considered lying to her and discarded the notion; his prevarication skills weren't at their best around her.

'Men like al-Mizan don't believe anyone. I rather like the fellow.'

'How broadminded of you. After all, he only wished to kill us both.'

'I don't think he was intent on blood—his brief was to find this book and bring you back to Boucheron so he could ascertain what you, I mean your brother, knew. His attempt at violence right there was sparked by personal pique and was a sore mistake. He is well aware of that. Hopefully once you, or rather your brother, leaves Egypt they will forget all about you. Now I need to find Birdie. I want him to run a couple of errands for me.'

She continued up the stairs.

'What errands?'

'I need some new…cravats.'

'Please don't bother to lie, or, if you must, at least make an effort at being convincing.'

'Yes, ma'am.'

'You don't intend to tell me?'

'No, ma'am.'

'You don't trust me.'

'Like al-Mizan, I don't trust anyone. For their own good. The more you trust someone, the greater the burden you place upon them. If I don't trust you, you needn't worry that you might let me down.'

'Another truly abysmal philosophy, Mr Grey.'

'Says the young woman who trusts not a single person on this fair earth.'

Her foot slipped on the step and he caught her elbow, steadying her.

He waited for her to proceed, but she remained where she was, staring at the floor.

'That is not true,' she muttered finally.

'Not true? You told me yourself you never truly trusted your father and we've established you don't trust your brother, not when it truly counts. Either tell me who you trust or stop denigrating my hard-earned right to mistrust everybody.'

'I trust you.'

She had to stop *doing* this.

He hadn't earned it; he didn't want it. Trust like hers demanded trust in return and if he let himself trust her... He had no idea what that even meant except that it had the power to terrify him, as if he held Pandora's box in his hands with warnings from the gods etched deep on to its surface. There would be no closing this box once opened.

She turned to him, chin raised. 'And Birdie, though I know you will say I should not trust either of you.'

'I have already told you precisely that. I don't enjoy repeating myself.'

'I trust you to do the best you can. Not for me, but because you think it is right.'

He put his hands on her shoulders and turned her, marching her towards her room.

'Stop this blathering mawkishness and go wash. I'll see about food. I'm hungry.'

Thankfully she didn't argue and he hurried away before he followed her. Lurching between lust and embarrassment was putting a strain on his ageing heart. The sooner he put her aboard a ship to England, the better.

Cleo sat on her narrow bed, listening to Rafe's receding footsteps. She rubbed her hands on the rough cotton of her robe. They were still shaking. *She* was still shaking. The sick jingling that had plagued her from Nubia to Syene and then quieted during the long days in the desert was back.

She unwrapped her turban and shoved her hands into her short hair.

Her bonnet...

She'd rescued it from the wreckage of their lodgings. And her dress and books and... They were all still there. Dropped on the floor when she'd seen the shadow move behind Rafe, the arm rising and the afternoon sun glinting off a dagger.

He was right. There hadn't been a coherent thought in her mind at that moment. Only images—the shadow, the dagger, Rafe holding a book, his back to his attacker. Then her own hands stretched before her as she found herself in mid-air.

It took being thrown against the wall to wake her mind to fear and denial, but by then it was all over.

Rafe's face had been utterly blank as he administered those two blows which stunned the man. Then he'd looked over at her, a quick look that was like a nail being hammered straight into her heart—sharp, painful, terrifyingly final.

At that moment he'd mattered more than life.

She'd done as he told her. Half her mind had listened to his interrogation of al-Mizan, but the other was still ringing with terror at what might have happened to him.

At some point it *would* happen. It happened to the best of them, he'd said. A moment's inattention. A mistake…

Today it had almost happened because of her.

She could not even think it. She was scared for Dash, for herself, but this felt different—almost superstitious. She *needed* him to exist and she did not even understand why.

'Supper!'

Rafe's call penetrated the door and her fog of confusion and her stomach grumbled hopefully.

In the small room that served as salon and dining room Rafe was putting plates on the table.

He glanced over at her, his pale green eyes sharp and alert.

'Sit.'

'I shall go bring…'

'Everything is ready. Sit.'

She was too tired to protest. She sat as he served her from another of Birdie's mouth-watering stews.

'Where is Birdie?'

'Out.'

'You are not going to tell me where?'

'It has to do with my brother.'

'You have news of him?'

He didn't look up from his plate, but smiled at the excitement in her voice.

'Only that he did indeed arrive in Egypt and continued south. Either on our trail or to my uncle's house in Qetara.'

'Are you not worried for him?'

'For Edge? No, not now he's here. He might be as pig-headed as a mule, but he was an excellent officer during the war. Until he was shot, that is.'

Her knife clacked against the plate and he glanced up.

She kept her own gaze lowered. She hated how shaky she still felt.

They ate in silence until he spoke again.

'Thank you.' His voice was low, resonant, like the rush of the Nile against the felucca's hull.

'For what?'

He leaned back, the cane chair protesting.

'I should have thanked you properly. For coming to my aid.'

'I'm certain you would have managed.'

He shook his head.

'Anyone can die, Cleo. I've seen skilled men make the most foolish mistakes. You should take credit where it is due.'

'I don't want to.'

'I know. And that is a bad sign. You can't go around believing I'm infallible. Until we get you safely on your way to England you need to remain alert.'

'I *was* alert. That is why you are sitting across from me and not dead or being stitched by a Cairene surgeon, which is not a fate I would wish on my worst enemy.'

He grinned and tapped the table with his palm.

'That's better. Moping does not suit you.'

'I was not moping!'

'Blue as a witch's…never mind. I keep forgetting you are a lady.'

'And I keep forgetting you're a grown man.'

'Excellent. Now throw something at me.'

'*Ladies* do not throw things,' she snapped.

'They damned well do. They can't easily throw a punch at me like a man might when riled. Though, like you right now, they might wish to. And my ragged face discourages slapping, so I've had the odd plate or tankard tossed at me. Go ahead if it will make you feel better.'

'Breaking something merely because one is angered or frustrated is childish and serves no purpose.'

'Says someone who's never done it. And you're frightened, not frustrated.'

'How precisely would breaking something alleviate fear?'

'I didn't say it would.'

'Then why are you telling me to break something?' Her voice was rising, shedding all pretence at calm.

'To distract you. It's working, too.'

'You. Are. *Infuriating!*' She ground her teeth, thumping her fists on the table. Part of her knew his object was not merely to distract her, but to break the strange tension that was binding them and that made her even angrier. She didn't want him to be flippant now, not when she was still shaking inwardly. She wanted something completely different and he knew that and that was precisely why he was trying to make her angry. Well, he'd succeeded.

If her plate had not still been half full of Birdie's stew, she might have succumbed and done just what he suggested. Smashed, shattered, razed, crushed it into tiny bits and stomped on them until they were dust. Until fear and need and confusion were consumed in the fireball of her fury. Until she was free of everything, including the most impossible man she'd ever met.

Rafe leaned back and watched the fire snap and crackle in her. It was there in the rush of colour up her face, in the narrowed gold fire eyes that were stripping layers from his skin, in the white-knuckled fists.

It was magnificent.

It was also singeing him inside and out. He mastered his breathing, but he couldn't stop his heart from going into a faster gallop than it had when that knife had slashed towards him.

That had been a very different kind of heartbeat. Fear was well and good, but terror was something he could not afford and that was precisely what had slashed through him as he'd watched her launch herself at the man.

That had been new. Icy. A shriek of denial.

Now she was sending his pulse out of control once more, except this time he wasn't cold—he was boiling inside. She looked like a queen about to cast him into the pits of hell and the madness was that he was as hot and hard as if she'd spent the past week seducing him.

Which, to be fair, she had.

If only he could do something about it.

He shifted on the uncomfortable chair, wishing his morals were significantly more flexible. He could only imagine all that fury and heat and frustration and determination in bed…

If only…

'Do I amuse you, Mr Grey?'

'Do you…?' He floundered.

'If you are going to sit there grinning at me, I will go elsewhere.'

She shoved to her feet, her chair squawking and teetering. He managed to reach the door before her.

'Cleo, wait, I am trying…'

'You *are* trying. I've never met a more *trying* man. If you try me any further, I might…' She appeared to physically struggle with her unfinished sentence and then tossed up her hands in despair. 'Kindly move aside, Mr Grey.'

Her glare alone would have been enough to incinerate a stack of papyrus scrolls. He leaned his full weight back against the door, not because he was afraid she would slip past him, but because he very much wanted her to come close enough to try.

'You are right. I meant well, but…'

'People always mean well, *but—*'

'If you would only listen to me.'

'I have done little else but listen to you this past week. I know full well what you wish to do. You wish nothing more than to deposit me on the first ship to England and have done with me...'

'I do not—'

'Yes, you do and I do not blame you in the least—I am just as tired of my problems as you are. However, that does not mean I will allow you to dictate my actions. Now, kindly step aside.' She reached past him for the doorknob and the opening door knocked him from behind.

It wasn't a serious blow, but the devil in him gave a yelp and he stumbled forward. Her hands shot out, steadying him.

'I'm so sorry, Rafe! I did not mean to hurt you!'

'When I advised you to throw something, I did not think you would start with doors. As usual you are highly precocious, Cleo.'

Her concern crumbled as swiftly as her anger and she burst into laughter and gave him a little shove. He didn't step back and she stayed there for a moment, her hands on his chest. Then she rose on tiptoe and touched her lips to his cheek.

Absurdly, that shock was on par with his earlier terror. His skin turned into a carapace of ice and his insides to a chaos of thumping heat. He didn't even realise he'd closed his arms around her waist, pinioning her to him, until she leaned back against their confining band.

She'd been flushed with anger before and the laughter was still there in her eyes, but also the softening, speculative heat she'd shown before.

She pressed upwards again, bestowing the same light kiss, but this time she stayed there, her lips parted against his skin, moving gently. He let his eyes close, his hand moving against her back, mirroring the motion of her lips.

God, it felt so good. Even her touch against his scars felt...

It was a sign of how addled he'd become that he only now realised it was his scarred cheek. He let her go faster than she'd charged at al-Mizan, but she'd already anchored her hands in his shirt and her mouth came to rest against the corner of his. She seemed to be gathering herself, either waiting for a signal or preparing to withdraw.

All he had to do was nothing. Ignore the warmth of her breath against his skin, the pressure of her body leaning against his, the heat trapped between them like a captured sun. The thudding, demanding, hungry, ravenous heat he was tired of shoving down.

He felt the tensing of her muscles as she prepared to push away and with a smothered moan he wrapped his arms back around her.

Not yet.

Just a little more.

Just an inch. Not even an inch. That was all it would take to bring her lips to his. He wanted so, so badly to kiss her. Properly, thoroughly. All of her, every warm living inch of her.

Step aside?

Like hell.

He turned his head, his lips touching hers. Hers parted just a little, fitting against his. She breathed in, sucking the soul from his body and setting the rest on fire. He heard the sound deep inside him and the answering buck of her body against him and he felt his reins slip from his hands.

Just a taste.

He let his lips move against hers, just gathering the feel of that warm, pillowy bow. He kissed it very gently, catching the corner of her mouth with the tip of his tongue, just where it hovered between smile and laughter. She gave a little moan and then her tongue touched his, a galvanic shock driving their bodies together, hard. His hand was suddenly in her hair and he felt it shake a little as her short feathery hair slipped like shattered silk between his fingers. God, he wanted to do that again and again.

He wanted…everything.

She had her hands in his hair now, too. Was on her tiptoes as she met his kiss, her breasts flattened against his chest. From a slight, brief embrace they were fast approaching combustion and he waited for the sword's thrust of conscience, he even went in search of it, hoping it might come to his rescue, but there was nothing inside him now but fire and the deafening thump of drums...

Not drums, someone was clumping up the stairs...

She must have realised it before him because she disentangled herself with the rapidity of a cat escaping a dipping.

'Birdie is back.'

'I don't care.' He moved towards her.

'We are in the dining room. He is sure to come here...'

Before he could even admit she was right the door opened. She was halfway across the room by then and Rafe scraped his hands through his hair, but clearly their attempts were unconvincing because Birdie stopped whatever he was about to say, looking from one to the other. Then at the plates on the table.

'Hungry, were you?'

Starving.

He didn't say it. He couldn't think of anything sensible to say and in the end it was Cleo who spoke, moving past them to the door.

'We were, thank you, Birdie. It was delicious. The stew, that is,' she added just before closing the door behind her.

Birdie placed the sack he was carrying on the table. When he spoke he pitched his voice low, but it did nothing to hide his anger.

'Sooner she's on her way to England the better, sir. Not like you to play fast and loose.'

'I am not doing anything of the kind.'

'Made her an offer, then?'

'What? No, of course I haven't.'

'Not well-born enough for the likes of you?'

'Birth has nothing to do with it. At least not hers. I don't even exist. Rafe Grey is nothing more than the figment of a boy's imagination.'

'Aye, but the Duke of Greybourne is real enough and that's what you are now, like it or not.'

'You know damn well I don't and that is precisely the point. With any luck Edge will have another son. I'm not going back to that place…that life. *This* life is all I know and all I'm good for, and it sure as hell is no place for a wife even if I wanted one, which I don't, so keep your opinions to yourself.'

'I will if you only keep your hands to yourself.'

'She kissed me first.'

'Jumped on you, did she?'

'No,' Rafe admitted. 'Hit me on the head with a door first.'

'Good for her. I might try that myself. Except you might kiss me, too.'

Rafe grinned in relief that Birdie's ire was fading.

'We had an incident with al-Mizan. At her lodgings. I was trying to distract her and I admit it got out of hand.' Far, far out of hand. 'I won't do it again.'

There wasn't as much conviction in his voice as he hoped, but Birdie's attention had been diverted by his previous comment, his ragtag brows climbing into his hair.

'You found the scoundrel?'

'He found us and almost introduced me to his dagger. That little hellion stopped him. The sooner we take her to Alexandria the better. With luck Chris and the *Hesperus* will still be in port.'

'She might take issue going aboard a privateer's ship.'

'Chris isn't a privateer. There's no war on that I know of at the moment.'

'Smuggler, then.'

'No one has ever accused him of smuggling.'

'Not yet.'

'If I see he has dubious goods aboard, we can find her

other means of travel, but you know she'll be safer on the *Hesperus* than travelling alone on a merchant ship.'

'That's the truth.' Birdie sighed. 'So, that's the plan? We hand her to Chris and wash our hands of the whole affair?'

Rafe poured the wine, but did not pick up his cup.

'No,' he said at last. 'Now I know Edge is safely in Egypt, it's time we returned to England ourselves. As you said—I can't run for ever. I need to take stock of Greybourne so I can get on with my life. That way we can see Cleo safely to England as well. With any luck her brother will already be there and that will be the end of that.'

He waited for Birdie to raise objections, but all he said was, 'Have you told her?'

'No. I don't think I should.'

Birdie picked up his glass.

'It sits ill with me to lie to her, Colonel.'

'With me, too, but we're between a rock and a hard place. Unless we prove that nuisance brother of hers is safely on his way to England, her conscience won't let her sail. But she's not safe here, Birdie. It's not al-Mizan that worries me any more, it's how he spoke about this Boucheron fellow. I don't want her in his domain any longer than absolutely necessary.'

'Very well. I'll pack our belongings. You go with Naguib to speak to the Captain of the *dahabiya*. Best not leave you here alone, just in case she throws herself at you again,' he added with a snap and headed into the kitchen.

Chapter Twelve

Cleo had not been to Alexandria since her arrival in Egypt. It had changed since then, but it was still rather a ruin of a town. Like many port cities she'd seen, there was a sense of miasmatic menace. Rootless people came and went and one knew little of them—perfect for the venal, the criminal, and the lost.

A small closed carriage drew them through the town and past the shattered structure of an old Roman tower. Behind it the sail-studded turquoise sea stretched away, and in front stood an obelisk, stark and tall and covered base to pyramid-pointed tip with hieroglyphs.

'*There* is my namesake,' she murmured and Rafe turned to her from his inspection of the view. With a word he motioned to the driver to stop.

'That must be some sixty feet tall,' Birdie mused and she nodded.

'It is called Cleopatra's Needle. I've seen illustrations in *Description de l'Egypte*, but I've never seen it myself. I wanted to come here when we arrived in Egypt, but my father said we hadn't time. It's…amazing.'

Rafe swung open the low door and held out his hand.

'Come along, Queenie. There is no one here but the camels and donkeys to see us and we can spare a few moments to pay homage to your birthright.'

Cleo had reason later to be doubly grateful for their short excursion to see the obelisk and climb the tower to look over the expanse of the Mediterranean. From the moment they reached their rooms in a lovely Mameluke palace overlooking the bay, her curfew began. She'd given Rafe her word she would remain indoors for the rest of the day as he and Birdie made enquiries, but the inaction sat ill with her.

By afternoon she was seriously contemplating going in search of her errant knights, but just then she heard voices from the courtyard. She hurried into the sitting room, but it was only Birdie, instructing a servant to place a large wicker basket on the table. He glanced up with a smile, but immediately shook his head.

'No news yet, miss.'

'Oh.'

'But we've set matters in motion. Tomorrow we'll go see Captain Carrington. This is not a large city and the Colonel's friend is still docked here, which is good news as he knows many people. If your brother is here, or if he has recently sailed, we are likely to know very soon.'

'Dash might not have travelled under his own name.'

'I hope he hasn't, but there are still ways to trace him. There cannot have been many ships sailing for England this past week so the options are limited.'

'Unless he sailed to another port...' Her heart constricted. That would make the possibilities multiply. And the risks.

'It is possible. Tomorrow we should know more. I've bought you some new clothes.'

She looked absently at the shirt he was unfolding, but her attention was elsewhere. 'Did Rafe not return with you?'

Birdie glanced up.

'Don't worry, miss. He stopped at the *hammam* and paid the fellow to have the place to himself. I'm off to prepare supper. Go rest. It will be a long day tomorrow.'

'I've been resting all day,' Cleo said in frustration.

'I know it isn't easy, miss, but you agreed it would not do for Miss Osbourne to be seen in public when we want it known she already left for England.' Birdie sighed and extracted something from his pile and placed it on the table. 'Here. This is from the Colonel. To keep you occupied.'

It was a rather beaten volume in ochre-coloured leather with most of the gilt worn off, but still enough to read the print on the spine.

Shakespeare. Vol. IX. Taming of the Shrew.

She snorted.

'Very amusing—and it is my least favourite comedy of the lot, Mr Grey,' she muttered and went to her room. She stared at the wall for a few long moments, cradling her farewell present to her chest.

Tomorrow was likely her last day with them. Whatever they discovered or not about Dash she knew she had to release Rafe to seek his own brother, by force if need be. So, if this was her last day of unfettered freedom, she should not be spending it moping in her room. She wanted an altogether different farewell present.

She wrapped her turban round her head and slipped quietly downstairs.

She'd seen the unobtrusive entranceway to the bath house on their arrival. It stood just a few steps from their lodgings and she gave herself no time to think before she plunged inside. Her heart, already rushing downhill at a swift pace, slammed into her ribs when a man in a long white robe stepped out of the overseer's room.

'The *hammam* is closed. Come tomorrow,' he said, shoo-ing her with his hands.

'I am the *hawagi*'s servant,' Cleo said in Arabic. 'I have an important message.'

The guard shrugged and went back to his little room.

Cleo proceeded, her heart thumping in her ears as she pushed aside the heavy curtain covering the entrance to the *maghta* and a burst of steam enveloped her.

'*Ijo de cabron...* Cleo!'

She stood frozen for a moment. He'd thrown a long cotton towel over his shoulder, like a Roman toga, but it did little to cover his steam-slicked body. She knew men were required to cover their hips with a *futa* in *hammams*, but Rafe was clearly taking advantage of his privacy.

'What are you doing here?' he demanded. 'Has something happened? Where is Birdie?'

She shook her head, gathering back her scattered thoughts.

'Nothing happened. Birdie thinks I'm resting.'

'Then what in the name of all the rings of hell are you doing here?'

'I wanted to see a male *hammam*.' She looked around, trying to sound casual and wondering why this had seemed a good idea. 'It's not very different from the women's. I thought it would be larger.'

He didn't answer and she went to look at the nearest portal. A small pool with stone steps stood as flat as a sheet of ice and several buckets of water stood beside a spout. Above her a murky light entered through the ornate glass pieces that studded a low dome.

It was almost dark outside and she was alone with a mostly naked man in an Egyptian bath house.

'You shouldn't be here, Cleo.' His voice was muffled by the steam.

Her heartbeats reverberated through her like the clanging of a deep bell but she unwound her turban and breathed in the hot, scented air. Once again her life was about to change, through forces beyond her control. But how she acted, what she did, was hers. Soon this man would be gone from her life. It felt absurd and wrong, but she knew it to be true. Therefore, she had to choose how to act now.

'I think I will miss being a man when I return to England,' she said.

He didn't answer, so she took off her robe, folded it and placed it on a wooden shelf by the room with the dipping pool. She gathered the skirts of her *gallabiyah* and there was a curse behind her as he grasped her arm.

'Enough, Cleo. Go back to the rooms.'

This close she could see every sinew and muscle. His skin shone, water tricking slowly over the landscape of his body. He *was* beautiful. Not just the force of his body, but remnants of his mistakes. He might be built like a Roman statue, but it was the damage that made him real. She knew she would probably never again see anything so beautiful.

'Cleo, *stop*.'

'I'm only looking,' she murmured and he groaned and dropped her arm, turning away.

'You're mad, you know.'

'I don't think it is mad to enjoy looking at you, is it? I'm certain enough women have done so before me. Why am I different?'

He gave a slight laugh and went to sit on a bench, his back to her.

'I told you I won't take advantage of you.'

'We are in Alexandria. Tomorrow we either find Dash here and you consign me to his care, or I will secure passage to England. Either way you are relieved of your protector's duties.'

She took off her *gallabiyah* and closed her eyes, breathing in the spice-scented air. Sage and mint. She would miss those scents. She would miss Egypt.

She would miss this man most of all.

Her breath shortened and she swallowed. There was nothing for it. She knew the world kept moving beneath them.

'I'm going to wash myself. You may leave if you wish. Or stay.' She went into the next room and poured the warm water over her. She'd washed in the small tub the servant had brought to her room, but this was different. With the steam all around her and the warm water streaming over her she closed her eyes to explore the image of Rafe's body, slick with steam, the pressure of his hands on her body, shaping her...

Rafe stood helplessly in the doorway. His code required he do as she suggested and leave, but he couldn't.

She stood with her back to him, her body shimmering like pale marble in the dimming light from the dome. She might as well have been a statue come to life, the line of her back and the rounded rise of her behind as she rubbed the soapy palm fronds over her arms.

He'd been right—she had a lovely body, generous and beautifully curved. Perhaps she was right, he was making too much of this. She was no virgin, no English miss. She was Cleo, a wholly strange and independent entity. If she wanted this, why not allow this temporary breach?

He picked up another ball of stripped palm fronds, lathered it with soap and moved towards her. He knew she felt his approach because her chin rose a little, but she did not turn.

'I'll wash your back,' he said.

She gave a little nod and straightened. He touched the slope of her shoulder and closed his eyes for a moment. He was as hard as the rock floor. All he had to do was one step closer and... He breathed in and out, clasped her shoulder gently with one hand and brushed the fronds down the curve of her back.

He went slowly, watching the lather slide down as he

worked, over her buttocks and down her legs. He let his fingers and knuckles graze her warm, slippery skin. It was addictive, this touch. He wanted to spread her out on the cold floor and do the same to every inch of her—look, touch, taste…

He swallowed and kept to his agenda, ignoring the howling need that pulsed in every cell and gathered into a ravenous demand in his loins. He didn't want this to end, not even in satisfaction. He knew what would follow then— regret and reckoning. No, he wanted to stay like this, his hands on her skin, standing so close to her he could see the wet spikes of her short hair clinging to her nape, a pulse just at the side of her neck, the curved line of her cheek between that determined jaw and the uncompromising cheekbones.

He didn't want to ruin this moment, not even with pleasure.

She turned her head, her eyes gleaming. She looked the way she had in the temple—shadowed, whisky-coloured eyes that were absolutely honest in their need.

She leaned her hand against his chest and he realised he'd let his own towel drop. He didn't have time to think before she moved, her arms around his back, pressing her full length against him. His body blazed like a molten sun against her cool skin, his erection pressing hard against her, their skin slick.

'Our lives could end in a flash and I don't want to regret not taking this. When we leave this room, we leave this behind if you wish.'

He shook his head at the absurdity of that, but it was such a seductive fiction. And at least one thing she'd said was true. Their lives could end in a flash. This was honest, this burning wish—it was just now. It, too, would pass, but right now…

He let his hands finally settle honestly on her skin, without the lie of washing her. He let them slip from her shoulders down to her thighs, fitting her to him as he went so he could feel the full pressure of her breasts, the tension of her abdomen on his erection, her legs shifting gently on his, so much softer and smoother. He slipped his knee between her legs and she hummed, letting her leg rub the length of his.

'Yes,' she murmured, rising to touch her mouth to his neck. He arched it to give her better access, urging her on with words while his hands talked to her as well. For a long while he explored her, watching every expression that flitted across her face as his hands travelled over her, tracing her lines gently as he felt her body relax into his touch. Her mouth moved along his neck, his chest, not quite kisses, just breathy answers that heated and cooled his damp skin.

He kissed her, teasingly light at first, drawing her to him until she rose into the embrace, her body moving with his as if to music, and she was humming gently, almost purring. His whole body reverberated with that sound, like the lasting shimmer of a bell.

Her eyes were half closed, gleaming amber and gold as she explored him as well, her hands shaping themselves over him, stopping to rest gently against his damaged skin in a way that made him clench hard around something he didn't want to open.

He slid a hand down the curve of her back, cupping her behind as he leaned back, tracing his fingers gently over the curve of her breasts. They were beautiful, round and warm in his hand, her nipples rose-coloured like her lips, but darkening as they hardened at his touch. He brushed his lips over them and she gave a little mewl, deep in her throat, her fingers threading through his hair and tightening painfully.

'Yes, I want that…' she whispered in her gravel and honey voice and he shuddered, resisting the beating rush of need that was demanding he act *now*. End it now.

He didn't want it to end. He wanted this to go on for ever. He kissed the tightening crown of her breast, flicking it with his tongue and revelling in the answering clenching of her body against his, in her soft encouraging murmurings. Her hands mirrored his, caressing his back, slipping lower to sweep tentatively over his behind in a way that nearly felled him, gaining in confidence and only faltering when he shifted to touch the soft skin on the inside of her thigh.

She tensed, reminding him that his desert queen might be devastatingly passionate and not an innocent in society's terms, but one lover years ago did not mean she was comfortable with the intimacies he took for granted. He slowed, taking his time until that hum returned. Then he brushed his hand very gently down her abdomen and over her wet curls.

'May I touch you here?'

She breathed in sharply, pressing her face into the curve of his shoulder, her arms tightening about his nape.

'Yes.' Her voice wobbled but her legs parted further as he trailed his fingers up and down her thighs. 'I like that, just like that…'

He pressed his eyes shut, hard. Every word she spoke was like a hand stroking him. Her skin was already slick with steam and it was so beautifully simple to slip his fingers over the silky skin of her parting.

He anchored his hand in her short hair, kissing her deeply, hungrily, as he touched her. She kissed him back with the same hunger, her breath catching in little helpless gasps, her hips moving now against his hand, searching, reaching… She'd dropped all her defences and he saw everything, every confusion and pleasure and that soft secretive smile that knocked his heart on its side. He pressed her against the tiled wall and her head fell back, baring her breasts to his mouth as she clung to him until she cried out her release in a series of long shudders.

They stayed like that for a long moment, surrounded in milky swathes of steam, his arm hard around her back, his mouth pressed to the thudding pulse in her temple, his palm warm against her. Then she gave a long sigh, her muscles relaxing.

'I'm so glad I came here.'

He gave a choked laugh against her hair, but he was in too much pleasurable agony to make the obvious glib remark. He drew away a little, but her arms tightened on him, her hips moving, rubbing herself against his erection.

'Cleo, perhaps we shouldn't…'

'Yes, we should. I want you to be glad I came here, too,' she murmured against his skin, her hands moving down his back with purpose. His heart, already beating far too fast, stumbled.

'It felt so, so good,' she continued. 'I don't remember it at all like that. William didn't…'

Rafe nipped gently on the lobe of her ear and she shuddered and mercifully fell silent.

'A piece of advice, Cleo. When making love to one man, never discuss another.'

He felt her smile against his skin. He took her hand, his fingers sliding between hers, and guided it to his erection. She gave a little sigh and wrapped her hand around it and he couldn't hold back a groan of sheer pleasure.

'It's so soft,' she murmured, sweeping her palm over its length.

'Soft?' he demanded in a choked voice.

'The skin.' She half laughed, her gaze on her hand as she explored. 'Underneath it's hard as stone, but here…soft…' Her voice was almost as much a torture as her hand. 'Like this? Do you like it?'

'I love it,' he answered, not caring about anything but that she not stop. He wanted to stay right there, in this pitch of agonised pleasure, with her body and mouth torturing him and her hand wringing his soul into ecstatic oblivion.

He guided her until she caught the rhythm, kissing her, stroking her head and back as she kissed his neck, his chest.

When her mouth stroked past his nipple he felt an explosion of joy and she paused.

'You like this as much as I did,' she murmured against him and he nodded helplessly, his mind pleading—*don't stop.*

She held him as he came and they stood afterwards in a hard embrace, the steam still rising in fluffy billows, but weakening. He could feel the cooler air snake about his legs. Everywhere she was not pressed against him felt bare, exposed. He detached himself carefully and went to fetch a bucket of the cooling water. He rinsed her off gently and dried her with a cotton towel and she stood there and let him.

They dressed in silence and left, passing the guard who was nodding at his post. Rafe placed another coin on his tray and followed Cleo out into the darkening evening.

At the bottom of the stairs to their rooms Cleo turned and smiled.

'Thank you, Rafe. I won't forget that.'

A burst of pain radiated through him and he didn't even know why.

'I don't think I will either.'

She hurried up the stairs and slipped into her room. He could hear Birdie moving around the kitchen-cum-dining room and he went to his own room and lay down to stare at the ceiling, torn between ebbing bliss and rising guilt. His conscience had already been flaying him about what was in store for her the next day; he hadn't thought he could feel any more culpable.

Apparently he could.

Chapter Thirteen

They walked along the stone jetty towards the rowboat rising and falling on the waves. Beyond it was the deep blue of the Mediterranean, blooming with sails. She slowed, her cracked heart lightening at the sight despite her sorrow. She remembered the salted breeze and the sound of the waves so well from those years in Acre—it was like listening to a heartbeat under a blanket.

Rafe had told her his friend might be able to shed light on Dash's whereabouts, but she knew the chances were slim. In a matter of days, she would probably have to leave for London and this wondrous sea would lie between her and her past, between her and her new friends.

She didn't want to leave. She was not ready.

Rafe stopped by the rowboat, holding out his hand peremptorily.

'Come.'

His voice was clipped, his eyes cold and distant, and her old instincts came to the fore. 'Why could this Captain not meet us on shore?'

'Because he's the Captain and he has other matters to attend to, Prudent Pat.'

'Stop calling me that,' she snapped. 'You called me Cleo easily enough in the *hammam*.' For a second before he withdrew his gaze she knew he was back there as well, steam wrapping around them, his body hard and hot against hers, his mouth…

She'd wanted a memory and now she had it…branded on to every inch of her.

A trickle of sweat ran down her neck and between her breasts and she was grateful for the sea breeze that cooled her as she stepped into the rowboat. It rocked and tipped as Rafe entered and she grabbed at the side.

'Careful. You'll tip it.'

'Now that is unkind. I've all but starved myself of decent food seeing you through the devil's desert and now you're complaining I'm fat?'

'I did not say that. You are merely big…' Her cheeks flamed in sudden embarrassment.

'You do look like you could use a cooling dip, Pat.' His hand rose and settled back on his thigh, but her cheek tingled as if he'd brushed his fingers across it.

'In these clothes I'd likely sink to the bottom like a rock.'

'I'd save you. Again.'

'I seem to remember saving you the last time we had a brush with danger,' she replied. Possibly it was the wrong thing to say for he fell silent, his almost-smile flattening out. She felt he was gathering himself for something and for a moment wondered what history he and this mysterious Captain had together.

They did not speak again as they cut through the waves to draw alongside a large two-masted brigantine. The sailor called up their arrival in French and there was a clacking and a series of thuds as the Jacob's ladder was unrolled for them. Rafe stood, his feet apart for balance, and helped her to her feet. But again his gaze seemed to slip away from her.

Once on board he moved swiftly and she had no more than a brief impression of a wide and impressively uncluttered deck before they entered the quarterdeck and proceeded down a corridor. He opened a cabin door and as she stepped inside she couldn't hold back a gasp of surprised pleasure.

She'd been on many ships in her short life, but she'd never seen such quarters. The bed was long enough to accommodate someone Rafe's size, there was a gilded sofa with embroidered silk cushions, a large rolltop writing desk, and two substantial-looking chairs framing the door like sentinels. The floors were covered in multicoloured rugs and the walls in cupboards and shelves stacked with books, crockery and rolled charts.

'What a beautiful room. It looks as though a sultan should be reclining on that bed eating sweetmeats,' she whispered. 'I've never seen anything like it.'

'That's because there is nothing like it. Chris is unique.'

'That sounds ominous. Are you certain he might know something of Dash's whereabouts?'

'He knows a great many things, the scoundrel,' Rafe replied and went to open one of the cupboards, taking out a bottle and two glasses. He unstoppered the bottle and sniffed at it, then poured himself a measure and took a deep swallow from his cup. His eyes closed and he expelled his breath on a groan that made her legs tense. 'Including where to find the finest spirits in the Mediterranean, damn his black soul. Try this.'

She took the glass cautiously and sipped. Her mind filled with sunset colours—deep burnt orange to purple-black cherries.

'It's wonderful,' she said hoarsely as it stopped exploding in her mouth and the fiery skies she'd swallowed settled into a soothing afternoon haze. 'What is it?'

'I don't know, but I agree, it's wonderful.' His voice was muted and she risked a glance at him, but he turned away again, moving towards a painting on the wall.

'Perhaps we shouldn't have drunk from it?' she said, looking into the innocuous-looking liquid. The ship was swaying gently, adding to the soft sensation left by the spirits. She'd heard of drugging potions used in harems. 'Are you certain it is wine?'

'Of course it is wine. Chris knows the best vineyards in Europe. He sells most of it to the highest bidder, but if anything makes it to his private chambers, it is tried and tested and true. Drink up.'

'If I drink up, I will likely fall down and I must still go search for Dash once we speak to your Captain.'

He took a deep breath and set his cup down. She tensed, setting her cup down as well.

'Rafe. I *know* there is something you are not telling me. Please…have you word of Dash?'

He squared his shoulders.

'Nothing yet. After I speak to Chris, I will continue with our enquiries. You will remain here.'

'I most certainly will not. I agreed to wait while you made enquiries yesterday and I came with you to see this Captain of yours, but our agreement ends there.'

'Boucheron is in Alexandria. I won't risk him seeing you.'

'Boucheron… You knew this yesterday.'

'Yes. You will be safe here on the *Hesperus*.'

'On a ship full of felons?'

'They aren't felons; they are…enterprising sailors. The point is they are loyal to their Captain and their Captain is loyal to me.'

'You cannot place me here like a trunk and expect me to sit twiddling my thumbs. I am not your property, Mr Grey.'

'You hired my services, Miss Osbourne. Now you are stuck with them. I've kept you safe so far and I have a distaste for watching my good work go to waste. So begin twiddling your thumbs. I will return soon. And don't drink all the wine, I'll want a glass when I return.'

'What? No!' She leapt for the door, but it closed with a

thick thump before her hand even touched the knob. Then there was a click as the key turned.

He'd locked her in.

It was so obvious and yet her mind struggled to accept it. In all their long journey together he'd never yet done something like this.

She rattled the knob and gave the door a kick, cursing Rafe in every language she could summon.

How *dare* he. Like hell she would stay there. She turned and spotted another door and strode towards it, but it merely led to the Captain's quarter gallery. It comprised a dressing room, then a room fitted with a large copper bath and finally a small latrine. They were all as pristine as the Captain's quarters, as if they had only now been delivered from the shipyard. But since they offered no other exit other than the small windows that opened directly over the rolling waves, she was too furious to be impressed.

The waves were lazy and rhythmic, but large. She could hear their distant boom against the rocks. It would be possible to squeeze through the open quarter-gallery windows and try to swim ashore, but the ship was anchored well out of the bay—a long and dangerous swim with the current against her…or she might be taken up by one of the fishing boats and God only knew what they would do with her…

And when Rafe discovered her gone? He cared about the charges he took on. It wasn't merely pride—protecting his charges was a measure of his worth, of who he was. He would search for her just as she had searched for Dash, possibly putting himself even further in harm's way. Now she knew Boucheron was in Alexandria her foreboding escalated. Now she had not only Dash, but Rafe to fear for.

She returned to the cabin and sat down with a thump on the sybaritic bed and picked up a crimson cushion, hugging it to her. It was not natural—sitting here while they were out there.

If something happened to Rafe because of her…

At times like this she envied devout people. They would have their gods to pray to, to place their faith in, to blame if aught went wrong. All she could do was hug the tasselled cushion and wait.

She'd never expected to fall asleep. One moment she was seated, hugging her cushion, and the next she was lurching out of darkness into darkness.

For a moment she thought she'd been tied into a sack, but it was only a blanket. She twisted off the bed, misjudged its height and fell with a grunt on to her knees.

Hands brushed against her, closing on her arms and pulling her to her feet. She should have been scared, but she knew immediately who it was.

'Are you all right?' he whispered, his hands skimming down her arms. Rising to touch her face.

'I fell asleep,' she stated unnecessarily. 'What happened? What…?' She stopped speaking, realising something was very, very wrong.

'We're moving! Rafe, the ship is sailing. Oh, hurry, we must stop it!'

She surged past him, groping for the door; instead she found herself blocked by a large body once more.

'Rafe! Tell the Captain…'

'We sailed two hours ago.'

'What?' Her voice faded. She could hardly see his face, but she could feel him and not merely through her hands, which were fisted in his shirt. He was stone again. Grey.

'It's Dash.' She forced the words out. 'You've discovered he's dead.'

His hands grabbed her arms, tightly this time.

'No. No, I haven't. I don't know if he's dead or alive. We could not discover if anyone of his description sailed for England in the past couple of weeks. I bribed the harbourmaster to keep an eye out for him and to tell him his sister has sailed to England and that if he has an ounce of sense he'll do the same if he has not already.'

She let go of his shirt. Her hands were burning, her face, her chest. There was a boiling blaze at the centre of her forehead. It wasn't the heat of lust that had carried her into a dreamful sleep. It was rage.

Fury.

'You *bastard*.' It was like the hiss of a kettle. She could barely part her teeth to let the venom through.

He laughed.

'Chance would be a fine thing.'

'You had no *right*. Oh, God, if I were bigger I would… I would… How *dare* you! You tricked me! You might very well have left my brother to die!' She groped around in the dark, searching for something, anything, to wield. She bumped into a chair, wrapped her hands around its back and raised it, but it was absurdly heavy. She threw it anyway and it dropped, narrowly missing her foot.

She bumped into the shelves and glass clinked on glass. The bottles! She stroked upwards, over the wooden shelf guard to the smooth glass. She grabbed a bottle by the neck and hoisted it.

She knew it was pointless and pathetic, but she couldn't stop. She was choking with something, suffocating with it, and he just stood there like a lump in the dark while they moved further and further from the *only* person who mattered, leaving him to whatever fate awaited him. Alone.

Because she'd trusted this man. Hadn't she learned anything from her feckless father? From William? She'd walked into this trap without a second thought, like the blindest of the blind, smitten, fools. She'd learned *nothing*.

She'd wanted so desperately to trust him not only with her fate, but with Dash's, too. She *had* trusted him. Despite everything, she'd felt lighter, happier these past days than any time she could remember. She should have known it was too good to be true.

She hated him, but she hated herself far more.

Her eyes were better accustomed to the dark now. He was still an outline against the door; watching her. He'd done nothing to stop her frantic search for weapons. His face was blank, but his shoulders were slumped. She knew he wouldn't move if she threw the bottle, which was stupid. She didn't want him to accept her anger. She wanted him to toss it right back at her and tell her the truth. That he was only doing what mercenaries do—she was to blame for trusting him. That she'd known all along what he was, but she'd closed her eyes and dreamed. And while she'd been dreaming they'd cast off their moorings and sailed and left Dash to his fate.

No hurled bottle or chair would turn this ship back. She had nothing to threaten him with or bribe him with. It was done.

She replaced the bottle and pressed her hand to the lump of blazing coal embedded in her forehead.

'No.'

'Cleo…' His voice was husky and he pushed away from the door, but she raised her other hand, palm out.

'Go away. You win. Now go away.'

He shook his head and righted the chair.

'I'm staying.'

'I don't want you here.'

'I'm staying and you're listening.'

'No.'

'Yes. It was the right course of action. The only course of action. For you *and* for your brother if only either of you are intelligent enough to understand that.'

'Don't you dare belittle him.'

'Or what? I'm sick and tired of you endangering yourself as if he's a five-year-old lost in the forest. He's a grown man and if he has an ounce of the integrity you claim every time you sing his praises he'll be thanking me for getting you out of Egypt.'

'*If* he isn't killed by al-Mizan. If he hasn't already been killed by him.'

'He hasn't.'

'You can't know that—'

'I can. Boucheron is no fool. I told him—'

'You *told* him…you spoke with him?'

'Shh. You've already woken half the ship. Do you want to wake the other half? Yes, he owns a palace in Alexandria and was in town awaiting a ship to France, or so he said. Al-Mizan must have sent him word of our encounter because he wasn't in the least surprised when I arrived. Boucheron might be a dangerous man, but he's no fool. I made clear that whatever idiocies your father engaged in, your brother had no part in it. As long as your brother leaves Egypt swiftly, Boucheron will let him be.'

She swallowed her bile and lowered her voice.

'That sounds like quite an amicable discussion you had.'

The chair squeaked as he leaned forward and the gleam of the night sky turned his eyes luminescent, like foam on the sea.

'I negotiated with an enemy, that is what I do. Hopefully Boucheron will now be wary of interfering with your brother knowing he is not unprotected. What the devil do you think would have happened if you stayed in Egypt? Even if your brother discovered you were still there, he could not contact you for fear or putting both of you at risk.'

'Why did you not tell me any of this?'

'Because I knew you wouldn't wait here simply because I asked. So I told Chris to sail as soon as I came back aboard. There is a trunk with some of your clothes over there by the wall, by the way. We rescued them from your lodgings.'

She gave the trunk no more than a cursory glance. She had more important issues at hand.

'Did you drug me?' she demanded, thinking of that wine

and her dreams. Perhaps that explained why she'd so lowered her guard to fall asleep while effectively a prisoner.

'What? No, of course not! You can lay quite a bit on my doorstep, but don't blame me for falling asleep.'

'It was convenient, though.'

'It damned well was. Believe me, I wasn't looking forward to…this.'

This.

She reached for her anger and found there was nothing there. Not anger, not fear, not anguish, not…caring. Nothing.

He was probably right about everything. Even that she was a risk to Dash as long as she remained in Egypt.

It didn't matter anyway. They had sailed. *That ship had sailed.* What a silly little phrase. Nothing you can do, that ship has sailed. And here they were. On their way to England. And nothingness.

'I hate that you went about this without me. Without telling me anything.'

'I know,' he answered.

'You told me I could trust you.' She couldn't stop the words or her voice from shaking.

'Trust me to do my best to keep you safe. Not actually trust *me*. Those are two different things.'

'Apparently.'

He didn't answer. He was just another bulk in the gloom. Like the cupboard and table. She wanted her anger back. Something to make her tilt her head back and howl at the skies; she wanted to find Dash—safe, alive. She wanted to turn the clock back six months and make everything go away, including Mr Rafe Grey. Now she was on her way to England, to a world she no longer knew and a future she couldn't imagine.

She lay down on the bed, turned her back on him and stared at the whorls on the wooden wall.

A night breeze was slipping in through the galley windows along with the sound of the waves lapping against the hull. A fast, sleek ship suspended between two worlds and she belonged in neither. Perhaps it would never reach anywhere and they would sail and sail, the two of them with a band of pirates.

It was a mark of her confusion that she could consider that fate the best of all possible outcomes.

Rafe stayed where he was, watching the slow rise and fall of her shoulder and arm. She was curled up tightly and he wished he could wrap himself around her, absorb her confusion and fear until it drained away.

A fantasy even more likely to remain a fantasy now he'd made her hate him.

The swift collapse of her justifiable anger didn't re-assure him in the least. He'd have preferred the storm to stay high.

He considered leaving the cabin so she could have the privacy of her misery. But he didn't fully trust her either, so he shifted a chair so that it blocked the door and sat down. He didn't know what Cleo might do, but he couldn't leave her here alone with her pain and frustration. She was still his responsibility, whether either of them liked it or not.

Chapter Fourteen

He had no memory of falling asleep, but the next he knew the bed was empty and the daylight was bright in the open windows.

The open windows…

He surged out of the chair with a strangled sound. She wouldn't. She…

The door to the quarter gallery swung open and Cleo entered. Rafe sank back into the chair, rubbing his face and waiting for his pulse to slow. His tumbling, panicked mind struggled to right itself.

He was too old for this. Not that anything in his past was truly equivalent to *this*. *This* was proving far too much of a strain on his tattered soul. He watched warily as she moved towards him. He searched her face for the volcanic anger that had welled out of her last night, but her face showed nothing but weariness.

'Please let me pass. I would like to ask where I may prepare some tea. I am thirsty and there is nothing here but wine.'

He half stumbled to his feet, shoving the chair to one side.

'I will fetch it.'

'There is no need, thank you, Mr Grey.'

'Cleo…'

'Miss Osbourne, please, sir. We are no longer in the desert,' she said haughtily as she swept past him into the narrow corridor.

The sailors Cleo came across as she passed through corridors and crowded holds didn't seem shocked to see her, but they did tend to melt away, as if unsure whether she posed a threat. When she reached what must be the sleeping quarters—a space hung with hammocks, some still populated by snoring sailors—her steps faltered and a luckily slim man of indeterminate years approached her, his deep black eyes reflecting the light of the lamps.

'Mees? I help?'

Yes, please. Help. Take me back to Alexandria and help me save my brother.

'I'd like some tea. *Thé. Shai.* Please,' she answered, the last word a little wobbly.

He smiled and beckoned her to follow and to her surprise he led her on deck. The wind held the sails taut and the air was filled with the sound of water slapping against the hull and the creaking of ropes and masts. The view all around was the same she had seen from the window of the Captain's cabin. A blue, liquid, anchorless desert.

The brigantine was far swifter than the heavy merchant ships she'd travelled on and she could feel the gentle burst and skip of the ship as it cut through the low waves. She felt a strange detachment—she was suspended between England and the East, the two halves of her past. She wished she could stay here—all she needed was tea and a book and she could sail like this for ever.

'You rang for tea?'

Rafe stood before her holding an elaborate silver tray, his feet braced apart for balance and his expression that of a punctilious butler. She wanted to hate him, knock the tray out of his hands and let loose the howl inside her. She let the image come and go and even that tired her.

All she wanted now was tea.

'Thank you.'

He hesitated, watching her as if waiting for something else. Then he placed the tray on the table before her. The ship shifted and the tall, elaborate coral-coloured teapot with delicate paintings on either side teetered.

'Goodness, careful!' She steadied the pot, inspecting the gently drawn landscape rising from a river to jagged mountains along its side. 'This looks like it is Qianlong. Or more likely a marvellous fake. If so, my father would likely have brokered a deal with the forger on the spot.'

She poured the tea into both cups and the scent, as fine as the crockery, mingled with the salt air. Rafe sat on one of the wooden chairs. It was a little small for him and he shifted uncomfortably.

'Knowing Chris it's not a fake. He's too finicky.'

'Not finicky; *discerning,*' said a deep voice and she turned. The man did not in the least resemble the image conjured by a wine-loving Captain with a taste for luxury. He was quite tall, though not as tall as Rafe, but it wasn't his stature that was the source of his impact. His hair was a deep shade of mahogany brown, gilded at the edges into fire by long exposure to the sun, his eyes as blue as the sea, shading to dusk around the pupil, and he was one of the handsomest men she had ever seen.

Rafe grunted and stood, confirming his superior height, if not manners.

'*Finicky.* Chris, this is Miss Osbourne. Cleo, this is Captain Christopher, or Chris. They don't use surnames on this vessel of knaves. And whatever you do, don't call him Kit.'

Their host shot Rafe a look that could have felled a forest, but by the time he turned back to Cleo he was smiling and she smiled back without thinking.

'You are quite right, Miss Osbourne. It is Qianlong. You have a good eye.'

So do you. Two of them, even, she almost said before she recollected herself.

'I apologise for commandeering your cabin and now your chair, Captain Christopher.'

'They are both honoured. I am sure if they could speak they would be thanking you for the improvement in their terms of employment. Besides, I owe this ugly fellow a favour and this allows me to discharge it while enjoying the company of someone who appreciates beauty. Any chance you can go read a book somewhere and leave us to discuss the long and convoluted history of Chinese crockery, Grey?'

'No. And fetch your own cup. That's mine.'

The Captain's mouth curved up at the corners, but he put down the cup and beckoned to the sailor who had helped her earlier. When that was done the Captain leaned back in his chair and began the tale of how he had acquired the Qianlong teapot. It involved actual pirates—rather than *faux* pirates, as Rafe disdainfully called Chris—a beautiful Chinese princess, a malevolent wizard, a dragon's egg and the daring rescue of the princess's beloved Shih Tzu puppy.

Meanwhile a sailor brought more cups, tea and delicious little almond-and-hazelnut-filled cakes sprinkled with cinnamon which Cleo devoured without even realising.

'If you like I will show you a collection of Sèvres *théières* I'm transporting for a friend, Miss Osbourne. Did you find the book, Benja?' he asked as the sailor who had brought the tea returned.

Benja handed a book to Cleo with a little bow. It was all very ceremonial and she had to resist the urge to bow in response.

'I am quite certain you will enjoy this,' said the Captain as he rose. 'If you will excuse me?' His smile shifted from her to Rafe and deepened into a near grin as he headed towards the bridge.

'One day he'll hang,' Rafe said just loud enough to be heard.

'Shhh… I thought you were friends.'

'Of course we're friends. Doesn't mean he doesn't annoy the cr— the hell out of me. He probably invented that story.'

Cleo sighed, licking a sliver of hazelnut from her fingers before wiping them on her handkerchief and picking up the book.

'I don't care. It was a wonderful tale. Oh, look, it is *Captives of the Hidden City*, the fourth of the *Desert Boy* books! How marvellous.'

She was struck with sudden guilt. Just an hour ago she was railing against fate and here she was enjoying tea, laughing with her nemesis and blissful at the prospect of sinking into this wondrous book.

'Ah, don't go that way again, Pat.' Her face must have shown her thoughts, because Rafe leaned forward, his hand rising, but falling back on to his thigh. 'You're alive. If your brother hasn't already left Egypt, with any luck he'll do so soon and will find you in London.'

Don't go that way.

He was right, it wasn't like her to become maudlin. She leaned her head against the back of the armchair and met Rafe's storm eyes straight on. He smiled a little.

'That's right, Cleopatra. No asps for you.'

'Of course not. But there is no comparison. Cleopatra likely believed wholeheartedly in the afterworld where she would reign as queen and goddess. Death was merely a rite of passage.'

'Still a mad thing to do. I'd rather stay and fight.'

'Evidently.' She smiled. 'You and your Captain Krees are of that breed. Taking on life headlong and making the most of it. I'm envious.'

'You're not that different, sweetheart. I don't know a handful of women, or men, who would have made it this far from Meroe. Whatever misguided vision you have of yourself, take it from someone who has seen a little of the world—you have a deep, strong core. You'll survive and thrive.'

She couldn't stop her mouth from wavering out of shape or her eyes burning. She didn't want him to say things like that.

'I've said the wrong thing again.' He sighed. 'Have some more tea.'

She shook her head.

'Tell me about our Captain, instead. How do you know him and why does he owe you a favour? And why does he hate being called Kit?'

'More bedtime tales?'

She shivered a little, remembering lying on the desert floor, watching the stars shimmer as he spoke. Amazingly she wished they were back there. Foolish.

'No tales, just the truth.'

'They aren't my tales to tell. But he's a good man and a better friend, that's all that matters. Is this general curiosity or are you smitten already?'

She smiled. She would not have thought someone with Rafe's looks and physique might be envious of the handsome Captain, but there was definitely a sour tinge to his voice.

'Not yet. I shall inform you when it happens.'

'Very amusing. I've seen women fall prey to his charms more times than I can count. I don't want to bear that burden of guilt as well.'

'I shall try and spare you, then.'

'You can laugh all you want, but it was evident you were enthralled with his pretty face, admit it.'

'I was enthralled by the teapot as well. And the sunset

over the cliffs in the desert and a host of other beautiful things. But that doesn't mean I want to stare at that sunset for ever. There is a vast difference between appreciating and wanting. Once he began telling that story I forgot how he looked and, in truth, I liked him better then.'

He picked up the book, leafing through it.

'Just be careful. His charm runs deeper than his handsome face. I didn't consider...just be careful.'

She wanted to tell him his concern was absurd. Even a little insulting. Only the day before they'd shared an intimacy that to her at least had been utterly transporting, and today he was suggesting she might become infatuated with another man.

Perhaps this was how his world operated. Perhaps he was used to falling in and out of lust with women and thought little of it. She wished she could do the same. She would be quite grateful if Captain Chris could inspire a tenth of what she felt towards Rafe. She didn't want to be stranded with these feelings, whatever they were—lust, need...love...

'I'm in no danger from Captain Chris.'

He shrugged again. Sometimes he looked and acted like an overgrown boy, uncomfortable in his rough frame. She wanted to take the book from his hands, take them in hers and tell him that she wanted *him*, not handsome Chris. His vanity might enjoy the tribute, but the rest of him would shy away, raise that barrier even higher.

Just be careful. His warning had come too late and she wondered if such warnings were ever effective.

'You're angry at me again, Cleo-Pat.'

She met his gaze and told him the truth.

'I'm...worn and worried and, yes, I'm still angry at you, Mr Grey. You may have thought you were acting in my interest, but your chief concern was *your* peace of mind and *your* conscience. Now go away. You are blocking the sun and I wish to read.'

* * *

It cost Rafe, but he did as he was bid and went away. He'd known she would take it ill, but somehow he'd hoped she'd understand.

He found a frowning Chris in the map room with Benja.

'Trouble, Chris?'

'No. A few Barbary pirate ships have been harassing merchant seamen south of Malta. Just marking their possible route so we can avoid it. What's on your mind? Disembowelling me?'

'The thought did occur to me, yes. Don't toy with her. She has been through enough. The last thing she needs is you charming her into a broken heart.'

Chris straightened, directing a very peculiar look at Rafe.

'I don't think I can, but in any case I shall try to rein in my desire to charm my way into the heart of every female within twenty leagues of me.'

'I didn't mean it like that and you know it.'

'You're in a foul mood. I've never seen you so worried about your customers. You've fulfilled your brief. She's alive and on her way to London. What more can you do?'

'Nothing,' Rafe grunted.

'Is she even paying you?'

'There's this great big horror of an emerald. Like the ones we used to see in the mountains in South America.'

'A fine payment. You're not taking it, I presume.'

'She'll need it once she reaches London. I doubt she'll make much from her writing, even assuming they'll accept articles from a woman.'

'Hmmm.' Chris stared off at the wall, his fingers tapping on the map. 'I like her.'

Rafe straightened in alarm.

'There's no currency in that, Chris.'

'What? Oh, not in that way. I meant I like her and she'd

best find a position that can support her. I think I shall have a word with my Aunt Mary when we arrive.'

'Anyone ever tell you what a useful fellow you are?'

'Never the ones that matter, Grey. And what will you do while I am relieving you of your burdens?'

Rafe almost objected to his calling Cleo a burden, but stopped himself. He'd probably revealed too much already. How had he become so enmeshed in all this? He wished he could just…disappear. Run away again and escape this tangled confusion. Perhaps that would be best. He'd done it before and been perfectly fine. Happy. Content. He could do it again.

'Whether Edge returns to England or not once he digs himself out of Egypt, I'm afraid I can't put off going to Greybourne any longer. If my mother refuses to continue to manage the estate, I'll need to make arrangements to administer the place from…wherever.'

'Why not from Greybourne?'

'No, thank you.'

'Your father's dead. It's yours now.'

'I'm aware of that.'

'And you're getting too old to play this soldier of fortune game.'

'Say's the gentleman smuggler.'

'I don't smuggle. I trade.'

'You just admitted you're still smuggling.'

'What, Boucheron's antiquities? That doesn't count as smuggling. The crates were marked for customs as marble and building materials. That was close enough. Besides, that was a year ago.'

'So you've turned respectable? What are you carrying now?'

'Cotton, spices, quite a bit of excellent wine, a damsel in distress and the very ugly Disappearing Duke.'

Rafe raised his hands, hushing his friend, and Chris sighed.

'Very well. I won't reveal your silly secret. You're just Rafe Grey, mercenary. Still ugly, though.'

Rafe rubbed his scarred cheek.

'Thank you, I find being ugly quite useful. Adds mystique and ups the price.'

'Except you just said you aren't taking a fee this time.'

Rafe kept his hand on his scars, grounding himself in them.

'No, every so often one has to do an act of charity to balance out the rest. This is mine.'

'I thought tricking Edge into travelling to Egypt was yours.'

'That is different. Edge matters.'

'And she doesn't?'

'She…' Rafe waited out another of those annoying flashes of tingling heat as it headed inexorably for his groin. Blast, he hated being sixteen again. The sooner they were off this ship the better. 'She is different, yes. But she doesn't matter, not in that way. Perhaps this whole Greybourne thing is throwing me off balance.'

'Ah, is that your excuse for kissing her?'

'I never said a word about…anything of that sort.'

'True. I was merely guessing. Now I know.'

'You blasted devil. Besides, it isn't true—*she* kissed *me*.' And quite a bit more.

'Of course you resisted wholeheartedly.'

'It might surprise you that I did…initially. She's lost her father, mislaid her brother and has no future to go to. What kind of cad would I be if I took advantage of her natural need for comfort? All she wants is a little solace in the midst of chaos,' he continued doggedly. 'Right now I'm all she has, but she'll land on her feet.'

Chris made a mark on the map. 'Useful trait to have. Are you worried she might develop expectations if she knows of your title and fortune?'

He considered it. 'No. Not in the least.'

'You sound almost disappointed, Grey—' He broke off as Benja returned and Rafe jumped at the opportunity to escape, leaving the two men bent over their charts, plotting the course to England and to a life he did not want.

Chapter Fifteen

'Hallo, Birdie,' Cleo said as Benja left her by Birdie's bunk in the sailors' hold. Birdie grunted and hauled himself into a sitting position. 'No, don't rise. Captain Christopher said you are feeling poorly so I brought you some tea.' She looked around the surprisingly clean hold.

'Don't worry, now. It's always the same when I first come on board.' He rubbed his beard, inspecting her over his cup. 'You're looking a little peaked yourself. The Colonel said you're angry.'

She shrugged. 'Not at you, Birdie.'

'It was the right thing to do, Miss Cleo.'

'He should have asked me.'

'Should he? And saying he told you we thought your brother might still be in Egypt, you would have come quietly?'

'Of course not. He is my little brother.'

'Well, there you have it, miss. Captain Chris couldn't wait any longer in Egypt.'

'I would have found another ship.'

'Not one where we could know you were safe. It is only fools who turn their noses up at an offer of help. I don't oft think you're a fool, but...'

She sighed. 'You are probably right, Birdie. I am mostly

disappointed in myself. I should not feel so relieved to have had choice taken away from me. But why did you and Mr Grey also leave? I thought he meant to find his brother?'

Birdie sipped his tea, considering the ceiling.

'The Colonel has business to see to back home. He'd done what he set out to—tempted his brother to Egypt; Edge will have to find his own way from there.'

'I hope both our brothers do. I should not have been so angry with him.'

'He expected nothing less. But don't make him suffer long.'

'Don't exaggerate, Birdie. He's hardly suffering.'

'I've known him a few days more than you, miss.'

'Devil take you, Birdie. Now I feel guilty myself.'

He gave a jaw-cracking yawn.

'Good. So go tell the lug you don't wish to feed him to the crabs.'

Rafe lowered the book at the knock on the door. Bunking in the map room meant he had to accept interruptions with good grace, but he was in a particularly foul mood at the moment and would have appreciated some privacy. He put down his book.

'Come in.'

'Mr Grey? May I have a word?'

He stood, his simmering anger at Cleo transforming within seconds into a different heat altogether. These shifts of mood were happening far too swiftly for his liking.

'Is there anything you need, Miss Osbourne?'

'I did not mean to interrupt.'

'You aren't. What do you want?'

His question was both ungracious and childish, but he felt a snap of satisfaction at her blush. Still, she stepped into the room and closed the door. He was suddenly absurdly conscious of the bed behind him. His hands curved of themselves, as if they were already closing on the cool sweep of her skin, and his mind conjured the image—Cleo in his bed, her short hair tossed into charming chaos by his hands just as it was now by the wind…

For the hundredth time his body scrabbled at his control, cursing him for taking what she'd offered and branding all those sensations into him. Odysseus's sirens he could deal with, but Cleopatra Osbourne was another matter entirely.

She shifted her weight. He was probably making her nervous. Good, she was making him writhe.

Finally, she drew a long breath and plunged in.

'I wished to apologise, Mr Grey.'

'Ah, yes. I heard you went to speak with Birdie. Did he instruct you to apologise?'

'Yes. He told me I have been monstrously unfair to you and that you are huddled in a corner, weeping and smiting your brow at the injustice of it all. I presume that is what the book is for. You couldn't possibly be reading it.'

Damn her.

He planted his tingling hands on his hips and managed not to smile.

'Naturally I wasn't reading the thing. I keep one by me in case I need to chase off a rat.'

Her dimples appeared before her smile did.

'Thank you for the warning. I had a close escape, then.'

'Very. The only thing that held me back was that it was one of your friend Shakespeare's and you'd probably have snatched it and scampered off.'

Her eyes went wide and bright. 'Oh, how marvellous! Which one?'

'I'm not telling you. You will ruin the ending.' He caught her sleeve as she moved towards the bed.

'No. Do stay away from my bed unless invited, Queenie.'

She stopped immediately. She'd flushed before, but now she turned as crimson as Chris's cushions. He had not meant to ruin their tentative return of rapport, but there were limits and sometimes her naivety sent her hurtling over them. He'd never thought that gaining her trust would become such a burden.

'I am sorry. I think… I know I have been living in my own little world for too long. I was angry because you imposed your will on mine, though I knew you did so because you felt I was at risk of real harm. Yet I did the same to you and can't claim that defence. That day in the *hammam*…' His heartbeat shot ahead, but she wasn't looking at him, her hands twisting into each other as she struggled with the words. 'I keep pushing you into a corner, don't I? I wanted something and I…oh, I am no good at explaining myself. I don't think I have had enough practice.'

He breathed very carefully, as if a flickering butterfly had settled on his hand.

'I think you are doing a fair job of explaining yourself, Cleo, but you have nothing to apologise for.'

'Yes, I do, Rafe. I never thought myself particularly impulsive, yet I have been doing all manner of impulsive things since I met you and every time it is you who must pay the price.'

He half held out his hand.

'I think it is more a case of honesty than impulsiveness, Cleo. And I prefer you be honest, even if it tests my fortitude at times. Friends…' he tried the word tentatively '…should be able to allow themselves more latitude with each other. I shall take it as a compliment that you allow yourself that latitude with me. I show Birdie sides of me I would never show the world and I trust him not to run in horror if I misstep.'

'Then thank you for not running in horror.' She pressed her hands together and to his surprise he saw they were shaking. He resisted the urge to touch her cheek, to make her look up so he could see the shifting storm of thoughts he knew were pounding inside her.

'You mustn't lay my weakness at your door, Cleo. I

could have been stronger and sent you on your way. I didn't.'

'But you would never have done anything had I not forced you into that situation.'

'Probably not. I don't have many codes, but the ones I possess are important to me. But I don't… I can't regret that it happened. It was…beautiful.' He wanted to say so much more, but his own thoughts were chaotic and jumbled, as if his mind had begun to speak a foreign language. 'I'm sorry, I've never had a conversation like this before.' He laughed a little and she smiled and heaved a hefty sigh of relief.

'Neither have I. I rather like it, though. Thank you.'

'I declare a moratorium on apologies and thanks for a while, Cleo-Pat.'

'Very well. I still feel quite guilty, though,' she said as she went to the door.

'Still? I told you…'

'No, about something else entirely.'

He knew he shouldn't ask. He knew it. And yet he did. 'About what, then?'

'Your bed. It is so much smaller than mine.'

The door closed behind her.

Even passengers on a smuggler's ship are ruled by routine.

After a week at sea Cleo woke, dined, and went to sleep to the tune of the ship's bells like everyone else on board. She particularly waited for the bell calling them to dinner. It wasn't the surprisingly excellent food she looked forward to, it was that Rafe was most relaxed with her when in the Captain's company.

Her apology had defused much of the tension between them, but Rafe seemed to have traced a circle around himself, like a druid's mark of protection. She could not tell if he was shielding her or himself; if it was her, it was failing miserably.

At least during dinner and sometimes seated with them on deck she felt utterly, vividly happy. Rafe and the Captain had clearly known each other long and enjoyed the peculiar and rare camaraderie of men who were completely comfortable with one another and therefore enjoy outdoing each other in pointing out each other's foibles.

The Captain was also more than willing to indulge her love of Shakespeare, especially when he realised how much it goaded Rafe. One dinner he brought his collection of the plays, all dog-eared from frequent reading.

'I'll leave these here for you to take what you want. Perhaps you'll even convince this philistine to give them a try. He used *Hamlet* in school to even the table legs.'

'It kept wobbling when we were playing whist. Very distracting,' Rafe defended himself.

Cleo's attention sharpened. Rafe continued to parry all her questions about either his past or his future. She gathered any glimpse of his life like nuggets of gold from a river.

'What was school like?' Cleo took the opportunity to ask.

'Rafe was very instrumental in making sure I survived my first two years in school.'

'I was also two years older and a head taller. It was no great effort to keep those damned bullies at bay.'

Captain Chris's smile twisted a little.

'It cost you a beating by the headmaster.'

'Only once. It was well worth it to see Barnsley and Greaves waist deep in the mud.'

'What happened?' Cleo demanded.

'Curious, Cleo-Pat?' Rafe grinned and Chris leaned his elbows on the table and told a tale which had Cleo laughing so hard she spilled her wine.

Rafe took her glass from her.

'Here, you may laugh at me all you wish, but I won't condone the waste of Chris's precious nectar.'

Cleo dabbed at a spot of wine on her dress with a napkin.

'I cannot afford to spill it either. This dress might be years out of fashion, but it is my most respectable one and I shall be needing it when I present myself to Mr Fulton, the editor of the *Gazette*.'

'What a pity I didn't know previously,' Chris said. 'We sold a dozen bolts of Chinese silk to a merchant in Alexandria. There was the most amazing embroidered orange silk that would have suited you perfectly, Cleopatra.'

'Stop flirting, you bacon-fed knave,' Rafe growled.

'Rafe! That is from *Henry the Fourth*! Oh, very good!' Cleo commended, taking back her glass.

'It's all your fault. Between the two of you quoting that mawkish pap at each other morning to night I'm surprised I'm not dreaming in Shakespearean blather. I'm only glad Chris doesn't share your fascination with mummies.'

Captain Chris raised his brows.

'Mummies?'

'You know, dead bodies wrapped in sheets.'

'I know what mummies are, Greybeard. Are you interested in mummies, Miss Osbourne? How wonderfully ghoulish.'

'My father was interested in them and only because they fetched a good price. Just before he disappeared he sent a shipment of three dozen mummies to a Mr Pettifer in London, who apparently unwraps them in front of an audience.'

'Ah. Pettifer.'

'You know him?'

'Yes. He's well named, that petty scoundrel. Opened what he calls a "Hall of Wonders" on Piccadilly. I don't advise you follow up on the acquaintance.'

'But I must. He is always late in payment and it is usually not until he wishes for Father to procure him something else that he pays his bill. I plan to demand he honour his debt when I reach London. Besides, if Dash did indeed succeed in leaving Egypt already, then Mr Pettifer might know where he is. Dash mentioned Pettifer's connections in the antiquarian world might prove useful.'

'If it is antiquarian connections he needs, I'll introduce him to John Soane. He is a close acquaintance of my aunt's and I often procure objects of interest for him. In fact, my aunt is an excellent person for you to meet. In fact, I think…'

He leaned back and stared at the ceiling, but whatever thoughts were being conjured in his mind were interrupted by Benja's appearance.

'Wind is changing, *Capitán*.'

'Hold that thought, Cleopatra. I shall return anon…'

He left the cabin, taking the carefree atmosphere with him.

Of late, each time she found herself alone with Rafe she had to rearrange herself, like the moment after stumbling on a perfectly straight road. He also appeared to find these moments a strain because he would usually hurry to make a remark, but this time it was she who rushed to fill the void.

'It is very kind of Captain Chris to offer his assistance, but I have imposed on him enough. He needn't go out of his way on my account.'

'Since he is certain to visit his aunt when we reach London, he will hardly be going out of his way.'

'You know what I mean. I cannot continue to hang on your coattails. When we reach London I must make my own way.'

'Oh, God, not that again. You have the rest of your life to make your own way, Cleo. But right now you haven't the tools to do so.'

'We must agree to differ on that head, Mr Grey.'

'If there is any phrase I dislike more than that, I cannot recall it at the moment. No, we will *not* agree to differ. This is a very simple issue, Cleo. Do you honestly believe I will deposit you on the dockside and go about my business? What the devil do you think I am?'

'The stubbornest man of my acquaintance, sir. You make me sound as if I will wander about the docks like a stray lamb just waiting for the first scoundrel to fleece me. I am neither an imbecile nor reckless.'

'I think you qualify for both those epithets if you refuse a perfectly reasonable offer of assistance.'

'I have already accepted a great deal of assistance from you. I cannot be forever hanging about your neck, like those fictional swooning damsels you so deride.'

He flushed.

'I never lumped you in that category. For pity's sake, you are the least susceptible female I have yet come across.'

'Somehow that does not sound very complimentary.'

'I was making a point.'

'That I am case-hardened and bull-headed. I should fare just fine on the London docks, then.'

'Don't twist my words, Pat. What great scheme of the heavens might be upset if you surrender your vaunted independence for a brief moment and accept our help? Is there some Greek curse that will be unleashed? Is the fate of civilisations at stake? Or is it simply your wish to give me more sleepless nights than you have already?'

She pushed back her chair and went to the windows and stared into the darkness. The waves were slow inky swells that rose and fell like the breath of a sleeping, slimy beast. In the distance she thought she could just see the glimmer of a light—perhaps another ship or even the shores of Portugal.

Soon, all too soon, she would be returning to a country where she knew no one. Why *not* accept Rafe and Captain Chris's help?

Not because of a Greek curse, but something far more mundane. She *knew* Rafe. He would not be able to walk away without making absolutely certain she was safe. It was simply the way he was. Her insistence on independence was rubbing on his conscience and his peace of mind… She almost smiled as the wheel finally settled into the groove.

How *petty* of her. She *did* want him to worry, she did not wish to be put away, score settled, like his past assignments. She wanted him awake at night, worrying about her fate. She wanted him thinking of her.

Petty and unfair.

She rubbed her eyes and returned to her chair.

'I'm too tired to argue with you, Rafe. Can we not resolve this later?'

'No. I refuse to have this argument with you in the middle of a dockyard, which is precisely what will happen if we don't resolve this now. The sooner you come to terms with it the better. We will be in London in a matter of days, Cleo.'

'I *know* that. Stop growling at me!'

'What are you two arguing about now?' Captain Chris asked as he re-entered, bearing a tray of cakes. 'On second thought, don't tell me. I might have to take sides and hurt the big lug's feelings. These will make you both feel better. Benja prepared it especially for you, sweet Viola. He is clearly smitten, which shows excellent taste on his part.'

'Is senility setting in, Chris? Her name is Cleo, not Viola.'

Chris settled into his chair and took one of the cakes himself.

'If you'd minded your lessons with the same assiduity as you spent trying to escape school, Rafe, you might realise it is perfectly apt.'

'Oh, God, not Shakespeare again.'

'Yes, philistine.'

'Which one was Viola? The one who lived in the forest dressed like a shepherd and made men run rings around each other?'

'That was Rosalind and I do *not* do that,' Cleo objected. 'Though I am flattered by the comparison—Rosalind is a fine heroine. Captain Chris was referring to Viola from *Twelfth Night*. She also dressed like a boy and is mistaken for her brother, but the resemblance in our tales ends there.'

Cleo considered the cakes and took a generous slice. She'd eaten better since boarding the *Hesperus* than she had in years. Any more of this and she'd be bursting out of her few dresses.

'Oh, there's more to her story, I think. A very resilient young woman, Viola. She thinks she has lost everything, but rather than abandon hope and bemoan her fate she takes on the guise of Cesario, becomes page to the Duke of Orsino, falls in love with him and, though he is a blind fool for most of the play, she ends up marrying him.'

Rafe grunted and crossed his arms as well.

'Sounds like the plot of a third-rate Haymarket play. No wonder I cannot remember it.'

'I agree it is not one of my favourites,' Cleo admitted, giving in to temptation and taking a second slice. 'I found Viola's devotion to Orsino rather tiring and his adoration of Olivia even more annoying.'

'The two of you haven't a sentimental bone between you.' Chris laughed. 'I find other parallels, though. There is the fact that Viola disguises herself as Cesario which, of course, is quite apt, given Caesar was Cleopatra's lover. And then Orsino means bear in Italian. You have a fascination for names, don't you, Rafe? I thought you might find that curious.'

'Do you mean because of the "bourn" in Osbourne, Captain Chris?' Cleo asked, perplexed by the exchange between the two men. This clearly touched on something that lay between them.

'There is that, too.' Chris nodded. 'I applaud all things symmetrical.'

'You are lucky you're pretty, Popinjay, because you are about as amusing as an arse boil,' Rafe snapped.

'We can't all be endowed with your ample measure of charm, Grey Bear... I mean Grey *Beard*.'

'Don't you have a ship to sail?'

Captain Chris laughed and stood.

'I do. And a storm to beat if we're lucky.'

Cleo glanced worriedly towards the windows. She'd seen no signs of storm clouds in the dark sky.

'Another storm?'

'A big one this time. Past the straits the sea is a different beast altogether. It will either speed us towards the Channel or make fish feed of us all. I'd better go ensure the former. I'd hate to follow literary parallels and have my Viola cast ashore in an untimely manner. Unless, of course, you find your Orsino in said manner.' He winked at her and left.

'Addle-pate,' Rafe muttered.

'What on earth was that about?'

'I neither know nor care. As for you—until you know your way about London you will accept whatever position Chris can conjure out of his family's ample hat.'

'Have a piece of cake, Greybeard. It might sweeten you up.'

'I'm serious, Cleo.' His tone softened. 'I need to know you will be safe. I would say you owe me that. Think of it as a way to erase your debt.'

'By owing you more?'

'By granting me peace of mind. I'm not asking that you commit yourself to a nunnery. Merely meet with Chris's aunt so she can see if there is some position she can secure for you. If her suggestions do not appeal to you, you are free to reject them. Would that be so terrible? You are not signing over your soul, you know.'

She looked down at Benja's cake. She'd already given Rafe a large portion of her soul. What difference would it make whether she agreed? Whether Dash survived or not—her life as she had known it was over.

'I'm sorry, Pat.'

She pressed the heels of her hands to her eyes. She hated how he could sometimes see right through her. He rarely called her Pat any longer, except to tease her, but he wasn't teasing her now. Soon he would no longer call her that, or call her anything at all.

'Pat is gone, Mr Grey. Henceforth I am Miss Osbourne. Whoever she is.'

'You'll find your way again. You have that…gift,' he said, but his voice was strained as if he was trying to convince himself.

'I might, but I don't particularly wish to.'

'I can sympathise with that. Life is not very considerate of our wishes, is it?'

'No. What do you wish for, Rafe?'

He turned his glass in his hand, watching the light from the lamps dig deep into the purple. His expression didn't change, but she could feel him slip away again. When he looked up and smiled she knew he'd marked the boundary between them once again.

'Oh, I'm easy. Good food, good wine, good company. At the moment I am lucky to have all three. What else would I need?'

Me, said the treacherous little voice inside her. She took a third slice of the cake and stood.

'Where are you going?' he asked, rising as well.

'To find *Twelfth Night* among the Captain's books. Perhaps I shall learn something useful.'

Chapter Sixteen

She would have done better to have read *The Tempest*.

At first she'd thought it was the Captain's wonderful wine that was making the room roll so alarmingly. But she doubted it would account for the ship behaving more like a barrel rolling downhill than a sea-going vessel.

She managed to change into her nightshift and lie down, only to find herself dumped summarily on the floor as the ship tipped on its side.

There were times when hammocks were definitely preferable to bunks, she thought as she grabbed the shelves, spreading her legs wide to battle the roll and pitch. She could feel and hear the waves lashing at the hull, the desperate creak and wail of wood being strained to its last fibre.

Then the worst happened. She could feel the ship rising, straining and shuddering as it was lifted up. She knew it could not last, any moment the laws of nature would have their way with them. When the inevitable drop came, it took the ship, but not her stomach. The latter lurched up into her chest only to be thrown down again as the ship tipped over on its side.

Any moment now and the Captain's prediction about them becoming a treat for the fish might very well come to pass. She clung to the polished wood, her heart slamming far faster and more brutally than the shrieks of wind and raging waves.

But her mind was amazingly quiet and clear. All she could think was—she did not want to die and she did not want Rafe to die.

She wanted him here, with her.

The door slammed open and something between a squawk and a shriek burst from her, but it wasn't the ship being torn apart. Rafe stood braced in the doorway as the ship rolled back. His hair and face were slick with rain and the coat he was shrugging off fell with a wet thump to the floor.

I've conjured him, she thought. Her relief was so great it took quite a bit of restraint and common sense not to abandon her grip and throw herself at him precisely like a Haymarket heroine.

The ship gave another mighty effort to shake her off. She lost her hold on the shelf, but managed to grab one of the solid chairs that was grinding sluggishly back and forth across the floor, dragging her as she clung to it.

Rafe came towards her, using the shelves as anchors.

'Stop dancing like a drunken goat and sit down.'

'I am trying! It's impossible to stay still.'

She was beginning to feel queasy. She couldn't remember suffering from seasickness before, but there was a first time for everything. Her first relief at his entry was dissipating fast. It was bad enough she must look like a fright in the oversized nightshirt; casting up her accounts in front of him would add injury to injury.

'I am perfectly fine. Go away,' she said, trying not to sound desperate.

'No. Not while you're rolling around like a billiard ball.'

'I'll sit down.' She aimed for the seat and promptly fell to the floor as the boat went the other way. The blow to her bottom was so sharp she lost her breath and sat gasping.

He helped her to her feet, planting his feet wide against the roll.

'Come, sit.'

'I think I am safer on the floor.'

He laughed, tucking her against him.

'You'll roll around the floor like a loose cannon, Queenie. Come.'

To her surprise he sat at the end of the bed and propped his boots against the cupboard. Before she could understand what he was doing he used the roll of the ship to pull her off her feet and on to his lap. His arm curved about her waist, his hand on her hip, flexing as he held her through the particularly enthusiastic roll.

'See? Nice and snug. We roll with the ship, rather than try to battle it. You can't win that one, sweetheart.' His voice was a rumbling purr against her side and his breath warm on her temple.

His warmth radiated through the thin, damp cotton of their shirts and her hands began tingling at the memory of sliding her hands over his chest in the bathhouse. How his muscles had hardened under her touch, bunching and flexing in that strange dance of invitation and rejection. Her hand was so close to his waist, a simple tug could separate shirt from trouser and...

The ship gave another leap and dip and she grabbed at his shirt.

'Ouch. Watch your nails, hellion.'

'You've been stabbed more times than a roast ham. I hardly think my nails will have an impact on you.'

'God, you'd be surprised.' There was a laugh in his voice, but also a rawness, and she leaned back a little to look at him.

He was half smiling, but there was tension there and demons in his eyes.

She released his shirt, gently rubbing the spot she'd abused, still watching him.

His pupils widened, turning storm into thundery dusk, and under her thigh she felt him harden. It was definite, immediate, and so was her response.

All fear of the storm, the queasiness and embarrassment just…evaporated. Her body shimmered with heat, expanded and woke into awareness of every point of contact, of the tingling warmth between her legs, of the need to *do* something…

Oh, lord, she was in trouble.

'Maybe this was not the best idea.' His voice was even rougher than usual, but he didn't remove her from his lap. 'I think you'd be safer on the floor.'

'But not as comfortable.' She was *purring*. She'd never purred in her life.

'Comfortable isn't the word that comes to mind,' he muttered, but his arms tightened around her. 'Just try not to move.'

The ship pitched again, as if rolling in laughter at their pretence at civility. His legs braced harder against the side of the cupboard.

She rubbed her feet together and tucked them against his thigh.

'Stop it. Or I'll drop you.'

'My feet are cold,' she protested. He dragged the blanket towards them and drew it round her shoulders. She snuggled into it.

'I'm so glad Captain Chris appreciates fine things like cashmere. Isn't it soft?'

His answer was more grunt than corroboration, but his arms closed around her again under the fuzzy cocoon, one hand warm and heavy on her hip, the other tucking the blanket under her feet and staying there.

She sighed. If this storm was the end for all of them, at least she would go down more comfortable than she had been in…in for ever. She snuggled deeper, flexing her feet. His hand tightened, his fingers firm against her instep. She smiled.

'Thank you, Rafe.'

'Please don't. Just…stop moving.'

'It's the ship, not I.'

'Liar. I know I deserve to be tortured for all my sins, but this is beyond my dues. Please try to sleep.'

'I don't think I can.'

'Try. *Please.*'

She did try. She tried not to think of how addictive and unique his scent was or wonder what it was about it that made her wish to fill her lungs with it and keep it with her always.

She tried, not very hard, not to take advantage of the rolling ship to expand her map of his body against hers. To be quite fair, he was not helping. His arms and hands tightened with each roll and pitch, his legs tensing and relaxing. He was no more still than she and she could not tell how much was necessitated by the workings of gravity and how much driven by the same demons that were hard at work undermining her control.

She kept waiting for the next wave—his hands would close tightly on her hip and foot, sending sweet waves of bliss through her like music from a chime. She risked flexing her foot against his hand as they rolled and his fingers pressed hard against her sole, sending a shiver all the way up to her scalp. It felt… Oh, yes…marvellous!

'And stop humming, blast it.'

'Sorry. I feel a little fuzzy. Can one become tipsy from being cuddled?'

'I don't know, but one can and is becoming addled by it.'

'Sorry,' she said again and kissed the side of his neck. He seemed to collapse like a house of cards, with a protesting groan that echoed the creaking of the boat. She was no longer cocooned but crushed—stretched out on the bed with a very heavy and warm giant on top of her, her arms still tight about his neck.

'I know this is my fault, but there are limits, Cleopatra, and we've just passed mine. I'm going on deck where it's safer. Now go to sleep.'

'I don't want to sleep. My future…my whole life is a great unknown, but this feels so right. How could it be so wrong?'

His breathing was deep and unsteady, his chest brushing against hers with each breath.

'It certainly is in the world you are heading to.'

'But we are not there yet. We are not anywhere yet. We might not reach anywhere if this storm worsens. Would it be so terrible if we take this pleasure?'

He raised himself a little. In the dark his eyes were even more menacing—twin shards of a northern sea. If she hadn't felt his heart thudding against her, she might have worried she was alone in this drugging need.

'You are under my protection…'

She unhooked her arms.

'Oh, God, not that again. I am no longer under your protection, but under Captain Christopher's. I am, however, under *you* and I like it here. If there is one thing I have learned in my addled life it is to take what pleasures come my way as long as they harm no one.'

He didn't answer immediately, but the muscles of his jaw were working away, making the scarred skin ripple.

'This isn't good. I'm far gone enough for you to be making sense, Queenie.'

'I *am* making sense. You said yourself lust is the manifestation of a natural need. Or were *you* prevaricating?'

'No, but it is different for you. You're…'

Her eyes narrowed.

'I am what? If you dare say *a woman*—'

'Well, you are.'

'You have taken others of my genus to bed, haven't you?'

'Yes, but they were…more experienced. Stop glaring at me like that. It matters. At least, it matters to me. Right now you are lonely and scared. Hell, I'm the same. I would like nothing better than to drown my mind for a while in this madness, believe me. Nine out of ten parts of me are hitting me over the head for not saying yes at the top of my lungs.'

'Those are the nine parts of you that I like, Mr Grey.'

He smiled, his hand coming up to clasp hers where it was still pressed to his chest.

'The tenth part is deeply wounded, but it likes you best of all and doesn't want to sacrifice our friendship for the price of pleasing my damned libido.'

'Tell Mr Tenth to keep its nose out of the other parts' affairs. And I mean that literally. What happened in Alexandria was not an aberration; I want this honestly.'

He sank his head on to her shoulder. She could feel the battle inside him, the rigid weight pressing down on her. She wanted to tell him the battle was for naught. She would never hold this against him, but despite his strange life, he had rigid standards and she was not certain she wanted to force him to break with them.

She sighed and turned to brush his soft dark hair with her lips.

'Just a kiss, then? And then I promise I shall stop torturing you.'

'Just a kiss?' He raised his head and she wasn't certain if there was relief in his voice or disappointment.

'Yes. That is all. For tonight at least,' she amended conscientiously.

'Then you sleep?'

'As best I can. Yes.'

He adjusted himself on his elbow, gazing down at her. After moment he gave a small, determined sigh and brushed his fingers from her cheekbone to her jaw, his thumb settling on her lower lip, brushing gently.

'Just a kiss,' he repeated and she nodded.

'Just a kiss. After what we did in the *hammam*, how much harm could a simple kiss do?'

'At this rate a simple kiss might burn me to cinders, Cleo.' His fingers were tracing the lines of her face, gliding over her cheek, the curve of her ear and the sensitive skin below it before returning to her mouth. 'This is probably not a—'

She slipped one hand into his hair and drew his head down into the kiss.

Just a kiss.

Just the whole world cracking open and revealing itself like a ripe fruit, just her body saying—yes, finally…more.

For a few moments he let her explore his lips with hers, doing nothing more than holding himself above her, his hand as gentle as a down feather against her cheek.

This was *hard* for him, this control, she realised with glee. She wanted it to be hard. She wanted him to *need* this. To be buffeted by it just like the waves outside, just like the forces inside her that kept pushing her towards him.

She wanted him to want *this* as much as she did. No, she wanted him to want her. Not her kiss or her body, but *her*. This was different from Alexandria. She didn't know how; she just knew it was.

He raised himself suddenly, his hand pressing into the cushions, his face taut.

'Hell, I want more than a kiss, Cleo. I want to watch you come like you did in the *hammam*. Just listening to you makes me hard…your voice, your laugh…it lights me up inside…' His voice was rough and shaky, his hand sliding down between her breasts, pushing aside her pendant, down over her abdomen and up again, splaying across her ribs.

Her pulse chased his warmth, but it was his words that were working on her now, his voice a drug pouring through her, pumping heat and need through her veins.

'You amaze me, Cleo,' he murmured against her skin, his mouth following his hand, his breath shaping the words over her breast, along the surprisingly sensitive curve of her waist. 'You hold so much inside. But you're so generous, so true.'

He kissed the softest point just beside her hip bone and her legs drew up in a convulsion of need. He was driving her to the brink.

'Touch me,' she urged, rubbing his shoulders, reaching as far down his back as she could without stopping his destructive, beautiful progress. He pushed back for a second, pulling his shirt over his head and tossing it aside and then did the same to hers, much more gently.

'I will,' he promised. 'Trust me.'

'I do,' she whispered and he went still for a moment and then very gently eased her thigh to one side, his breath warm on her skin as his mouth lightly brushed kisses from her hip downwards. It felt foreign and a little frightening for him to be so close to her there.

'I want to hear your voice when I touch you,' he murmured against the inside of her thigh, his tongue tracing slow circles that made her skin skitter and pulse. 'Tell me what you like.'

She shook her head. That was beyond her.

'Whatever you're doing, I like it. Just do it more.'

His laugh was its own torture, a puff of warmth that rushed up between her legs and she clenched her jaw. When he slid one hand under her behind, raising and adjusting her, she let him. When he pressed a trail of gentle kisses to the sensitive skin of her inner thigh she held herself still until he reached the soft centre of the thudding heat between her legs. Then she couldn't hold back a spurt of breathy laughter—embarrassment and pleasure and gratitude all clashing.

She draped one arm over her eyes, as if hiding from the world could protect her. Her other hand hovered near his head, brushing at his soft dark hair until he threaded his fingers through hers and brought her hand to her breast, his thumb catching at her nipple and making fireworks explode.

The sensation was sweet and sharp and as it met the rising pulses of pleasure at her core she knew it had to stop, but it didn't. She tried not to cry out as the pleasure whipped itself into a storm, but the sounds burst from her—soft, then urgent, and finally imploding in a long breathy moan as honeyed heat crashed through her, sweet, molten. She was drowning in it…

She went rigid and he stilled, just holding her as wave after wave swept over her, softer each time until she lay there, exhausted but still humming.

'Listening to you is better than any aphrodisiac, Cleo.' His voice was raw and she could feel the tension in him. She turned lazily to press against him, her hand slipping down to see…oh, yes, he was hard and hot, the skin velvet-soft.

His breath hitched and he tucked his head into the slope of her neck.

'Wait a little…don't hurry.'

'I'm not,' she said idly, her hand gently stroking—her palm, the back of her hand, testing each sensation, mirroring the swaying of the ship. She whispered, 'Look, the storm has calmed.'

'Has it? Doesn't feel that way.' His voice was muffled against her neck. He held himself very still and she turned to kiss his temple, his flushed cheekbone. He was big and warm against her and it felt so absolutely right to have their naked bodies intertwined like this. She nudged him on to his back and raised herself above him, her legs slipping against his, her breasts half pressed against his chest. She traced a long line down his chest, over his stomach and up his erection, resting her palm on its heat and slowly closing it into a gentle squeeze. His eyes fluttered closed and a rumbling groan caught deep in his chest.

She smiled and trailed her hand the other way, right up to the dip at the base of his throat and back again. As her fingers and nails travelled up and down his muscles contracted and goosebumps rose on his skin. She could feel the vicious control he was exerting, but he couldn't control the shudders that struck, especially when she reached a certain point just by his navel or when her hand brushed his nipple. And when her fingers closed on his erection, each time a little tighter, a little longer, his breathing began coming apart at the seams. It made her feel hot all over again, powerful...*happy.*

He might keep himself from her, but she felt so close to him she could not believe there wasn't at least part of him that cared, that wanted to take what she was so willing to give.

'I like to make you feel like this,' she murmured, brushing her mouth across his, in long slow sweeps just like her hand. He said something in reply, but it might have been old Norse for all she knew because he dug his hand into her short hair and kissed her—a long, drugging kiss that began spinning its own magic through her body. His other hand anchored on hers, guiding her until his head arched back on a hoarse groan, his body tightening in release.

The storm had released the ship and it settled into a gentle swaying, like a great hammock. Rafe held her close as their bodies cooled and pulses slowed.

As the wondrous warmth began to fade, one thought rose like a jagged rock out of the mist—he had to tell her the truth of his identity. He could no longer hide behind the cowardly fiction that there was no need to do that since they would soon be in London and each heading on their merry way.

She kept condemning his conscience and right now he

wished he could send it to the devil himself. But whether his bond with her went any further or not, he had to tell her who he was.

For the first time in his life he was about to voluntarily reveal his identity to someone other than Birdie. It terrified him and he did not know why. Perhaps he was more superstitious than he thought, as if revealing his title, his origin, would somehow unleash a curse he'd escaped when he repudiated his name. It was absurd, childish, but it made his stomach roil.

He had to tell her.

He stroked a hand down her arm and she gave a little hum, stretching against him. A greedy shudder ran through him in response and set his heart pounding, not with desire this time, but with fear. The web his body and mind were weaving around her was tearing down all his defences, all his control.

She pulled away, rising on her elbow. Her smile faded as she met his eyes.

'What is it?'

'Nothing… I used to have some semblance of control. Apparently not any more.' The words were wrenched out of him and she placed a hand on the centre of his chest. Now he could feel his heart slamming against his ribs—like a fool pointlessly throwing himself against a wall.

'Rafe. You keep telling me not to go that way. Now I am telling you—don't let your conscience ruin this moment.'

'I can't help it; this is who I am, Cleo.'

No, it isn't, said the mocking little voice of his detested conscience. *Who you are is Rafael Edgerton, Earl of Braden, Duke of Greybourne. Tell her the truth.*

He slipped her off him and stood, searching for his clothes. It was still pitch dark outside, but he could hear the men hurrying about the ship, no doubt righting the chaos of the gale. They'd weathered the storm outside, but he had no idea how he would fare in the storm ahead.

Tell her.

The coward in him dressed in silence. Once she was safely on her way to her new life he would tell her and risk whatever curse life chose to toss at him next.

'I must go help Chris. A storm like that was bound to cause damage.'

'Of course,' she replied and he cast her a quick glance. She sat curled into the corner he'd occupied only a few hours ago, the blankets cocooning her.

'Your hair is getting longer,' he said inconsequentially and her hand snaked out of the warmth of the blankets and touched it.

'It must look a mess.'

'It looks beautiful.'

She shook her head a little and he fought the urge to walk back to that bed, to her, and send the world to the devil.

'I must help Chris,' he said again and left the cabin.

Chapter Seventeen

The Thames, England

'Good morning and welcome to England. Land of horrible weather, worse food, and plenty of phlegm.' The Captain's morose greeting was a perfect echo of Cleo's sentiments. They stood for a moment watching the flat, reedy shores slide by as Benja steered the *Hesperus* up the estuary.

'It looks soothing, though,' she replied, trying for cheerfulness. 'All that green.'

'True. There is a great deal of green.' He looked up at the sky and wiped the mist of rain from his hair. 'And grey.'

'Speaking of which—where is Mr Grey?'

He turned to look at her. Evidently her attempt at nonchalance left much to be desired.

'He spent hours with us cleaning up after the storm and he looked exhausted, so I sent him to rest a little before we dock and must face the real world.'

'I wish we could keep on sailing for another month at least. I'm not ready,' she blurted out and Chris sighed.

'Neither am I. In fact, quite a few people on this ship are dreading going ashore for one reason or another, including your knight errant, Viola. Perhaps our concerted repulsion will send us back out the estuary. I can't very well wish my sister remain unmarried merely for my own convenience, but I do wish her letter had missed me in Alexandria.'

'I think it is very noble of you to honour her so.'

'Pure fear. She will complain to my grandmother and that formidable woman terrorises the lot of us.'

Cleo smiled, as he'd intended, but she could hear a dozen conflicting currents in his tone. He seemed so open and yet, like Rafe, he kept himself mostly hidden below his handsome surface.

'I hope it is not as bad as you think.'

'I hope the same for you, Viola. But meanwhile I want to make a suggestion. Until I speak with my aunt I would like to suggest you remain on the *Hesperus*.'

She pushed away from the bulwark.

'Captain...'

'Don't reject my offer out of hand, Cleopatra. Accepting help does not diminish you, quite the opposite.'

'You sound like Rafe.' She sighed. 'But I *need* to go back to managing on my own. I'm beginning to worry I will have forgotten how.'

'I gather your resilience has been challenged before and will likely be so again. It would be rash, even arrogant, to reject our offers, and you don't strike me as being either. Be sensible.'

'I once thought I was a very sensible person. Or perhaps that was merely in comparison with the world we inhabited with my father. I have recently come to realise I am not at all sensible.'

'I wouldn't go quite that far. I've known you to show glimmerings of good judgement.' Rafe spoke behind her and she stiffened, her body giving her ample proof of her utter lack of sense.

'Cleopatra is eminently sensible,' Chris intervened. 'She's agreed to stay on the *Hesperus* while we conclude our first round of enquiries regarding her brother, a position and that weasel Pettifer. Much easier to co-ordinate our plan of attack from here than from some busy lodging house with suspicious matrons on the watch. Correct, Cleopatra?'

The wind whistled past them and far into the distance she could see a farmer's cart moving along a straight, empty road. It looked as foreign and outlandish as Acre had appeared to her a dozen years ago.

She did indeed need to manage on her own, and soon enough she would, but for the moment these two men were offering to smooth her path. Cleopatra the Queen would have expected nothing less. In fact, she would have demanded it.

'I agree. Thank you, Captain. However, my agreement is conditional.'

She directed the last part to Rafe and a smile picked up the corner of his mouth.

'Conditional on what, Queenie?'

'On your promise that you won't do anything behind my back.'

'I rarely make the same mistake twice, Cleo. I promise.'

She sat down with a thump at the Captain's table and re-folded the letter. She had expected nothing else, but the moment Rafe returned bearing Mr Fulton's response from the *Gazette*, her heart had gone into a hopeful gallop. It was doing that far too often these past months and usually for the wrong reasons.

'I presume that means your editor has not heard from your brother?' Rafe asked as he watched her.

'No, he hasn't. He presents his compliments to C. Osbourne and informs *him* he is interested in continuing his association with us at the same rates as before when D. Osbourne arrives in England.'

'Well, that is good news at least.'

'The only good news we have.'

'A first swallow of spring,' he replied, hiking his voice up and waving his hand with a flourish, and she smiled.

'You are in a fine mood. Have you visited your mother?'

'I would hardly be in a good mood if I had. That joy yet awaits me. But I have two more swallows in my pocket.'

'News of Dash?'

'No, Queenie. Not yet. The first is courtesy of Chris— he spoke with his aunt and by a stroke of good luck a widowed cousin of hers is in need of a companion while she is waiting for her sister to return from India to come live with her. I told you that family is a source of endless surprises, good and bad.'

'Oh.'

'Don't sound so glum. She is staying with her relative, a Mr John Soane. According to Chris, the house is a veritable museum of antiquities. You should feel right at home.'

'I was thinking of swearing off antiquarians for a dozen years or so.'

'You may do so soon enough with my best wishes, but not quite yet. Which brings me to my other swallow, or rather pigeon to be plucked—Mr Pettifer. I will be meeting with him this afternoon.'

She surged to her feet, a martial look in her eye.

'You mean *we* will be with meeting him this afternoon.'

'I think it is best you remain here.'

'It is *not* best. This is not merely a matter of collecting on his debt to us. Pettifer and my father often corresponded and he might know something of what happened between my father and Boucheron. We might be in England, but until I am certain Dash is here and safe, I must have a clearer idea what my father was involved in so I understand the risks.'

'I can do all that. I'm quite a hand at subterfuge.'

'I know you are, Mr Grey, however—' She broke off, examining his careful lack of expression. 'Are you making game of me?'

'Ever so slightly.'

'So you *did* intend for me to come with you?'

'Not precisely. *We* will meet with him, but *you* won't.'

'That makes no sense.'

'You will meet him as Patrick, not Miss Osbourne. Miss Osbourne will only make her appearance in a safe and proper setting as Mrs Phillips's companion. And *I* will ask the questions. Now go change back into a boy. If you *please*, Miss Osbourne.'

He shot her a half-mocking smile as he left the cabin and she changed as swiftly as possible and was still arranging her cravat when she hurried down the gangway to the awaiting carriage.

Rafe watched her struggles with the starched linen as the carriage drew off, his scrutiny making her fingers clumsier than usual.

'I feel as though someone is strangling me,' she muttered. 'I hate cravats. Why can I not wear a neckcloth like you?'

Rafe clicked his tongue impatiently. He, too, had changed clothes and was dressed in a rough serge coat and simple waistcoat and scuffed boots, yet he still looked far more impressive than she ever would in her respectable gentleman's clothing. It wasn't merely his size and the scars, but a quiet yet undeniable potency that was even more apparent here in the dank heaviness of London than in Egypt.

'Chin up. I shall try and salvage that disaster.'

She did as she was told, trying to keep her eyes on the squabs behind him and not on his face as he leaned towards her. His lids were lowered and his silvery eyes intent as he unravelled her knot and set about retying it. The pressure of his fingers at her throat was gentle, fleeting, but it was hard to breathe. She had an overpowering urge to touch him, even just rest her fingers against his thigh that was so close to hers. She counted out her breath and gave in to the need to look at him. It was absurd to be so happy that he was so close when all he was doing was fixing her cravat, but she was gathering these memories like fireflies in a jar.

She could count his lashes from here, see the fine meshing of grey and green in his eyes, the pressure of bone beneath his cheek and the moonscape of his scarred skin. She wanted so desperately to touch it again. In her mind she leaned forward just a little more, pressing against his fingers, brushing her mouth against his cheek, slipping along his freshly shaven jaw, absorbing the tension of his mouth, soothing it with hers until it softened…

'There.' He sounded as strangled as she felt and when he looked up she stayed there like a beached boat—bare and helpless.

'Cleo… No!'

'I wasn't doing anything.'

'You were thinking it hard enough. Damn it, we are in England now.'

'Is it outside the law to think about kissing in England?'

He leaned back, shoving his hands deep into his pockets.

'You know what I mean.'

'Yes.'

She fell silent and turned to look out the opposite window. It wasn't raining, but it certainly did not look like springtime. She'd expected the city outside the boundaries of the docks to look more like her memories of her village or the murkier memories she had of Dover, but here there was no hint of the green shores they'd passed—just brown and grey buildings with dark, blank windows. The people were also dressed in sombre colours and walked swiftly, heads down.

Very soon she would be swept up into this world and Rafe would continue in his. He had fulfilled his task—she was in London and safe, at least for the moment. Today or tomorrow might well be her last day in his company.

It was over. The most harrowing, intense, terrifying, exhilarating, confusing month of her life was over.

She would have to make the best of this as she had always done before, but for the first time in her life she wondered if she could. With this strange friendship she'd let slip the protective shield she had not even realised she wore until it fell away. Without it she felt both weaker and stronger. She'd allowed herself to feel and show need for the second time in her life and, unlike William, she knew that Rafe was worth it. Whether or not he could love her in return, she loved him.

She'd known she was heading down this path, but somehow she'd hoped she might avoid the destination. It felt like another part of her come home. Another wing unfurling as she crawled out of her chrysalis. There was so much of her that was coming to life these past weeks she wasn't certain she recognised herself any longer, but she was certain it was right. All this—this unravelling and knitting back together was right. Even if loving Rafe led to pain, it was still right.

She hugged herself against a sudden convulsive shiver. Without a word Rafe unfastened his coat and draped it over her legs. She tried to hand it back to him.

'I don't...'

'You are freezing. I don't want you falling ill.'

His arms were a folded bar across his chest. The shirt was of rough cotton and the sleeves a little short, just showing the fine dark hair on his forearms. They were rising in goosebumps and she realised he, too, must be cold. She shifted close to him on the seat and spread his coat over both their legs.

'We'll share.'

His arms were shifting, rising and falling where they rested against his chest. Her leg wasn't quite touching his, but she could feel its warmth, as if he was reaching out to her despite himself. She eased a little closer still, stopping when the fabric of his trousers touched hers.

'Cleo.' There was entreaty in his voice.

She moved away a little and wet her lips, the words forcing their way through the sudden ache in her throat. 'I liked being close to you, that is all. I'm not asking for a cottage and a garden. Just…some warmth.'

'*Ijo de cabron.*' He slipped his arm around her waist, pulling her on to his lap just like he had during the storm, tugging the coat around them both. 'There. Now we're close. But it's only for warmth in this mud puddle they call English weather.'

'Fine.'

She leaned her forehead against his cheek, her stomach contracting at the transition between the stubbled jaw and the smooth but twisted skin. He didn't like when she touched his scars, but she did, it was almost a compulsion. It took her closer to that fear of what might have been—he could have died, just as she could have died in Syene. As her mother and father had died. As Dash might even now be dead. Life was fleeting and gave no quarter. There was no fate, no faith, no guiding force watching over her, either evil or good. There was only life—this moment before it passed into another and was gone. She would weather this, too, but for now she wanted to be close.

As the tension eased from her she sighed, letting her eyes drift shut a moment. His arms jerked about her, as if he'd been prodded, and he seemed to relax them by force. But his voice was as tense as his muscles when he spoke.

'This is madness…'

She nodded and they stayed like that, shifting with the coach, his fingers resting on the back of her hand, brushing gently at the soft skin just at the junction of her fingers. He had such a gentle touch, as if she were a little chick dropped from a nest. But it didn't mask the strength beneath. That was as evident as the arousal that pulsed into life beneath her thighs as the carriage rumbled on. A moan bubbled through her at that telling pressure. He wanted her, too. For whatever reason and for however long, he felt at least a little of this burning. She could feel the urgent pressure of the blood pulsing at his neck—warm and alive—and she turned to touch her mouth to it. He tasted of the desert, of open space and vast nights and…hers.

When she was like this it felt so absolutely true. That he was *hers*.

This man, this touch.

She arched her hand, slipping his fingers between hers and clasping them. She should have resisted the urge because he groaned, moving her off his lap and leaning his head back against the squabs as he addressed the roof.

'Blast it, I'm doing it again. This is too serious to be taken lightly, Cleo. When we've dealt with Pettifer and are back on the *Hesperus*, you and I are going to talk. There is…something I must tell you.'

Something I must tell you. That sounded as ominous as al-Mizan's voice coming to claim her in her nightmares. Or William's voice the last time she'd seen him—in the dark evening outside their lodgings in Greece, two furtive figures, one with a very furtive secret. They'd often met like that, but this time his message had said he had something to tell her. She'd been in seventh heaven, certain he meant to propose and they would marry and return to England together. She'd never considered 'something' meant a wife and three children back in England. She'd learned a lot that week.

'What *thing*?' she asked, her voice dull and flat.

'Not now. We've arrived.'

The carriage turned off a main thoroughfare and slowed to a halt. Rafe reached across for the door and paused.

'Remember you are not to speak, Cleo. I will do the talking.'

His voice was abrupt and it snapped her temper back to her defence.

'What am I to do if I have questions? Write you a note? Whisper in your ear?'

His shoulder rose as if she'd done just that and tickled him in the process.

'*Carajo*. Very well, but keep your voice low and let's hope he just thinks you're young and effete.'

'I will speak like this.' She dropped her voice into a husky rasp. 'Will this do, sir?'

He exhaled a harsh breath.

'It will if you're trying to find a position on the stage at Drury Lane, or worse. If you must speak, try mumbling. I will translate. I'm not being stubborn for the sake of it, Cleo. People like Pettifer are dangerous; they are always on the verge of capsizing and seize at everything they can to stay afloat. Let's make certain it is not you.'

Mr Pettifer was a small man with eyes like a curious calf and a halo of soft brown curls and a bright red waistcoat embroidered all over with birds and flowers. He looked… sweet. Cleo mistrusted him immediately.

Rafe rejected his offer of ale and asked the innkeeper for whisky. Cleo wanted to demand some for herself as well, but refrained. She watched as Rafe picked up his glass and inspected Pettifer with such leisure that the man slowly began turning red. He gave a little laugh and tilted his head to one side, rather like the robins on his waistcoat.

'Well, sir? Your…friend was most insistent I meet you and here I am.'

'So you are. We have a mutual acquaintance, Mr Pettifer.'

'We do? I mean…how wonderful. May I ask whom?'

'A Mr Arthur Osbourne, lately of Egypt.'

'Osbourne. Charming fellow, charming. Good eye. Very good eye indeed.'

'So I hear. You share a penchant for mummies, yes?'

'We share a fascination with all things extraordinary.'

'Have you heard from him of late?'

'Oh, not for a year, I think.'

Rafe set down his glass and leaned forward.

'Lying will only make this conversation longer and more painful than necessary. You corresponded with him and you recently took shipment of several cases of mummified remains. Nod if you agree with those facts.'

Pettifer's head wobbled before it settled into a reluctant nod.

'Good. You owe payment on that shipment, Mr Pettifer. I am here to collect it on his behalf.'

'I assure you, I dispatched payment...'

Cleo leaned forward, but Rafe raised his hand.

'I said do not lie. I haven't the patience.'

Pettifer's smile held, but his eyes darted from side to side as if surveying an internal inventory of lies. Finally, he sighed.

'I am certain some accommodation could be made.'

'*Will* be made. A man of mine will come to collect first thing tomorrow. Be certain to have payment ready or those mummies just might take on a life of their own and do a little damage to your exhibits during the dark hours.'

'Surely there is no need for violence.'

'That is completely up to you, Pettifer.' He paused. 'Now that we've settled that, tell me what Osbourne did to set Boucheron on his tail.'

Pettifer's cherubic face flushed from his shirt points to his carefully brushed curls. He flapped his hands.

'Pray lower your voice. Osbourne may have been so foolish as to challenge that man, but I am not.'

'Challenge him? How? Don't slide away now, Pettifer. Just answer the question.'

'I do not know for certain. Osbourne always had more ambition than sense. It was clear from his correspondence he did not enjoy taking part in supplying antiquities of… dubious origin to creditable establishments and collectors. It went against his fantasy of becoming respectable. In his last letter he asked me for the direction of someone trustworthy at the British Museum and whether I had heard who had acquired a large granite statue of Horus sent recently from Luxor.'

Cleo clenched her hands but Rafe gently pressed his boot on hers.

'And what did you reply?' he asked.

'I asked what he meant by trustworthy. He did not write back.'

'In other words you evaded his questions.'

'Well, I felt it best not to become involved. Boucheron has connections in my little world, even in England. I tend my little garden and keep out of others'.'

'Of course. So do you know who acquired this statue?'

'Not in England, though I did hear a statue of Horus along with a most excellent sarcophagus were acquired by the Louvre for well over one thousand pounds.'

Cleo swallowed. No wonder her father had begun to turn against Boucheron—she was quite certain he had never seen a fraction of those sums.

Rafe's gaze captured hers before turning back to Pettifer.

'Have you by any chance heard from Osbourne's son?'

Pettifer frowned.

'No. I have never had the felicity to meet him. Why?'

Cleo wished she could have heard a shadow of a lie in his answer, but she felt he spoke an uncomplicated truth. If Dash had arrived in England before her, he had not contacted Pettifer.

'Never mind why,' Rafe answered. 'Should you hear from him or of him you will place an advertisement in *The Times* saying Mr P. has an item for Mr G. and then watch the advertisements the following day for instructions. Do you understand?'

'I really don't see why—'

'Think mummies in the night, Pettifer...'

Pettifer sighed and nodded. '*The Times*. Mr P. has an item for Mr G.'

'Good.' Rafe stood and Cleo followed suit. 'Anything else, Patrick?'

Cleo shook her head. She felt deflated and weary as she followed Rafe outside into the drizzle. It wasn't merely what they'd learned from Pettifer.

We need to talk.

'Thank you for helping me, Rafe.'

'You are welcome. You had no idea those so-called souvenirs were being sold as actual antiquities, did you?'

'No. Boucheron must be mad, selling them to museums. The risk is enormous.'

'That depends. If a single piece was suspected, Boucheron could claim he himself had acquired it in ignorance. But if your father had intimated this was no innocent mistake, but a large-scale endeavour, his reputation would be ruined and no one would buy from him. I would wager the infamous book al-Mizan was sent to retrieve was a record your father was keeping of these items. Chris told me he heard Boucheron transported a large shipment of antiquities on a ship to Marseilles only a few weeks before we sailed. God knows how many of those were forgeries.'

'What shall we do?'

'I will have a word with Chris. He knows these people. I don't want you involved in this in any way... For your brother's sake.'

She had been about to speak, but his last words stopped her, as he must have known they would. It galled her to be shut out like this, but he was right. Clearly Boucheron had ties in London as well. Until she was certain Dash was safe, she must keep out of it.

He appeared to be waiting for her to say something, but the only words that came were, 'I wish I was a man. Being a woman is like running uphill with pebbles in one's shoes.'

His smile was weak and there was no sign of humour in his eyes—they were far more grey than green and the scars were grey-tinged as well.

'I wish you'd been a man, too. This would have been much easier. But you will be safe with this widow and sur-rounded by a host of mouldy antiquarians. For all you know you might discover you enjoy being in a household like Soane's. Whatever slurs you cast on them, I can see how much you love that world. I'll wager you'll all too soon be fending off sonnets and marriage proposals by the dozen.'

There was conviction in his words, as if he'd already settled her future in his mind and was casting her away on the current like a paper boat.

'Don't be foolish,' she snapped, struggling to contain the gnawing pain in her chest. But then the anger, too, faded away, a paper fire only, leaving her cold and ashen and resigned.

She'd known what he was—he was far more a nomad than ever Gamal was, because Mr Rafael Grey had no set route to travel. His very being was defined by chance—chance encounters with those who might need his services for a while before cutting themselves loose again once their objective was fulfilled. He was instrumental, incidental. He had no substance of his own to anyone except Birdie, his brother and, for a brief tragic while, his little nephew.

And for an even briefer while, to her.

Which was her mistake, not his.

Chapter Eighteen

Rafe followed Cleo out of the carriage and up the gangway, gathering his resolve with each step.

He could no longer avoid the inevitable. They'd crossed the issues of Cleo's finances, lodgings and occupation from the list. That meant she was safe. More importantly, she was no longer in his care.

It was time to tell her the truth.

She stopped in the middle of the deck, raising her face to the first drops of rain.

'I'd forgotten about English rain,' she said. 'It's so different from rain in Egypt or the storms at sea, but it feels like…home.'

Home.

He raised his own face to the sullen flicking of cold pins and needles and rubbed his chest. His pulse felt thick, as if struggling through a peat bog.

'Come inside.'

She followed without a word. Once inside the cabin, she went to stand by the table, leaning one hand on its surface.

He felt as anxious as she looked. The time of truth had come and he had no idea why this was so very hard. Why he had not just said it weeks ago. It was not such a great matter after all, was it?

My name is not Rafe Grey, though that *is* who I am… whom I have been for most of my life.

My name is Rafael Edward James Braden Edgerton and I happen to be the Duke of Greybourne and it is now time for me to face my past and my future and I would like to ask you to be part of it.

Perfectly sensible speech.

I am the Duke of Greybourne.

Just say it.

'Rafe? Are you well? You look…pale.'

'I…uh. My name is not Rafe.'

Her brows drew together.

'I know that. It is Rafael.'

'No, what I meant to say was…' Oh, hell, why was this so hard? It felt as though he was about to voluntarily walk off a cliff.

No, it felt as though he was about to kill Rafe Grey. Reach in and murder him with his own hands just as his father had once tried to murder that poor maid.

And he had no idea what would take his place.

He finally opened that door an inch wider. Time to let her in.

'My father was a violent man.' The words left him in a rush. 'My first real memory of my father was when he broke my brother's arm. I have no idea why. Not that there had to be a reason—it could be anything. That final time, before I left, we were in chapel and he tried to strangle Susan, our maid, simply because she laughed. I remember every second of that day except for the few short moments when I lunged at him to pull him off and was thrashed by him. Those moments are…gone, as if I'd slept through them. They've never come back. The next day I ran away to enlist and that's where I met Birdie. For years I tested myself to see if that strain of violence was in me. I was certain it would find its way to the surface sooner or later. So I became a soldier and a mercenary and—'

'It isn't in you, Rafe,' she interrupted with finality.

'You don't know that.'

'Yes, I do. I think you do as well; at least I hope you do. There is a different between using force when you must and being ruled by it or being blind to its effect on others.'

He gave a small laugh.

'Is there?'

'I believe there is. I don't think you allow yourself to be ruled by anything but conscience and caution, and you are certainly anything but blind to others. You must know you are not like your father.'

He breathed in and out. 'I prefer to believe I am not. I have never felt the pull of it, but the fact is that violence has shaped my life in too many ways to count. But that is not what I wanted to tell you...it is merely so you can understand why I did what I did...'

He rubbed his forehead, wishing the words would somehow appear out of the muddle. Now that the moment was here he wanted to stop it, delay it just a little further. Tell Chris to raise anchor and take them back into the emptiness of the ocean so she would have time to absorb the truth. Not when the very next moment she must go play companion to a widow and her lapdog and he must go confront his living ghosts.

He'd made ill use of his time with her, hemmed in by conscience and pointless convention, just as she'd said. He might not wholly be his father's son, but perhaps he was more his mother's son than he'd hoped.

He breathed deeply, searching for that elusive streak of valiance that would propel him forward. Cleo came and took his hands; they felt clammy in her warm clasp.

'Rafe? Something is wrong. I can see it is. What is it? Just *tell* me.'

He'd known this was coming the moment he'd received the letter informing him of his father's death. Rafe Grey, all of twenty years old, was about to be extinguished. Rafael Edgerton, Duke of Greybourne, had to step back on to the stage and he had not the faintest idea who he was.

Just tell her and make it real. Rafe Grey is no more… He'd never truly existed.

Just *tell* her.

'Cleo. I'm not…'

There was a clumping as someone ran along the corridor and Cleo dropped his hands. Rafe hoped whoever it was stopped before they reached Chris's cabin, but then the door swung open and Birdie strode in, a letter in his hand and his usually equable countenance twisted with anxious tension. Cleo moved towards him, her eyes wide with concern.

'Birdie, what is it?'

'It's a letter from Paul, Elmira's brother.'

Rafe caught Birdie by the shoulders and felt them shaking. If he'd ever wondered how much Birdie cared for Elmira, he knew now.

'What happened?'

'She's not dead. But he writes she's ill. This letter was sent three weeks ago, Rafe. Three *weeks* ago. I must leave *now.*'

'Of course. We'll ride out as soon as we find horses.'

'You needn't—'

'I'm not letting you go alone. It's a long way to the Lakes and you'll need someone to see you don't ride yourself into exhaustion and a ditch. You'll be in no state to help Elmira if you do.'

'You have your own affairs—'

'They've waited until now; they will wait a little longer. Go pack and I'll hire the horses.'

Birdie nodded, his mouth a tense downward bow. He cast a quick look at Cleo.

'I'm sorry, Miss Cleo.'

To Rafe's surprise, and Birdie's as well, Cleo hugged him fiercely.

'Don't be foolish. Godspeed, Birdie.'

He mumbled something incoherent and hurried out.

'Is there anything I can do?' Cleo asked. Rafe considered and discarded blurting out his admission. Cleo was safe for the moment and what he had to say was something he could barely manage when he was coherent, let alone with Birdie's fear hanging over him.

'Yes. Go with Chris to this Mrs Phillips and wait for your brother. When I return London we will finish this conversation, but now I must go with Birdie.'

'Of course you must. Please be careful, both of you.'

He nodded and made it to the door before turning back, almost by compulsion. He had no idea what to say that could be said in the minutes ticking by at Birdie's expense, so instead he crossed the room back to her. He raised her and placed her neatly on the table before clasping her face gently between his hands. They were still cold and now also shaking a little as he brushed the feathery hair back from her cheeks and brow. He wanted to take her with them, have her ride by his side and Birdie's. He had no clear idea what he was doing, but he didn't want to leave her here. He didn't want to leave her.

She smiled and brushed her hands over his, slipping her fingers between his.

He kissed her hard and she opened to him with her warm generosity, her hands threading through his hair and over his nape before drawing back.

'You must hurry.'

'I know. Stay out of trouble, Pat.'

Chapter Nineteen

Lincoln's Inn Fields, London—two weeks later...

The tall arched windows of Soane House were bright with candlelight though it was only just turning dark. It seemed to stand forward from the row of rain-drenched, dark-windowed and dark-bricked houses, a happy invitation to enter and be amazed.

Rafe shoved his hands deeper into his pockets, gathering his resolve. Somewhere behind that cheerful façade was one Miss Cleopatra Osbourne, companion and thorn in his side. He'd rehearsed his admission *ad nauseum* during the interminable ride north and back, but now the moment of truth was upon him he felt the words fizzle and fade once more. It wasn't the words that would matter in the end; it was Cleo.

In a matter of minutes Cleo would decide which path his life took. There had been times when others held his life in their hands, but strangely he'd never felt as powerless before fate as he did now.

He'd missed her every moment of these long, long two weeks. All his faculties for gauging danger, for scanning the future for pitfalls, had been engaged with her. His mind had populated the dank grey skies and muddy roads and indifferent posting houses with an accounting of the past weeks from the first moment she'd appeared in his room in Syene. He'd leafed through every image, fixing it in his memory as if it was already fading in the damp of his new life.

It scared him because that was what he'd done after Jacob's death as he'd tended to Edge's misery, holding his own inside. He'd held each memory of his nephew like a drop of dew, willing it not to break and spill. And now he was doing the same with her as if she'd already turned her back on him and begun walking her own path, without him.

Sometimes he was convinced she must care for him as he did for her. That it could not merely be friendship and gratitude and the physical fascination of an undeniably passionate woman. But he couldn't get past the fact that, despite all that had happened between them, he recognised in her that strength that would allow her to move on despite tragedies and loss. She might already be consigning him to the trash heap of her past, determined to make the best of what she now had.

He'd thought…he'd truly believed he was the same, but she'd snatched that fiction from him. He knew he could manage if he had to, but for the first time in his life, he didn't want to. He needed her—her love, her hands holding his, her eyes telling him she wanted to be with him. He wanted to make her smile and keep her safe. With him.

He should be happy for her if she was settling into her new life. It was unfair to want her to be as confused and agonised by this separation as he was, yet he wanted precisely that.

He wanted, quite desperately, for her to need him.

He squared his shoulders and brushed the drizzle from his face, preparing himself. He'd just stepped on to the path when the door opened and a figure stepped out, leading a small mop of a dog. Rafe shifted back into the shadows and watched as they crossed the road towards the square, his heart picking up speed as if in the presence of danger.

The storm had left leaves all over the path and the dog snuffled happily at the damp debris, its long hair gathering samples as it went. With her face hidden by a bonnet, a pelisse most likely borrowed as it was both too large and too short, and her purposeful stride reduced to the dog's shuffle, he might easily have walked by her on the street without even noticing.

But then she looked up at the sky as if out of a deep hole and it was like waking up in the vastness of the desert, the soft halo of a sunrise behind the hills. Again he felt the same blessing of being alive that had begun to unfurl in him since he'd met Cleo. Those weeks in the desert and on the *Hesperus* he'd felt…content.

He rubbed his chest, trying to still the nervous thumping. Then he took a deep breath and came up the path behind her.

'Hello, Cleo-Pat.'

Both she and the dog jumped. The dog gave a throaty cough, but after its first outrage came to snuffle at his boots. Rafe crouched down to pet the tubby ball of hair, buying time.

'How does he see where he's going?' he asked, pulling the soggy skeleton of a leaf from its fur. 'What's your name, little fellow?'

'Perseus, but we call him Percy.' Her voice was muffled and it was a moment before she spoke again. 'Thank you for sending me word so promptly that Mrs Herndale was recovered. I was worried for Birdie.'

He risked looking up and wished her face was in its expressive mode. It was unfair that just when he needed her to show something, she could flatten everything out. Her skin was still darker than the approved English complexion and strands of her short hair were escaping the confines of her bonnet, feathering on her forehead and cheeks.

He scratched the dog's head, took another deep breath and stood. Now she had to look up to meet his gaze, but it gave him no real advantage. Her uptilted face and the sweep of her throat were so familiar he felt his throat tighten with something between pain and relief. It was still Cleo.

'You look tired, Rafe.'

Definitely still Cleo.

'I have just arrived from the north.'

'Have your affairs not gone well? Is aught wrong with your family?'

'I don't know. I haven't seen them yet.'

Her brows took wing.

'Why not? I thought that would be your first order of business.'

My first order of business was to see you.

He didn't say it because she was right. Once he told her the truth, going to Greybourne should be his first order of business. He had to face his demons and discover precisely what he was about to offer before he did. She deserved a home, stability…the promise of her own pack of jackals. If he could not find it inside him to offer her that, he should not offer her anything at all. She must be able to trust him and that meant he would have to trust her.

He waited for the slap of fear and it didn't come. Of all the shifting, roiling chaos inside him, that was solid—he might not know who the Duke of Greybourne was, but he knew who Cleopatra Osbourne was and he trusted her.

'You needn't answer me if you don't wish,' she said, cutting into his thoughts and hurrying on before he could recover his wits. 'Chris wrote to me yesterday. He has been very good at following your orders to keep an eye on me. He has even offered to review the article I am writing for the *Gazette*.'

'Has he? Kind of him.'

Her brows rose slightly at his tone.

'It is kind. He is a good man.'

His unwelcome burst of jealousy faded.

'He is. The very best. I'll be happy to review it, as well, if you like. What is it about?'

Her dimples finally appeared.

'It is an account of my journey to Nubia and back. Expurgated, of course.'

'No mention of scarred mercenaries, I hope? I prefer to operate in the shadows.'

'You are very inconspicuous, indeed, Mr Grey. And, no, you are not featured in my article. I knew you wouldn't appreciate the notoriety. I am writing about al-Mizan, however. I wish I knew more of him; I find myself regretting I did not speak with him after all.'

'I find myself grateful you didn't.'

'I thought you liked him.'

'I do. I appreciate sensible people.'

She smiled, but her tone was wistful. 'I don't think I am very sensible, not truly. If I were, I wouldn't be talking to a man in a darkened square within sight of my employer's window.'

'I'll amend that. You are part-sensible, part-impulsive, and an assemblage of several dozen other conflicting parts.'

'Goodness. I sound like a mad aunt's quilt.'

'Hardly. More like one of those Dutch paintings with everything happening all at once, but at the centre there's a joyous, steadfast core.'

It was hardly a gallant compliment, but she flushed and looked a little stunned. He had no idea where that strange thought had come from and it wasn't until he'd spoken the words that he realised how true they were. All those conflicting parts might turn him into a confused, lustful boy, but it was that deep, calm core of hers that made his breathing ease and settle when he was with her. It was a strange feeling and he hadn't noticed it until he'd felt its absence these past two weeks.

God, he'd missed her.

Leaves skittered along the path around them, whispering against the damp earth. Above them the trees were rustling with growing impatience.

Make a move, man! Just tell her.

He shoved his hands into his pockets, encountering the little parcel there. He fished it out and shoved it at her.

'I brought you something. I saw it in the market in Ambleside and remembered the story you told me. It's nothing. A jest.'

She took it with a quick glance at him and unfolded it to reveal a rolled length of blue ribbon.

'Rafe! It is just like the one I stole from Annie Packham.' Her voice was muted, but he could feel that welling of emotion in her she fought so hard to keep at bay. He felt absurdly accomplished that he'd found something that could do that to her. He wanted to wrap his hands around hers and cocoon that silly strip of ribbon between them.

He took a step forward.

'Miss! Miss!'

They both turned to see a small figure bundled in a shawl and mobcap hurrying up the path.

'That's Betsy, Mrs Phillips's maid,' Cleo said with resignation just as the young woman came to a stop several paces away, eyeing Rafe warily.

'Is this fellow bothering you, miss?'

Cleo's dimples quivered.

'No, Betsy. He is a friend of the family and, despite appearances, he is quite harmless.'

Betsy's face hid none of her scepticism.

'Mrs Phillips saw you from the window and sent me to fetch you and Percy back so you can be ready in time for the guests, miss.'

'Thank you, Betsy.'

If Cleo's quiet words were a hint, Betsy ignored it. She

stood, arms folded, all five feet of her radiating disapproval.

'It's coming on to rain, miss,' she added pointedly. It was true—the heavy clouds were succumbing once again to their weight, dropping big melancholy drops through the leaves.

Cleo sighed and looked back at Rafe.

'I must go. I'm glad Birdie and Mrs Herndale are well.'

She hesitated and he pushed back his frustration, but there was nothing he could do.

You're not in Egypt any longer, fool. This is London.

'I will come by tomorrow to make a more formal entrance, Miss Osbourne. Will you be here?'

She smiled, brushed away a drop of rain that splattered on her cheek and gathered the snuffling dog in her arms.

'Where else might I be?'

Chapter Twenty

'**W**ell, about time you returned to London,' Chris said as he handed Rafe a towel. 'And in the nick of time, too. Cesario has come on stage.'

Rafe dried his rain-soaked face and hair, but his mind was still in the windblown square, kicking him for having once again let the moment slide away. If ever he'd needed proof of his cowardice, his fear of putting his fate to the touch was conclusive evidence. It should have been the first thing out of his mouth: 'My name isn't Rafe Grey. It is Rafael Edgerton, Duke of Greybourne, and by the way—will you marry me?'

Well, perhaps not quite like that...

'Are you even listening to me?' Chris demanded. 'I said Cesario is here.'

'Who is where?'

'I'll translate. Dashford Osbourne is in London.'

That finally penetrated Rafe's self-flagellating fog.

'Are you certain?'

'Benja has been keeping an eye open on new arrivals and when he heard the *Nightingale* was arriving from Egypt he went to watch the disembarkation and spotted him right away. He said the resemblance to Cleo was unmistakable. He followed him to the Four Bells where the boy took a room. Gave his name to the innkeeper as Thomas Mowbray.'

'Don't tell me. That's the name of some Shakespearean fool.'

'Of sorts. In the play he's a nobleman loyal to King Richard the Second who banishes him for a crime he himself committed.'

'Hmph. Clearly he has issues with the deceased Mr Osbourne.'

'Fathers do appear to be a bone of contention of late.'

Rafe cast him a malevolent look.

'Don't tempt me to strike back, Chris.' He tossed the towel over the back of a char. 'Let's go there.'

'Unfortunately, he's no longer there.'

'You lost him?'

'I didn't know you were in London so I went there, but the room was empty. Apparently the boy used it as a decoy. Benja and the others are out searching the other inns.'

'Come along, then. I want the young pup secured as soon as possible.'

'Where will you take him? Here or your place in Lambeth?'

He hesitated.

'I'd best take him directly to Cleo. Then…we shall see. I need to see Edge, too…' He hesitated. 'I've had my contacts keep track while I've been up north. Apparently he is back and he is married.'

'What? Good Lord, when did he manage that?'

'In Cairo, apparently. To Lady Samantha Carruthers.'

'Lady… Isn't that Lucas Sinclair's sister?'

'The same.'

'Is that good? Bad? Horrific?'

'It is excellent. I hope. The timeline worries me. Three years he stays in Brazil scribbling away, then in a few weeks he apparently traverses Egypt, marries Lady Samantha and returns to England. He's being impetuous and that's out of character. I don't want to see him hurt.'

'Then put him out of his misery and tell him you're alive and well.'

'Once we find Cleo's brother I'll go see him and hope he doesn't plant me a facer. I'd hate to have to pay my visit of ceremony on Cleo tomorrow with a black eye.'

'Your visit of…well, about time. All the more reason we should find Dash before he absconds again.'

'Damn and blast the fool.' Rafe stood in the middle of the Eagle and Crown's courtyard, glaring at the shuttered windows. The room let to Mr Mowbray was as empty as the one in the Four Bells. 'Where the devil has he gone now?'

Chris yawned and wound his scarf tighter against cold air.

'I thought you said he was a scholar? He's being damned cautious.'

'He is a scholar, but he's also Cleo's brother. Clearly mistrust runs in the family.'

'Well, we'll pick up the trail tomorrow. At least we know he's alive and on dry land. Go tell Viola. That should please her.'

He wandered off and Rafe headed in the other direction, staring at nothing as he wove through the alleys towards the main thoroughfare.

Of course he had to tell Cleo right away. Perhaps her delight would melt those careful barricades she'd mounted. Perhaps enough to… To what? She was not the type of woman who would accept a proposal because he'd produced her brother. Or a title and fortune. She would either accept him on his own merits and her own feelings or not at all…

It was the faintest of sounds, but what caught his attention was that he'd heard it before, just after leaving the Eagle and Crown.

One of the most distinctive sounds was that of a man walking with unnatural caution. The denizens of the docks bent on mischief knew better than to make such a mistake.

He paused in the centre of a crossing. There was not enough light for anyone to cast shadows and he did not bother trying to trick the fellow into revealing himself.

'Dash Osbourne, you're lucky Cleo is fond of you because I'm tempted to break your leg so you'll stay put and not cause us any more headaches.'

He waited.

A figure moved out of the alley and the faint light from the tavern down the road raised a reddish glint off the man's dark hair. Rafe felt an absurd, almost painful relief. Finally.

'You're the one who left the message for me in Alexandria?' the man asked.

He even sounded like Cleo. Rafe was so tempted to grab the boy and truss him up safely before something happened.

'Yes. What the devil are you about, setting up lodgings at half the taverns in London?'

'I thought I noticed someone following me when I disembarked. I thought perhaps there'd been someone on the ship with me after all and I needed to be certain I was wrong before I went to look for Cleo. Then I heard you speaking with that man about me.' He took another step closer, but there was still a good six yards between them. 'Do you know where Cleo is?'

'She's companion to a Mrs Phillips at the house of Mr John Soane in Lincoln Inn Fields.'

'Companion? *Cleo?*'

'I know, it doesn't sit well, but for the moment it serves its purpose. I will take you there now. I think under the circumstances we will be forgiven for the late hour.' He moved forward, but the younger man stepped back, holding up his hand to stop him.

'I shall go on my own.'

'Cleo will have my hide if I don't see you there safely.'

'I'm going on my own. I've heard of Mr Soane and can find my way.'

'This is ridiculous. I'll follow you, you know.'

'If you insist. Waste of a cab fare.'

Rafe debated actually trussing the fellow up, but though delivering him to Cleo held an appeal, delivering him bruised and hog-tied didn't. Instead, he followed at a reasonable distance and when Dash Osbourne waved down a hackney on a busy thoroughfare, he did the same.

When his hackney stopped before the distinctive house of Mr Soane, Dash Osbourne was already on the steps. He looked back as Rafe descended from his cab and gave him a slight salute of the hand. Then the door opened and light and the sound of company poured into the cool street.

Rafe cursed beneath his breath as he paid the cabbie—he'd forgotten Soane was entertaining that evening. He stood on the other side of the road until it began to drizzle once more. England thus far wasn't proving very welcoming and he wished once again he could somehow transport himself and Cleo back to the desert. Back to travelling with Birdie and Gamal, helping her evade Kabir's jealous nips and talking into the night. Knowing what he knew now, he would make better use of his time with her.

He wished he could see the look on her face when Dash appeared, but he had no intention of walking into a social event. He could hardly present himself as Mr Grey to people who might already be Cleo's friends and certainly not as the Duke of Greybourne. That was not how he wished for Cleo to discover the truth about him.

He turned westwards, walking swiftly. The frustration that had been plaguing him now for weeks was reaching fever pitch. He should be happy, delighted even. He'd brought her safely to London, found her a position, found her young fool of a brother. But he wasn't. He didn't know what he was any longer. He was becoming soppier than Hamlet—swinging between antic moods and melodrama. He was becoming ridiculous.

And careless.

On the docks he'd been cautious and alert, but as he headed through the drizzle on to Duke Street, his mind remained by that well-lit house on the square. When he felt the oh-so-gentle tug he acted out of instinct to disarm the pest. He couldn't even blame the cutpurse for what happened.

As he knocked away the hand trying to separate his purse from his person, the pickpocket gave a surprised squawk, lurched backwards and slipped on the slimy cobbles. Rafe had just managed to grab the man's coat and haul him upright when he felt the sting to his thigh.

He was acquainted with that sensation through long experience with the wrong end of a knife. He shoved the man against the wall and pinned his knife hand. It wasn't a large knife, but sharp enough to slit a man's purse from its strings without being noticed. The man stared wide-eyed at Rafe and then down at the darkening stain on Rafe's trouser, visible even in the dark.

'Gad's truth, I didna mean to—'

'I know, you fool. Blast it. I don't have time for this. Go away.'

'Ye'd best bind it...'

'I don't need barber's advice from a cutpurse. What the devil were you thinking, going after someone my size?'

'The big ones are oft the slowest...begging your pardon, sir. I didna ken you was a blooming soldier. I don't go after swads less they're boozy. I'm no Tyburn blossom.'

Rafe let him go, untied his neckcloth and wound it around his thigh.

'I was in the rifles, not a redcoat, but you've made certain I've a set of red breeches now. What are you still doing here? Waiting to see if I drop dead from this scratch so you can turn scavenger?'

''Tis more than a scratch, that is. Ye might be needing a crocus.'

Rafe gritted his teeth as he tightened the knot.

'I don't need a blasted surgeon. You've done a fine job of cupping me already. You sound like a soldier yourself.'

'Aye, sir. Invalided at Ciudad Rodrigo, sir.'

Rafe sighed and opened his purse. The world could always be depended upon to remind one to count one's blessings.

'Here, take the night off from knuckling.'

'I can't take that, sir!'

'Why not?'

'*Why not?* I've pinked 'ee. T'wouldn't be right.'

'Don't quibble. I deserve to pay for lowering my guard. Try not to guzzle it in one night.'

The man drew himself up. 'I don't indulge in spirits, sir.'

'You're a better man than I, then.' Rafe tested his weight on his wounded leg. Pain slashed up and down like a dozen razors had been sown into his flesh.

There would be no visit to Sinclair House tonight. He would be lucky to reach his rooms.

'You can earn it by finding me the closest hackney, Soldier.'

'Fair enough. Pitch yourself at the corner there and I'll nab one for 'ee.'

Rafe had no idea how old his attacker was, but he was undeniably swift on his feet. By the time Rafe dragged himself to the end of the road, there was a hackney waiting, the driver squinting at him suspiciously.

'I don't want trouble with the Watch, see?' he growled, waving his whip, but the pickpocket merely snorted in disdain as he helped Rafe into the grimy vehicle.

'Pipe down, Jarvis. He's a flash swell and well equipped.'
And then to Rafe, 'Best see a barber, anyhow, sir.'

Rafe shook his head and shoved the coin into the man's hand and after a moment's hesitation the pickpocket melted back into the dark. Rafe gave the hackney driver the direction of the rooms he kept for his use in London, leaned back carefully and prepared himself for a long, painful ride.

Chapter Twenty-One

There were benefits to living, however temporarily, in what more closely resembled a museum than a home, Cleo thought. It wasn't merely Mr Soane's wondrous collection of antiquities that filled every corner of his house, but the fascinating people it drew like moths about a scholarly flame. They were very different from the dubious characters in her father's circles. Right now, for example, her employer Mrs Phillips was happily engaged in a heated discussion about the origins of the myth of Medea with two scholars and a few moments ago Cleo had a fascinating discussion regarding the latest news on the decipherment of the hieroglyphics.

Dash would undoubtedly enjoy himself in such a setting. Usually so would she, except she was...distracted. Her thoughts returned stubbornly again and again to the dark square and to Rafe. She could almost feel the blue ribbon burning a hole in her reticule.

A strange, gleeful, hopeful ball of warmth kept appearing somewhere deep in her chest, like a bubble struggling to rise.

He'd brought her a ribbon and would visit her tomorrow. A formal visit.

His tale of his father's violence made sense of so many

things about him and had even given her hope… She knew he liked her, was attracted to her. She'd seen it even in those brief moments in the square. She didn't know if there was more than that, if he felt any of the harsh, deep-cut need that struck her every time she thought of him or saw him or woke to a day empty of his presence.

She knew so little of his history and he knew all of hers, yet she felt she knew him better than she'd ever known a person, perhaps even better than she knew herself, for she was discovering she was not at all as she had thought all her life. Not cold, not wholly self-sufficient, not accepting of her fate.

She was alive and bursting with a need to be with him. Not just for what he might give her, but because more than ever she felt she had so much to give him. She was right for him.

He'd brought her a ribbon and was coming tomorrow. All she had to do was make it through this evening and the night and…

The crowd before her parted, creating a temporary path between her and a tall, dark-haired man who stood speaking with Mr Soane. Her heart catapulted up into her throat and for one joyous moment she thought Rafe had decided to act sooner than anticipated on his promise to visit.

But then her heart fell to the floor, flapping like a landed fish. The resemblance was uncanny—the slightly aquiline slant of the nose and the determined chin, the sun-warmed skin and that slow curve of a smile… But this was not Rafe. It was the jaw, bare of scars, that which made her chest contract and her eyes burn as they had each time loneliness caught her these past weeks.

Mr Soane's footman was just passing and Cleo rose quietly and stopped him before he entered the servants' passageway. 'Who is that tall man speaking with Mr Soane, Henry?'

The footman glanced over her shoulder.

'That is Lord Edward Edgerton, miss. He is here with Lady Edward.' His nod indicated a tall woman with laughing blue eyes and dark hair.

Cleo knew from his tone Henry had more to tell her so she motioned him towards the back stairs leading to the kitchens. It was no doubt not at all the thing to gossip with the servants, but she *had* to know.

'What do you know of them, Henry?'

'Well, miss, they are new back from Egypt and newly wed, too. She's a Sinclair,' he said and she nodded though it meant nothing to her. 'Everyone's talking about how it's he and Lady Edward that wrote those *Desert Boy* novels.' Henry allowed himself a gratified smile at her expression of shock. 'It's true, miss! They appeared tonight quite by surprise, too. Not that they would be turned away, not in a million years. Not the authors of *Desert Boy* books and brother to the Disappearing Duke, to boot. I don't doubt Mr Soane is right pleased they've come.'

'The Disappearing Duke?' she whispered.

'Yes, miss. Everyone knows the story. Lord Edward's elder brother, heir to the Duke of Greybourne, he ran away to the army when he was a boy. He's the new Duke a year now, but there's been not a peep from him. There are even rumours he's dead, which means Lord Edward will be the next Duke. Now if you'll excuse me, miss. I must bring these downstairs.'

She nodded and stood aside, staring at nothing.

Was this what Rafe had wanted to tell her? Her mind had taken her fears quite a few places these past weeks—a wife, children, an engagement, an illness, a crime... She'd imagined them all.

Or at least she thought she had. She hadn't imagined a duchy. It should be a relief compared with all the scenarios her mind had conjured, but it wasn't. And just now in the square...

That was what he'd meant to tell her. Not her foolish dreams, just his conscience giving him no rest once more.

No wonder he'd tried so hard to keep her in her place all this time. He was no fool, he must have seen she'd begun to weave him into her dreams…her cottage and her pack of jackals… He done his best to gently dismantle the bridges she kept insisting on building between them.

He might not be a scoundrel like William, but she'd been as blind with him as she had been ten years before. And of the scenarios she imagined, this revelation set an ocean between them as solidly as if he *were* already married.

Perhaps this was what it would feel like to suddenly discover the secret of the hieroglyphs—signs that had been before her all along were blindingly suddenly clear. Discussions between Rafe and Birdie, Captain Chris's taunts… Bears and Dukes and Viola and Greybeard…

Greybourne. Grey. Bourne.

She welcomed the anger, opened the door for it and dragged it in by the collar.

He and Captain Chris had talked over her head as though she was a child. All along he'd treated her a little like a child, hadn't he? Stay here, Cleo. Eat. Sleep. Be good, Cleo.

Throwing plates was too good for him! She should drop a pyramid on him. Feed him to Kabir and toss the remains to the Nilc crocodiles.

She shrank back into the shadows as a group came through the passage. It was Mr Soane and the woman Henry had pointed out as Lady Edward. They headed to the display room which was filled floor to ceiling with prints and paintings.

It was impulse that sent Cleo after them and made her wait until Lady Edwards remained alone in the room. When Cleo entered, the other woman was looking through framed drawings that filled a specially made cupboard that opened like pages of a book, each one hung with framed prints.

'You are Lady Edward Edgerton, are you not?'

Lady Edward turned at Cleo's overly brusque question, surprise and wariness evident on her attractive face.

'Yes. I'm afraid you have the advantage of me, Miss…?'

'Miss Osbourne.' Something flickered in the other woman's eyes and curiosity turned to intentness. Without a doubt her name meant something to Lady Edward. So Rafe had discussed her with his brother, perhaps even consulted on how best to deal with her. 'Are you here because of me?'

'I beg your pardon?' The woman's eyes widened.

'I knew the moment I saw Lord Edward that he must be closely related to the man I knew as Mr Grey. He did mention a brother and, if that is the nature of their relationship, I can understand why he did not see fit to share his true name with me. But that is hardly the point. If you are here by coincidence, I apologise, but if you are here on my account, pray tell him I do not need to be watched like a newborn lamb. He has done enough already.'

Lady Edward hesitated before answering.

'The Greybournes are a stubborn lot. They mean well, though.'

'So I have noticed on both counts. Truly I am grateful for his help thus far, but there is nothing more to be done. And if he is indeed that… Disappearing Duke everyone is gossiping about, clearly he has his own affairs to see to.'

'I find that Edge… Lord Edward has a fixation with seeing things through. Perhaps his brother suffers from the same weakness?'

Cleo snorted.

'That is putting it mildly. I am grateful for his help—I know I might not have succeeded in returning to England without him, but I could have secured a companion's position without his interference. Mrs Phillips might have agreed to employ me as a favour, but she might yet decide to find someone who is not accosted at night by a giant with no manners and a dubious sense of humour.'

'Are you quite certain there is nothing more to be done?' Lady Edward enquired cautiously and Cleo turned to fiddle with the latch on the cupboard, breathing carefully.

Nothing more to be done. Those simple words ripped another hole in her tissue of hope. This revelation meant she had well and truly lost Rafe. Perhaps soon she might have to accept she'd lost Dash as well. Perhaps it was best to accept it all at once. There was no Rafe, no Dash. Time to grow up once again and move on. She dropped the latch and raised her chin.

'Since my brother may have suffered the same fate as my father and I do not believe in the occult, then, yes, there is nothing to be done. Gone is gone.'

She couldn't hold the woman's compassionate gaze. Any moment now she would break and she did not want Lady Edward to report back to Rafe that Miss Cleopatra Osbourne was a hopeless watering pot.

'I had best return to Mrs Phillips before her argument with Mr Thorpe regarding the true nature of Medusa comes to blows.' She tried to smile and went to the door, but compulsion made her turn and the words tumble out of her. 'I do hope Rafe keeps out of trouble. He was very kind and helped me, though I was nothing but trouble for him. I hope to repay the favour some day, though I cannot see how.' On a final impulse she added: 'I dare say you will think it forward of me to say so, but I do hope you and Lord Edward are working on another book. I cannot tell you the pleasure they gave me and my brother while… Never mind. Thank you for listening to me, Lady Edward.'

She didn't return to Mrs Phillips. She couldn't face anyone else just now.

She'd barely sunk on to a chair in Mrs Phillips's small parlour when there was a tap on the door and Betsy poked her head in.

'There you are, miss. I didn't see you downstairs.'

Cleo rose to her feet guiltily. 'Is Mrs Phillips looking for me, Betsy?'

'No, miss. A man. Not the big fellow from the square, another one. Very polite. Says he's your brother…'

The darkness welled up like sinking into a pool of ink and the air rumbled with the galloping of at least a hundred horses, but when the light returned the maid was still in the doorway, waiting.

'Dash.'

'Shall I show him up, miss?' the maid asked hesitantly.

'Show him…? Oh, yes, please, Betsy. Yes.'

When Dash entered she was standing, her hand braced on the table, still prepared for disillusionment. But it was him—her little brother, smiling. She stood, spread her arms and he walked into her hug. They stood like that a long while until he squirmed out of her arms just as he had as a little boy. But he was grinning.

'I'm honoured I merit a few tears, Sis. I can't remember ever seeing you cry.'

'I'm becoming soft in my old age. I'm so happy you are here and safe, Dash. I was so afraid.'

'So was I,' he replied, inspecting her head to toes. 'When I saw the damage to our rooms I was frantic until I found your letter saying you'd left for England. I wasn't certain you would have. I took what I could and left for Alexandria that same day.'

'But then why did you not leave for England immediately?'

'Because our friend Boucheron was in Alexandria and he controls everything there. I decided to lie low and wait for him to leave, but the blasted fellow looked set to stay there for a while so I finally risked coming into port, only to find myself waylaid by a sailor who knew my name. I almost had an apoplexy, but he just gave me this and disappeared. I realise now that your large friend with the scars must have set him on to me.'

Her breath hitched at the mention of Rafe, but she merely took the worn and limp piece of paper Dash handed her and unfolded it. Rafe's voice filled her mind immediately.

'I'm seeing your Patrick safely to London. Your friend B. is serious about retrieving whatever your father took from him, so if you have it I suggest you find a *safe* means of returning said property—I find it's always best to hide a needle in a haystack and make a great deal of noise about the hay. Whatever you do, don't turn your back on him— make sure there are other people about if you speak with him. And if a fellow named al-Mizan finds you, tell him *nadab* will make it well worth his while to send you safely on your way. I have a feeling he will show me that courtesy, one mercenary to another. Don't dither.'

Cleo rubbed the paper a little as if she could feel him.

'Who is he?' Dash asked, watching her closely, and she sighed. There was no point in telling Dash the truth about Rafe, at least not yet.

'His name is… Rafe. It's a long story. First tell me the rest of it. What did Father take from Boucheron?'

'I don't wish to show disrespect for the dead, but our fool of a father kept a notebook listing all of Boucheron's transactions. He listed which antiquities were sold where and there were markings which I think showed which were real and which forgeries. Farouq must have seen the notebook.'

'Oh, no. No wonder Boucheron wanted Father back under his thumb.'

'Yes, he must be well pleased he's dead.'

'Did you find the notebook among his belongings?'

'I did, though I had no idea of its significance until I read your friend's note. I only took it because it was Father's and I wish I hadn't been so sentimental. If I'd left it there for Boucheron's people to find, none of this would have happened. I returned it to Boucheron, though.'

'Dash! That wasn't wise. Now he might think you know about the forgeries!'

'I wasn't that obvious, Sis. I took your big friend's advice and gathered a stack of Father's most recent notes about the pyramids of Meroe, bought some books about Upper Egypt and was lucky enough to find a volume called *Hidden Treasures of Nubia* in an Alexandrian bookstore. I put it all in a parcel and waylaid Boucheron at the Ptolemy Club in Alexandria so there would be other people around. I think I played the wide-eyed innocent to perfection. Told him I presumed Father stole his plans to find a treasure cache in the Nubian pyramids and conveyed what I hope was the right amount of scoffing disdain at the idea. Then I proclaimed I was only too delighted to finally be able to leave Egypt for England. He said how delighted he was to recover the books, but it was the notebook that he slipped into his coat pocket as I was leaving. You know what he's like—a damned clever fellow. He was even so kind as to offer to put me in contact with some friends of his in London if I needed occupation. He assured me he had excellent connections here.'

'How sweetly ominous.'

'Exactly. I thanked him, but said I was looking forward to taking up an offer of a fellowship in Edinburgh. I felt that was far enough away to calm his concerns.'

'I'm so proud of you, Little Brother. But mostly I'm just happy you are finally here. I've missed you.'

He grinned and gave a jaw-cracking yawn.

'Same here. Now about that giant of yours—'

'He's a mercenary and he's not mine. Now you are safe he will no doubt consider his obligation fulfilled. He must return to his family.'

'Pity. I wasn't very gracious just now.'

'Just now? You saw him?'

'By the docks. He had people on the lookout for me. I thought they might be Boucheron's people who somehow followed me aboard the *Nightingale* and to England and was a little rattled.'

'Oh. What did he say?'

'That you'd have his hide if he didn't deliver me safely.'

She smiled, pressed her hands over her face and burst into tears.

Chapter Twenty-Two

Rafe leaned on the hackney door, giving his leg a moment to adjust as he looked up at the imposing façade of Sinclair House. Even after a day lying abed he was not yet well enough to be up and about, but his conscience was causing him more grief than his leg. He'd put off this moment far too long; it was time to see Edge and face his future. At least his injury might soften his brother's well-deserved ire.

The door to Sinclair House was opened by a butler almost before he'd released the knocker.

'Mr Grey to see Lord Edward,' Rafe announced and the butler opened his mouth but then paused, his eyes widening. 'Lord Edward is in residence, isn't he?' Rafe asked cautiously.

'He is, Your Grace.'

Ah. He'd forgotten how alike he was to Edge. Though given his current state, he would have thought it would take a man longer to make the connection.

Thankfully the butler said no more, merely stood back.

'This way, Your Grace.'

Rafe limped in his wake, concentrating on his steps. Each one was an adventure in discomfort. He was used to pain, had lived with it for quite a long time after the fire.

But strangely he felt this cut even more. He was not as resilient as he had once been. He just wanted it to be over. He wanted…

He wanted Cleo to be there and hold his hand and scold him for his stupidity in wandering around London at night without paying attention to his surroundings and to tell him that only an idiot tended to a knife wound himself. He wanted to see her frown and her smile and he just… wanted her.

Oh, hell, he was a mess.

'In here, Your Grace. I shall fetch your brother.'

He hesitated as Rafe lowered himself on to a sofa, biting back a groan of pain, and then hurried out.

Edge burst into the drawing room and Rafe smiled, far more relieved than he would have believed possible to see his brother. He looked fit and well. Far better than he'd looked the last time he'd seen him in Brazil. Apparently he didn't return the sentiment for his gaze swept over Rafe and his frown deepened.

'Good God, Rafe. You look like hell. Are you ill?'

'Blunt as usual, Edge. No, I had a little altercation with a cutpurse. I wasn't paying attention. My stupidity entirely.'

Edge seemed to waver as if contemplating pulling his brother into a hug, but then he strode over to the bell cord and gave it a tug. 'You need a doctor.'

Rafe sighed and nodded.

'I hoped to manage without a blasted surgeon, but that was probably optimistic. I think I might need a few stitches'

Tubbs appeared promptly at Edge's summons.

'We will need a doctor, Tubbs,' Edge said and the butler nodded.

'I know just the one. What shall I tell Lady Edward? She is worried.'

'Ask her to wait.'

'Not your run-of-the-mill servant,' Rafe commented

when the door closed behind Tubbs. 'I've heard the Sinclairs have their little battalion of efficient minions.'

'Yes. And, knowing him, that doctor will be here in moments so I suggest you take that time to explain why you have put me through hell these past months. I thought you were *dead*, Rafe.'

Rafe winced at the mix of fury and pain in his brother's voice.

'Don't look like that, Edge.' He tried to rise. He was not comfortable facing Edge's justified anger stretched on a sofa like an ailing aunt. But his leg, having carried him thus far, gave a shriek of outrage and buckled. He sank back down, breathing heavily. 'Damn this leg. I know you're furious and you've every right to be, but I knew it would take something drastic to drag you back into the land of the living. Every time I told you to return to Egypt you told me to jump off a cliff. So I did, figuratively. A contact of mine forged that letter from the embassy claiming I was presumed dead. I knew you probably wouldn't believe it, but you couldn't ignore it. I planned to leave clues along the way and wait for you in Luxor and have you finally show me this precious Egypt of yours.'

'So what happened to that charming little plan?'

Rafe shifted his leg with both hands and wiped his forehead.

'I came across someone who'd become separated from her family in a very inhospitable corner of the world.'

'Miss Osbourne,' Edge confirmed.

Rafe looked up with a grimace.

'I was wondering about that advertisement in *The Times*. It wasn't quite accurate so I knew it wasn't that unctuous little worm Pettifer. Still, it was clever of him to change the text to warn me. At least this saves me the need to visit him to find out why. How did you figure it out, by the way?'

'We had some help. But what has that to do with being stabbed?'

'That was purely my foolishness. I thought I had a lead on finding her brother.'

'Brothers appear to be disappearing at an alarming rate recently.'

'As amusing as ever, I see. I never really disappeared. I always knew where I was.'

'As *annoying* as ever, I see. You do realise you are now the Duke of Greybourne and have been back in England for several weeks and have not yet even contacted the lawyers, let alone the brother who you led to believe was now about to assume your title?'

'I planned to do so once I resolved this little issue. And I made sure that fellow you paid to look out for me in Cairo followed me to Alexandria so you would know I was alive and well and on my way to England.'

'I would have appreciated a note to that effect. The fact that you disappeared again once you reached London wasn't precisely encouraging.'

'Yes, well, I was distracted. I needed to arrange some matters.'

'Yes, meeting with fraudsters and convincing them to pay debts they'd never considered paying and then securing a companion's position for Miss Osbourne. I can see why your only brother's peace of mind would rank below those.'

Edge set to pacing the room, following the geometric design of the rug, regimented even in his anger.

'I'm sorry, Edge. If it's any consolation, you dealt me quite a shock when I heard you had somehow managed to marry your Sam while chasing me down. Good for you. I don't know quite how, but I feel I ought to receive some credit.' Edge continued his pacing and Rafe hesitated. 'That is good, isn't it, Edge? I mean, you've wanted her for ever, as far as I could tell. We've never talked about it, but devil take it, man, I would have had to be blind and dumb not to realise how important she was to you. The only times I've ever seen you light up were around Jacob or when you re-

ceived the drawings she made for your books. And when
I came to haul you out of Chesham after the funeral you
were quite voluble about—'

'I was drunk,' Edge snapped, not stopping.

'*In vino veritas*, as they say. When I heard she was widowed as well I thought…if Edge had an ounce of sense he'd
go see the lay of the land. But, no, he stays stuck in Brazil like a barnacle. So I decided to scrape you off and see
what happened. You can only write love letters so long,
Brother mine.'

Edge snorted in disdain. 'I've never written a love letter in my life.'

'No? I've read four of them so far and so have thousands
of other adoring readers. Damn long ones, too, but at least
there's some adventure and excitement and history along
the way while we all wait for Gabriel and Leila to come
to their senses and admit they are batty about each other.
That's why this last book has everyone swooning, from
what I hear. I've been damn busy these past few weeks,
but even I've heard the raving. I managed to leaf through
my housekeeper's copy and those last lines, on the cliff?
"It was only ever you." Damn romantic. No wonder Sam
agreed to marry you. She finally discovered the romantic
pudding under that dour exterior.'

Edge shook his head and sank into a chair, suddenly
looking as shaky as Rafe felt.

'My God, I'm pathetic.'

'Damn it, Edge, that's not what I meant. Any woman
would kill to have someone write masterpieces about her
and for her. Don't tell me Sam doesn't appreciate them—
her illustrations are a work of love in themselves.'

'Not to me. She had no idea I was the author. That is
just the way she is.'

'But…you told her, didn't you?'

'She found out a week ago. In a book store.'

'Oh. Well. That must have been…uncomfortable.'

Edge shoved his hands through his hair.

'Yes.'

'Do you mean to say you proposed to her, but didn't think of telling her the truth?'

'I didn't propose. She did.'

Rafe couldn't hold back a sigh and Edge gave a bitter laugh.

'I told you I am pathetic.'

'No. Stubborn. Wary. And luckier than you deserve. What is wrong, then? You should be in seventh heaven.'

Edge laughed again.

'I was on fourth and climbing, but I've fallen a few rungs. I knew from the beginning Sam wanted to marry me because she wanted a family and a home and I was willing to make that devil's bargain. This shouldn't make a difference, but it does.'

'What shouldn't?'

Edge scrubbed his hands through his hair once more.

'It's a damn long story.'

'I've nothing better to do until the sawbones arrives… Ah, hell.' He broke off at the sound of voices approaching. 'He could not possibly have found—'

'Mr Haversham, Your Grace. A skilled and discreet man of medicine,' Tubbs announced and stood back to allow a short man with unruly white hair to enter.

'Your Grace, Lord Edward,' the man said hurriedly, as if in a rush to dispense with niceties and get to the business of carving up his patients. 'What have we here? Bullets or swords?'

'A knife. To the thigh,' Rafe admitted.

'Excellent. Bullets are a nuisance. Give me a good clean cut any day. We'll need a bed, hot water, linen and a good fire. And some brandy if there's stitching to be done so we can celebrate a job well done when I'm through. Not for you, Your Grace. You look feverish enough as it is. Gruel for you, I'm afraid.'

For the first time since he arrived Edge grinned outright and Rafe was too pleased at the sight to resent it.

'Her Grace, the Duchess of Greybourne, is in the drawing room, Your Grace. I thought you might wish to know.' Tubbs stood in the doorway to Rafe's bedroom at Sinclair House, a distinct twinkle in his eyes. Rafe lowered his brother's book.

'Ah, hell.'

'Precisely, Your Grace. Your brother and Lady Sam are with her already. Here is your cane.'

Rafe debated claiming he was too ill, but that would not only be cowardly, it would leave Edge to face the dragon's wrath alone. Besides, he'd slept most of yesterday after the doctor was done with him and needed to get back on his feet. He had a visit to pay that was already overdue.

At the thought of Cleo, a surge of yearning coursed through him and he took the cane and let Tubbs help him to his feet. They had not gone three steps in the hallway when Edge came striding towards them, his mouth so tightly held it looked as though his jaw might shatter.

'Rafe...'

'Tubbs already told me she's here. Bad luck.'

'I know. Come. Before she says something to Sam I might regret.'

'You left Sam alone with her?'

'Hurry.'

The drawing room door was ajar and Sam's voice carried towards them, tight with fury and pain.

'I am sorry, Your Grace, but you must excuse me for a moment. I... No, I am not sorry. I am so very, *very* grateful to you. You will never know how much.'

'Grateful, Lady Edward?'

Rafe flinched a little at the sound of his mother's voice, as cool and distant as ever. Edge surged forward but as

Sam's voice rushed on, Rafe caught his brother's arm, stopping him.

'Yes, grateful, Your Grace,' Sam answered. 'I did not understand how you could have given away your child, a boy of six, but it was the very best thing you could have done. His uncle and aunt loved him with all their enormous hearts, unconditionally. They helped make him the marvellous, unique man he is. It broke their hearts when your…when *their* grandson died. It broke their hearts when Edge went even further away and they had to let him go and hope he would return. I saw their faces when he arrived in Egypt. *That* is love. And that is why Edge will always turn to them when he needs to see what he is really like. Not to you.'

'Yes. I know. And now to you. So, if you refuse to call my son by his given name Edward, what *do* you call him when you wish to annoy him?' the Duchess asked, her tone tinged with absolutely unfamiliar amusement. Rafe felt the jolt of surprise run both through him and Edge at the same time, finally propelling them into the room. Sam turned to them, her cheeks blazing, but her eyes confused and searching. Rafe took pity on her and spoke.

'Yes, Sam. What do you call this lug when you wish to annoy him? I could use some leverage. Hello, Mother. I admit you have succeeded in surprising me.'

'I dare say I have. You are not looking well, Rafael. The years have not dealt kindly with you. Do sit down before you fall down.' She patted the sofa by her, but Rafe eased himself into an armchair. Edge took Sam's hand and sat with her on the sofa opposite, turning to their mother.

'What game were you playing just now, Mother?'

'Game?' Sam asked.

'I do not indulge in games, Edw… Edge. I was curious about your wife, that is all. She is nothing like Dora.'

'No. Thank God.'

'Yes. Dora was a charming girl, full of light and laughter as long as the sun shone, but not built for hardship. A delightful lapdog to your current lioness.'

'You were *testing* me?' Sam's voice squeaked in outrage, but the Duchess turned to Rafe and Edge.

'I am aware my choices when you were young mean I will always have but limited access to you and I have accepted that. I still believe it was the best decision under the circumstances after the effects of your father's accident became apparent. Now that Rafael has little choice but to assume the responsibilities of his title...' she glanced at Rafe as he shifted in the armchair '... I will remove to the Lancashire property. I have only remained until now to ensure Greybourne does not fall into disrepair and I hope I have not done too ill a job. I know neither of you will voluntarily seek my company in future, so naturally I wished to take what is likely to be a singular opportunity to see if this woman will make you a good wife. I see that she shall and I was wrong to worry.'

Something flickered in Rafe's mind at her words, but it was Sam who asked the obvious question.

'What accident? And what has it to do with sending Edge away?'

'I am surprised you have no memory of this, Rafael,' the Duchess replied, her grey eyes fixing on him now. 'You were, after all, seven years old at the time. The Duke was thrown from his horse and suffered a severe injury to the head. For a long time, we thought he would not survive. He did, but it soon became evident he was no longer the same man. He became most pious and intolerant and...occasionally violent. After the incident when he broke your arm, Edw... Edge, Dr Parracombe and I decided it was judicious we limit his access to the children. There was no question of having him confined. The scandal would have stained the Greybourne name beyond repair.'

Edge clasped his left arm.

'He broke it? My father broke it? How?'

'That day…you were reading to me and Greybourne walked in and tried to take the book from you. You were always stubborn, my boy, and unfortunately you held on. Before I could even think he threw you against the wall. By the time Dr Parracombe treated you and sedated him I had made a pact with myself. I would protect my children by whatever means possible and that meant removing you from danger.' She smoothed her dress again, but as no one broke the silence she continued. 'I could hardly expect the Duke to condone sending his heir to Egypt, Rafe, but I ensured you spent most of the year at school or up by the Lakes, and the girls lived with the governess in their own wing. Naturally we could allow no taint of madness to cling to the Greybourne name and as far as I know there have never been rumours. Rigid religious beliefs served as a fine excuse for his…spells. Now he is dead we need no longer be concerned with discovery. Dr Parracombe is completely trustworthy.'

'Trustworthy… Mother, why did you never say a word of this? We have not been children for a long while. We *deserved* to know.'

'I thought it the best course of action.' She turned to Rafe. 'Greybourne is your cross to bear now, Rafe. I do hope you find someone to share it with who will make it a happier place.'

Rafe shook his head, feeling utterly shattered. He wanted to be angry at her for having kept the truth from them, for having them live in doubt and fear and loneliness. He could see now she'd meant to protect them, but this…

And just as quickly came a slashing sense of loss. A completely different life had been snatched from them, from all of them, through no one's fault but fate and a bad fall. Had his father understood anything of the tragedy? He hoped he hadn't. He didn't wish that on anyone.

What a waste. His whole life could have been different. Edge would not have been sent to Egypt and he would not have run away.

And neither of them would have met the women they loved.

He met his mother's gaze as it moved over his face. Her fingers reached out, hovered within reach of his scarred jaw.

'I hope…no more of this for a while, Rafe?'

He shook his head again. No. No more of this. Time to go home.

'Good,' the Duchess said briskly as she rose and fastened her dove-grey pelisse. 'I have promised to visit with some friends while I am in town and then I must prepare for my departure to Lancashire now I have seen all is well. Do ring for my carriage to be brought round.'

Chapter Twenty-Three

'A Mr Grey to see you, miss.' Betsy's voice held more than a smidgen of disapproval.

Cleo's pen stuttered mid-word, the ink creating erratic constellations over her description of Cairo.

Mr Grey.

She'd expected him to arrive yesterday, as he'd promised, and she'd resolved to show her gratitude and not a hint of all the other emotions crashing about inside her like billiard balls in an earthquake. But as evening fell she'd come to accept he was not coming. She'd even kept Percy out longer on his evening walk, scanning the darkening square, but it remained stubbornly empty. She could only surmise that he'd heard from Lady Edward that Cleo was now aware of his true identity, and was too much of a coward to face her until she absorbed the news and calmed down.

Well, she had not calmed down in the least.

Mr Grey.

No matter how many times she repeated to herself he was not like William, not like her father…that he owed her nothing and had promised nothing, yet had done more for her in the short time she'd known him than anyone since her childhood world fell apart…that she could and did trust him…that he owed her nothing in the end…even that he had every right to keep his identity to himself—she *knew* all this, but it still hurt to her core.

No wonder he'd tried to keep her at bay. He'd probably realised that despite all her protestations that she did not want anything beyond the moment, she was weaving him into her foolish dreams of cottages and her little pack of jackals.

The Duke of Greybourne, even returned from the wild, could have no part in that fantasy. Whether he wished it or not he was about to be swept back into a world in which she had no part.

What is in a name?

A chasm. A line as deep and treacherous as an ocean.

She knew why he was here. She knew his subterfuge weighed on him, she'd seen it every time he'd been on the verge of telling her the truth. Now it was time for him to complete his confession.

Third time unlucky.

The only thing that should matter was that he had helped Dash. Everything else *must* be put aside. She tried to clear her mind from everything but her gratitude, but there was quite a great deal to clear.

'Shall I send him away, miss?' Betsy said hopefully as the silence stretched.

'No. Show him in, Betsy.'

The first thing she noticed when he entered was the pallor that gave his sun-warmed skin a grey tinge. She'd not noticed it in the square, but then it had been dark. Surely it was not the result of merely two weeks in the rainy north? Her anger began to fizzle and she tried to pull it back about her like a slipping shawl. For all she knew he was feeling the weather after a round of dissipation. Perhaps that was what had prevented him from calling on her yesterday. She was not at all certain it was better than cowardice.

Her anger received another blow when he took a step

into the room and she noticed he was leaving heavily on a cane.

'Rafe! What happened? Was it Boucheron? This is all my fault!'

His mouth quirked for a moment. 'Hardly. You attribute far too much omnipotence to that French fraudster. I had a disagreement with a cutpurse, that is all. My mistake.'

'When?'

'When?'

'When did this happen? Yesterday?'

His eyes fell from hers.

'The day before.'

'After you saw Dash. It *is* my fault.'

'No, it is mine; I wasn't paying attention. I meant to write you a note, but I was a little…indisposed yesterday after the doctor stitched me. I slept most of the day. It isn't serious, just uncomfortable.'

'Then why are you on your feet?' she demanded. 'You should not be standing, I am sure.'

'Well, you haven't yet invited me to sit,' he said reasonably and despite everything she found her mouth curving.

'Besides,' he added as he limped towards the sofa and eyed it, 'sitting down has become something between ordeal and penance.'

She had no integrity at all. Her defences cracked and she hurried forward, taking his arm and weight as he lowered himself into the chair with a grunt, his leg extended. His arm was hard and warm under her fingers and as she reluctantly let it go he brushed the back of her hand briefly with his fingers, sending fire up her arm.

'Thank you, Cleo.'

She returned to her seat and folded her hands in her lap.

'You're welcome, Your Grace.'

He stiffened, a slight flush spreading over his cheekbones. Guilt personified.

'Edge mentioned you spoke with Sam that evening. I wasn't certain if you'd realised… I'd intended to tell you…'

'It is said hell is paved with good intentions, Your Grace.'

'Shakespeare?'

'Samuel Johnson. And don't think you can distract me.'

'I don't intend to. I know I was wrong not to tell you. Not initially, but certainly on board the *Hesperus* I should have told you the truth.'

'Why?' she challenged. 'You owe me nothing. I hired you to help me, which you did. There was never a requirement of honesty, as you made clear several times.'

Her words wiped all expression from his face. He looked his full ducal self now—hard and cold. She was being childish, but she couldn't help it.

'Nevertheless,' he continued, his voice as flat as his countenance, 'my name…my origins have always been an issue. When I ran away I decided to turn my back on them so when I enlisted I gave my name as Rafe Grey. At the time it felt fitting, a reminder of what I was turning my back on and a reminder that I had to be watchful and unobtrusive.'

His mouth twisted at the absurdity of that, but Cleo held herself still, her hands firmly in her lap, and he continued, 'I knew as long as I was Rafe Grey I could have no…permanence in my life, and I accepted that because I knew that as my father's son it was probably best I not inflict any more Greybournes on this world. I know you told me I am not like him, but I lived most of my whole life under the cloud of fear that I might be, or that, God forbid, that strain would manifest in my children if not in me. I did not want to willingly embrace a legacy of uncertainty and pain.'

'I told you before, Rafe. You are not like your father. I *know* that. Whatever happens, please don't let this rule you.

I've never met anyone more deserving of being happy and living your life to the fullest. You *aren't* like your father.'

She reached out and clasped his hand, trying to anchor him with her certainty. But she could not do that for him any more than she could be anything but what she was, Cleopatra Osbourne, daughter of a rootless fraudster.

He drew his hand from hers very gently, fisting it on his thigh before he spoke again.

'The mad thing is that I've just learned it wasn't like my father either.'

'I don't understand.'

'I'm not the only one making confessions. I've just come from a meeting with my mother...'

As Cleo listened to his account of his mother's visit, more and more layers peeled away from her flimsy defences. She didn't want to abandon the defence of her anger, but it was slipping away from her, leaving only a sense of oppression and loss.

'What a sad story,' she said when he fell silent. 'Your poor mother. I cannot imagine what she must have felt. To have your world ripped apart...the poor woman.'

'I suggest you don't say that to her face. She's likely to freeze you with a glance. She's as tough as an old boot.'

She smiled at the return of some colour to his voice, but shook her head.

'No, she isn't. Perhaps outside, but not inside. I'm so sorry you had to experience any of this, Rafe.'

He shifted uncomfortably.

'It's old history.'

'No, it isn't and you know it. I wonder if your father even understood the change that came over him. In a way I hope he didn't. To be cut off like that from yourself... to be aware in any way of what you've become. I cannot imagine a worse fate.'

His mouth finally softened, though not quite into a smile.

'You'll be making me feel guilty I wasn't more compassionate towards him.'

'I dare say you might have been if your mother had trusted you enough to tell you the truth. But she must have felt as though she was clinging to a branch in a flood. How sad.'

They fell silent and once again the truth rolled back to fill the void.

His Grace the Duke of Greybourne. Her little dream of a family with this man would remain just that. She didn't even have grounds for anger. He'd warned her, tried to avoid her, worried about hurting her. He was no William, as much as she might want to cast him in that role so she could cauterise pain with anger. He was Rafe. The man she loved with all her heart and soul and body.

'I hope knowing this will make going back to your home easier, Rafe—' She broke off and managed a smile. 'I can't quite call you Your Grace, you know. It just doesn't feel right.'

He waved that away, his gaze fixed on her face. 'I didn't come merely to tell you my name, Cleo, long overdue though that was. I came to offer it to you. Will you do me the honour of marrying me?'

The words came out in a rush, as if he was forcing them out before a door closed. Cleo sat very still. The mantelpiece clock tut-tutted away.

'Well?' he demanded. His hand was still fisted on his thigh and the other held his cane in a death grip. She tried several times to form the words, pulling in air only to have it slip out again, as shapeless as her thoughts.

Her fingers began to ache and she looked down at them. As he'd talked she'd wound the blue ribbon he'd gifted her tightly about them without even realising. She unwound the ribbon and the blood rushed back, beating hard.

'Did I ever tell you what happened after I stole that ribbon, Rafe?'

He shifted impatiently but his voice was flat when he answered.

'No. You didn't.'

She wet her lips and smoothed the ribbon on her lap. 'I kept it hidden in my drawer and agonised over it for days and days. I made myself ill worrying about it. It wasn't that I believed in damnation or sins, it was merely that I *knew* it was wrong to have taken something that did not belong to me. In the end I went to Annie and told her.'

'What did she do?' The words sounded as though they, too, were wrung out of him.

'She was angry. And hurt. She said, rightly, that I had no right to take what wasn't mine simply because I wanted it.'

'If you don't want the damned thing, then toss it on the dung heap. It is only a ribbon.'

'That isn't what I meant and you know it. I think you are the bravest and most wonderful man of my acquaintance, Rafe Grey. Which is why you must understand why I cannot accept your proposal—it would feel like stealing for me. I don't take marriage lightly.'

'You think I do? Then how the devil did I manage to avoid it for thirty-seven years?'

'With your soft heart? I have no idea.'

He smiled reluctantly, but it didn't show in his eyes.

'I am serious, Cleo.'

'I know. So am I.' She leaned forward and touched his arm and his hand closed over hers, warm and large and so inviting.

'You deserve so much, Rafe. I'm honoured that you are willing to overlook the difference in our births, but even if your conscience is telling you it is the right thing to do, it isn't. You are my finest friend and you deserve to love and be loved and so do I. If I agreed to enter into such an uneven match—'

'I don't give a sainted damn about my title,' Rafe bit out and she shook her head.

'I wasn't referring to differences in birth, but in sentiment, Rafe. It is a burden when one side loves and the other doesn't. I saw that all too well with my mother. If I said yes, I would be robbing you of that possibility and I cannot do that. Don't you understand?'

His hands rose, as if warding her off. For a moment he remained with his head bent, silent and frozen.

'I understand…' he said at last, but his voice scraped to a halt and he cleared his throat. 'God knows I wish… more than anything…that I could make that true for you. You deserve that more than anyone. Obviously I haven't that power.'

She watched his lowered head, her chest a knot of pain and her eyes filling. She tugged her chair next to his and took his hand. She hadn't realised her tears had slipped free until he raised their clasped hands to her face and his knuckles grazed her wet cheek.

'Don't cry, sweetheart. Damn your soft heart. I won't break. I promise. I refuse to have you pity me. I'd rather love you and have you kick me to the curb than be a cause of hurt to you. At least I've had the good sense to give my heart to someone worthwhile, even if she cannot love me back. I won't… I can't give up your friendship and, if all we can be is friends, I shall have to make do with that. Perhaps one day you'll…feel more. I won't badger you, though. And if one day you…find a man who will give you what you wish, I will do my damnedest not to make a fool of myself or strangle the life out of him. I want your happiness, Cleo-Pat. I wish it could have been with me, I will always wish it, but I wish for your happiness above that.'

Cleo's mind fiddled with his words like a child racing to complete a puzzle against the clock of doom. Surely it was impossible the picture that was forming was correct. She had misheard…he had misspoken…she had finally allowed sentiment to overpower sense…she…

Rafe loved her.

Not conscience, charity, not even lust…

Rafe *loved* her.

Rafe loved *her*.

She pressed their joined hands to her lips and his hand tightened convulsively on hers.

'No, Cleo… I don't want pity.'

'Pity! You ought to pity *me* for a blind fool, Rafe. And you are one, too, to so completely misunderstand me. I *love* you. I have for weeks. My poor heart has been cracked so many times it's a wonder it is still beating, but it is.' She pressed his hand to her chest. 'Can't you feel it? It's spilling over with love. I *love* you, Rafe Grey.'

Rafe felt as though he'd walked straight off a cliff, but forgotten to fall. He just hung there, in a strangely silent world, even his own breathing far away, as if he was seeing this all from a distance. But beneath his palm her heart was beating a matching rhythm to his.

He could not remember ever seeing real joy, he certainly had never felt it. Now he saw it in her face—in her smile, her eyes, in the pressure of her hand that held his to her heart. And he felt it—in the centre of his chest, expanding and making it hard to breathe.

'You mean it,' he said a little absurdly, his voice rough. Her hand pressed harder against his.

'Of course I mean it. I've meant it for ages. Why on earth do you think I have been gathering every moment with you, every touch, and begging for more?'

He touched his fingers to the corner of her beautiful mouth, to that tugging smile that ruled his soul and senses.

Cleo.

'You've never begged. You demanded,' he replied and was rewarded by her warm laugh.

'Because you are absurdly stubborn. If only you'd told me you loved me sooner…'

'A brave man might have. I told you I was a coward, Cleo.'

'I won't have you calling yourself that, it isn't true. You are cautious and caring and so giving to others that you forget to take. And I *love* you.' Her voice shook, deepened. 'I love you, Rafe. You told me I was one of those who… who manage and it's true, but I don't *want* to manage. I want to feel the way I do when I am with you. Alive, and happy, and myself, even when it hurts. I'm even happy being miserable with you.'

He knew well what she meant. He didn't understand the alchemy of it, but there it was—love had replaced a part of his soul with something that twined the two of them together. She was part of him now and he needed her. This.

'I only wish you didn't have this stupid title, Rafe. Otherwise I would throw caution to the wind and ask you to marry me. But even if we cannot wed, I want you to know I am yours in every way that matters.'

'Do it, Cleo. Throw caution to the blasted wind.'

She stilled, her eyes fixing on his.

'I don't expect it, Rafe.'

'You should. You should demand it. I've let the Greybourne name and legacy shape too many things in my life, Cleo. I won't let it ruin the best thing that ever happened to me.'

Her hand hovered over his chest, just brushing his shirt, and she took a deep breath.

'Rafe Grey. Will you marry me?'

'I will,' he said, capturing his hand against his chest. 'Today if I could. But two hasty marriages in our family might be a little much. My mother can finally begin atoning for her mistakes by helping us do this properly.'

'I doubt she'll be happy about this.'

'She will be ecstatic about anything that ensures I settle down, sweetheart. Not that she'll show it.'

'I shall just have to show it instead of her,' Cleo said as

she pulled the long chain with the emerald pendant over her head and placed it round his neck. 'There. I haven't a ring to give you, so this must do.'

The emerald lay heavily against his chest. He could feel his heartbeat against it, as if trying to reach through a cage and grab.

She leaned back to inspect it.

'I should say it matches your eyes, but they are much prettier.'

He half laughed and managed to force the words through his clogged throat. 'I cannot take it. It's yours.'

'You aren't. You are safekeeping it for our daughter. You promised I would have daughters, didn't you?'

'Yes. And sons. A wild pack of jackals.'

She touched his cheek lightly, her smiling eyes seeing right through to the pain that was still lodged in his stomach.

'And sons. You promised and you are a soothsayer, after all.' She snuggled against him, careful of his leg as she tucked her head into the curve of his shoulder as she had on the *Hesperus*. 'Do you know; I think I am going to be a very demanding wife.'

'I hope so.'

'And spendthrift, too. You *are* wealthy, correct?'

He leaned back a little, warmed by the laughter in her gold-flecked eyes.

'I am. What are you plotting? Building a pyramid on the front lawn at Greybourne?'

'No, a *hammam*. All marble and with a dipping pool, but with something to lie on right in the very middle so I can lay you down and wash you all over...' Her voice trailed off into a husky rumble, her hand slipping under his coat and down his chest.

He felt as though he'd been shoved into a steam room right now—the heat was spiralling through him like steam, half melting him, half turning him as hard as the emerald pressed between his chest and her glorious breasts. Mrs Phillips's parlour was *not* the place…

'And then…?' he prompted.

'And then I will take you on an adventure you will never forget, Mr Grey.'

Epilogue

Greybourne Hall—1824

'**W**ell?' Cleo demanded as she removed Rafe's blindfold. He stood for a moment squinting at the sight. The spring sun outside was powerful, cutting through the milky glass windows and transforming the marble and granite surfaces to cream and gold. The light caressed the cushions that lined two *chaises longue* and then sped on, dancing off the flat surface of the raised stone bath.

His mouth quirked—he reckoned the bath could comfortably accommodate four people, or one large scarred mercenary and his pregnant wife. Only last night he'd had a delightful time bathing Cleo in the brass tub in their dressing room, taking his time soaping her beautiful breasts and the taut skin of her stomach.

The thought of being able to join Cleo in the warm waters of this hedonistic corner of paradise and then move their exploration to the generously large *chaise longue* was…

'Well? Do you like it?' Cleo prompted, impatient at his silence.

'Good God, Cleo. *Like* is a very weak word to describe what I'm feeling at the moment. Full to bursting is closer.

Dangerously aroused is even more accurate.' He slipped his hands into Cleo's hair, threading through its warm silk. She often wore it down around the Hall, the chestnut waves covering her shoulders. Sometimes he missed her short hair, but playing with the warm tresses more than compensated for his occasional nostalgia. Like now, as he imagined it covering her bare breasts as she slipped into the water. 'Is the water warm yet? Actually, I don't care. Lock the door...'

'Bah!'

They drew apart and Rafe turned to face the wide grey eyes of his niece and the equally wide grey eyes of his sister-in-law and the very amused green-grey eyes of his brother.

'Bah!' little Charlotte announced again, waving a glistening fist towards the water. Edge shifted his daughter from one arm to the other, his other hand closing around Sam's as they entered the *hammam*.

'No, Charlie, I'm afraid you'll have to wait your turn going for a swim. Your uncle and aunt look as though they need a cooling dip first.'

Sam laughed, her eyes taking everything in.

'This is amazing, Cleo! Oh, Edge, look at the hieroglyphs!'

'I'll be damned,' Edge said, a new light entering his eyes as he strode over to the wall with his daughter.

Rafe sighed with resignation, shelving his fantasies, and followed his brother towards the far wall. As he inspected the carving on the wall the memory returned of an evening two years before in a half-fallen temple in Kharga. There were the Pharaoh and the Queen, arms extended, each standing on a royal cartouches, and surrounded with lotus flowers, palms, and a row of...jackals?

Rafe smiled and laced his fingers through Cleo's, drawing her against his side, his throat tight.

'I can't remember. Are those the symbols from the temple in Kharga?' he asked Cleo, pointing to the cartouches, but Edge shook his head as he inspected them.

'Not unless you believe in colossal coincidences. Have you been studying Champollion's *Precis*, Cleo?'

She laughed, brushing her cheek against Rafe's shoulder.

'Dash is in Paris and sends me all the latest news on the decipherment of the hieroglyphs. But I put this together myself. What do you think?'

'Do you mean these squiggles actually mean something?' Rafe demanded. 'All I can see is snakes, lions and falcons. It looks like a menagerie. Actually that looks more like a slug than a snail.'

'A slug for a great big lug,' Edge said. 'That's you, Rafe. The empty eye, the slug and the lion. R-F-L.'

'Huh. And this?' Rafe asked Cleo.

'The one with the lion and falcon is my name, Cleopatra. And this…' she murmured, pulling him to a row of the hieroglyphs between the cartouches showing a crouched figure and a long-tailed snake. 'This part reads *iu-meri-y-chu*. Together it says Rafael and Cleopatra love for ever. At least I hope it does. It would be very embarrassing to discover it says Rafael and Cleopatra like snakes.'

'Rafael and Cleopatra love for ever,' Rafe repeated, tracing the symbols. 'Carved in stone.'

'Greybourne stone. I had this quarried from the same stone they are using to build the new school in the village, which is a rather worthier project than the *hammam*,' she added guiltily.

Rafe turned and brushed his fingertips down her cheek, resting for a moment on her dimple.

'I find this project eminently worthy. At least I think I will if only I am allowed to assess it properly…without an audience.'

Sam laughed and slipped Charlotte from Edge's arms, pulling her husband away from his inspection of the carvings.

'Come along, Edge. Charlie is also in need of a bath, though I doubt she will enjoy it quite as much as her uncle.'

'Finally,' said Rafe as he locked the door behind them and turned to look at his wife. She wore a low-cut, loose-fitting morning dress gathered below her beautiful breasts, showing the growing bulge of their child. Her head was slightly to one side as she watched him, her smile warm and loving.

'Come here, Rafe.'

'You're looking rather dangerous at the moment, Cleo-Pat. What have you in store for me now?'

'Another great adventure, Mr Grey.'

* * * * *

If you enjoyed this book, be sure to read
The Sinful Sinclairs miniseries by Lara Temple

The Earl's Irresistible Challenge
The Rake's Enticing Proposal
The Lord's Inconvenient Vow